THE GOOD NANNY

Fiction

The Plagiarist

The Partisan

Famous After Death

Nonfiction

Selling Ben Cheever: Back to Square One in a Service Economy

The Letters of John Cheever (editor)

The Good Nanny

A Novel

BENJAMIN CHEEVER

BLOOMSBURY

Published by Bloomsbury, New York and London
Distributed to the trade by Holtzbrinck Publishers

Library of Congress Cataloging-in-Publication Data
Cheever, Benjamin, 1948-
The good nanny: a novel/Benjamin Cheever.—1st U.S. ed.
p. cm.
ISBN 1–58234–122–2
1. Fiction—Authorship—Fiction. 2. Writer's block—Fiction. 3. Ex-convicts—
Fiction. 4. Kidnapping—Fiction. 5. Novelists—Fiction. 6. Nannies—Fiction.
I. Title.
PS3553.H34865G66 2004
813′.54—dc22
2003020907

First U.S. Edition 2004

3 5 7 9 10 8 6 4 2

Typeset by Hewer Text Ltd, Edinburgh
Printed in the United States of America by
Quebecor World Fairfield

For my beloved wife

The intellect of man is forced to choose
Perfection of the life or of the work
—*William Butler Yeats*

CHAPTER 1

"You're in the country now. Safe at last."

Experience the river views that inspired a famous school of art. Live in the grand estate neighborhood where Frank A. Vanderlip (First National City Bank) played penny poker with John D. Rockefeller (Standard Oil). This is Tara on Hudson. Full air. Stunningly appointed Great Room with fieldstone hearth. EIK. 4 BRs. Jacuzzi. A prestigious gem on one secluded acre. Special and unique. Walk to train. Maid's quarters with separate entrance. $850,000.

Sotheby's had placed the ad in the *New York Times Magazine* section. Joy Gainsborough-Orsini had spread her Gore-Tex parka on the sod, gone down on her belly to shoot the picture. And so the building—large enough in life—seemed to pierce the very skies.

Shown now in the last rays of a watery March sun, the edifice towered amid immature plantings. This was on the Albany Post Road and directly across Scarborough Station Road from the Scarborough Presbyterian Church. Although substantially smaller than the church, the house seemed to vie with that structure as to which was to be the more preposterous demonstration of man's aspiration to transcend practicality. Both buildings were designed

I

to excite awe. Both were far too large to justify their purposes as shelter.

The church was substantially bigger than its competitor, but the Cross residence had the Gothic windows once reserved for places of worship, and a three-car garage mahal. It outgunned the sanctuary six toilets to one.

Featuring the largest lawn in the development, the wedding cake of a house was bordered on the left by a replica of Washington Irving's Sunnyside. A miniature of the dome of Jefferson's Monticello took the right flank. The builder's motto and slogan: "The Grandeur and Genius of the Past; the Comfort and Convenience of the Future." The development: Heavenly Mansions.

This was Saint Patrick's Day in the New Millennium, and Tara's owners were hosting a party. The invitations had been cardboard shamrocks with "You survived Y2K, now come toast Andie," and then this line from Housman: "Malt does more than Milton can to justify God's ways to man." Although few of the guests were drinking malt. They were drinking Frascati, and a fruity Chardonnay. All purchased at The Art Of Wine in Pleasantville.

The host, Stuart Cross (no relation to the pens, thank you), was heading into the great room with a fresh tray of oysters. The hostess, Andie Wilde (no relation to the famous playwright and pederast, alas) was at the granite-topped island in the kitchen, taking the Saran Wrap from a bowl of guacamole. Stuart was 59. Andie was 32, a small, slender brunette now wearing an ankle-length suede skirt, which snapped up the front, and a black cashmere turtleneck. Andie always gave the impression of having just finished an exhaustive crying jag. Perhaps it was the too-generous use of mascara; perhaps it was something more fundamental to her character. This melancholy cast had rendered her irresistible to a certain type of male, many of whom were powerful or rich.

She'd grown up bookish in bookless Vandalia, Ohio—Dayton's airport town. "Raised in a bowling alley, but with the soul of an English maiden," Stuart had said, casting the first of the honeyed barbs that snagged Andie's heart. "If I weren't so old and shrewd, I never would have gaffed her," he said once when quite drunk. "I paid attention. Pay attention, and you needn't be kind."

Andie was half-Irish, but the party was being held to celebrate, or at least acknowledge, her promotion to the enviable but not entirely respectable position of top film critic for the *New York Post*. "Yes, I love my job," she said when asked. Everybody asked.

Stuart heard a cry of tires, and then what sounded like a collision, but by the time he put down the oysters and reached the window to look out, a red van was moving through the intersection. A green SUV, which was on his lawn, reversed back onto the road and followed the van.

"What happened?" Andie asked. "I felt just as if somebody had walked over my grave."

"Nothing to do with your grave," said Stuart. "Looks as if there was an accident at the crossroads."

"Doesn't that mean tragedy?" asked Wallace Stevens (not that Wallace Stevens). "An encounter at a crossroads?"

"Traditionally, it means tragedy," said Stuart, going back to the kitchen to get the oysters.

"Can I have another?" asked Stevens, when the host reappeared.

"You ate the last tray," said Stuart. "Let's give somebody else a chance."

"You didn't want me here at all, did you?" asked Stevens. "It

3

was Scarlet's idea, wasn't it?" A tall, ungainly creature who might have been Lincolnesque if it weren't for the weak chin and a terrible comb-over, Stevens—a book agent—had been the last guest invited and the first to arrive.

"He'll try and do business," Stuart had said. "And he's a spitter."

"He's had us to dinner twice now in the city," countered Andie. "You may not like him, but he is a brilliant agent. The man can ask the baldest questions and somehow get away with it, or almost. There are a half a dozen writers we admire who never would have made it without him. Besides which, we *are* celebrating the patron saint of outcasts."

"We're also honoring the man who cast out the snakes," said Stuart.

"If we don't include Stevens," said Andie, "he'll hear about the party from your old friend Loose Lips Solon at Random House."

The agent had arrived a half an hour early—Andie was still in the shower—and presented Stuart with a one thousand, one hundred-page manuscript titled *Gone With the Wind*. (Not that *Gone With the Wind*.) "Random House despised it, but I think it's perfect for you," he explained.

Now Stevens was making Andie blush.

"Is Tom Hanks here?" he asked.

"I didn't invite him," said Andie.

"He would have come," said Stevens, moving his face unnaturally close to that of his hostess. "Doesn't he want good reviews?"

"It doesn't work that way," said Andie, backpedaling out of range of the spray.

"Then how does it work?" asked Stevens. "I told Loretta that he might be here."

"I judge the movie on its merits," said Andie.

"Isn't that a bit subjective?" asked Stevens.

"Yes," said Andie.

"But you don't pay for your tickets, do you?" asked Stevens.

"No," said Andie, "not usually."

"Which right away puts you in a different position than all the rest of us," said Stevens. "Loretta asked me the other day if you got free popcorn. I didn't know. Do you get free popcorn?"

"No," said Andie, "not usually."

Stevens nodded pensively. "Did you ever try and figure out how much they pay you per review?" he asked.

"No," said Andie. "I never did."

"Loretta was saying they should wire a keypad into the seats," Stevens continued. "After the movie, everybody could push a button for thumbs-up, or a different button for thumbs-down. The results could be tabulated and published. That way we'd really know what to see."

"Enough charming chitchat for now," said Stuart, inserting himself between Andie and the agent. "How about a house tour? Anybody who wants to admire the Jacuzzi," he said, "queue here." Half a dozen late arrivals responded to the invitation, and Stuart started up the stairs. "The real estate agent promised a seasonal view of the Hudson," he said. "I don't see it. Unless she was talking about the nuclear winter."

"Where do you write?" asked Wallace Stevens, when the party reached the top of the stairs.

"Actually," said Stuart, "I haven't written a word since we moved in, but I have picked the spot."

"I think the places where creative people work are sacred," the agent said, looking into the faces of the other guests for confirmation. None was forthcoming. But Stuart led the group into a small bedroom off the hallway. This had a dark oak table with one center drawer and a chair with a cane bottom.

Stevens went to the desk. "Do you mind?" he asked, looking back over his shoulder at Stuart.

His host said nothing.

The agent opened the drawer, found it empty, took a card out of his wallet, wrote something on the back, put the card in the drawer, and closed it. Then he backed away from the desk and brought his face close to Stuart's "That's my home number," he said.

"Thanks," said Stuart, wiping spittle from his cheeks as he turned and went into the hall.

"Instead of the river view," he said, "we have a master-bedroom-suite-to-die-for. That's what the realtor was always saying, 'a master-bedroom-suite-to-die-for.' "

"Die happy," one of the guests chimed in.

"Somehow I don't think Joy will die happy," said Stuart, "but I accept the compliment."

He led the group down the hall and into the bedroom. This was large and with floor-to-ceiling windows on one wall. An ebony sleigh bed stood in the center of the room. A small, clever wooden desk with pillars, cubbies, and a Hepplewhite chair was set in a corner. "It's a reproduction," Stuart said, before moving out of the sleeping area and through the first phase of the bathroom—two sinks, and a long mirror lined with light bulbs, in a style reminiscent of a theatrical dressing room.

"It's fabulous," one of the guests enthused. "The dream house for the dream couple."

"And we dream big these days," Stuart said. "Five people, four thousand square feet. Lucky Karl Marx has been discredited. Else we'd all be murdered in our beds."

6

"Would they murder the nanny?" asked Rick Massberg, a colleague from the city and Stuart's protégé.

"I think she'd be the one to let them in, while we slept," said Stuart. "Or that's my understanding of class war. We've got the walk-in closet," he continued, leading the party deeper into the bathroom, "the Jacuzzi, steam shower . . ."

"Do you ever really use the steam shower?" asked a cleft-chinned blonde named Heather who worked for the Bathos Literary Agency in Manhattan.

"Yes, of course," said Stuart, as the party retreated down the stairs. "So far we've *really* used it only twice." The group crossed the kitchen, descended a set of bare wooden stairs and came into a large basement. Stuart hit the wall switch, and there was an appreciative pause as the guests spread out and took in the huge space, entirely empty and with a ceiling seven feet high.

"The hot water is heated right on the oil burner," Stuart said. "One fire instead of two. Cellar floor is as dry as a bone," he said, tapping at the cement with the toe of one tasseled loafer. He extended his arms and turned once in a slow circle. "Imagine a gym, a wine cellar, a prison."

Solidly built and of moderate height, the host moved with surprising grace. He wore his curly gray hair long, in a style more befitting a musician than an editor. Despite his age and sedentary profession, he was still slender and carried himself with the grace and assurance of a natural athlete.

After the third glass of wine, he'd begun to tell everybody who would listen—and some people who would not listen—that with Andie's increased income, he was now finally prepared to resign his editorship at Acropolis Books "and write the novel that's been eating at my guts since I first achieved consciousness." Wearing chinos and a white button-down shirt with blue pinstripes, no tie, but fastened at the collar, he was standing now, with one hand on the mantel, talking intently to a knot of guests. "I'm tired unto death of delivering other people's children. Delivering them, and washing off the blood and sputum."

"He's blotto. Snockered," said Herbert Pipes, a friend from the city and the couple's tax lawyer. "They'll take you out of that elegant office of yours in a pine box," he told his host.

"Stuart couldn't quit back then. He was the sole support of his widowed mother," said Andie, angrily.

"Maybe," said Pipes turning back to the other guests. "But you all should know that the very first thing Stuart told me when I met him was that he was going to leave his job and write the great American novel. That was twenty years ago."

"Might quit," snapped Stuart. "And while I'm making changes, I might also engage a lawyer who doesn't tread on my dreams." This was delivered in tones that were clearly meant to sound lighthearted, and just as clearly failed. The host opened his mouth again, perhaps to make amends, but he was cut off by the rising clamor of police sirens. The large Gothic windows at the end of the great room had a commanding view of the Albany Post Road. Stuart and several others moved to look outside as two squad cars raced north toward the Village of Ossining, followed by an ambulance, and then a third police car.

"Move to the country," said Stuart. "Escape urban brutality."

"All right, all right," said Kika Campion-Bourne. A friend of Andie's since Kenyon, Kika had lived in Scarborough for a decade. She was the individual most responsible for convincing the couple to abandon that cramped apartment in Chelsea that Stuart had shared with his mother. Kika was tall for a woman—five feet eleven inches—and had naturally blonde hair, which she wore to her waist. "Your pal might be sexy," Stuart had told Andie once, "if her hips weren't so generous and her bust so ungenerous. Girls frequently pair off in college, with one being beautiful and moody, the other ordinary but reliable," he told his wife. "I bet Kika was reliable."

"You're only trashing her because she's my best friend," said Andie. "And you don't like to share."

"There's that," said Stuart, "but even you can see how plain Kika is."

Andie never aired her husband's poisonous remarks to her friend, and so they had the desired effect, which was to weaken the connection between the two women. Kika was not a dunce, though, and sensed the hostility. She treated her pal's distinguished husband as if he were a naughty little boy.

"Now, now. Don't get your knickers in a twist, Stu. You're not in Manhattan anymore," she said, wetting the index finger of her right hand and tucking hair behind her ear. "The police in Scarborough are like Maytag repairmen. Half the department turns out for a busted taillight."

As she spoke, another squad car pulled up to the intersection, paused, made a hooting sound with its siren, and ran the light.

"I don't care how bored the police are," said Stuart. "That's not a minor accident. Sounds like a race riot to me. Isn't Peekskill north of here? A mob tried to murder Paul Robeson in Peekskill."

"Now we *are* showing our age," said Kika.

"Time out," said Andie, stepping between her friend and her husband and putting a hand on each of them, trying to draw the charge of malice into her own body and then to ground.

9

"As for the many police cars," said Kika, shrugging off her friend's hand, "your husband's trying to judge the response by city standards. Can't do that. There was a story in the *Ossining Citizen Register* yesterday about a woman who thought she was being sniped at in the parking lot of the Arcadian Shopping Center. The police closed off the Albany Post Road for an hour."

"Sniping is my idea of serious," said Stuart.

"It was three little boys," said Kika. "A Briarcliff dowager had left her grocery bags lined up in the cart, while she went back into the store for more Bloody Mary mix. You know how that market has a target on its bags? There were three children out there with as many BB guns. I wouldn't have been able to resist it myself. A jar of relish was slain."

"I can't help but feel that the city was safer," said Stuart.

"You forget that your beloved wife was very nearly raped in the front hall of the apartment building you're so mawkish about?"

"No," said Stuart, "I'm not forgetting that. But *four* police cars?"

"You'll read all about it in tomorrow's paper," Kika said. "Don't worry, big boy. You're in the country now. Safe at last."

CHAPTER 2

The Trouble with Nannies at All

"Speaking of safe," said Andie. "I'm genuinely worried about the girls." Jane Wilde Cross (six) and Virginia Woolf Cross (nine) had been taken out with the new nanny to buy six large bags of fat-free pretzels and one of "nude" popcorn. "It's in the health-food section," Andie had explained. "You put it in a bowl and pour a little melted butter over it. No candy for Ginny. I don't care how she begs." The nanny (Louise Washington, a small—no, tiny— black woman of thirty-seven from Yonkers, New York) had come to work for the first time that day at noon.

Stuart glanced at his watch. "I wouldn't worry yet," he said. "The vaunted Miss Washington doesn't know the neighborhood. She might easily have gotten lost."

"On the way to the grocery store?" asked Andie. "It's a straight shot from here to there. I don't think so."

Stuart sighed. "You're always anxious about your precious girls," he said. "And we haven't lost one yet. Let's give the child-care professional another twenty minutes. Then we can call out the National Guard."

"You have a new nanny?" asked Pipes.

"Brand spanking new," Stuart agreed.

"And?" asked Pipes.

"And she's an odd bird," said Stuart. "The girls are encouraged to call her 'Sugar.' We're encouraged to call her 'Miss Washington.' I'm not even sure she graduated from high school. And you know what she wants to be? A painter," he continued, not waiting for Pipes to respond. "Not a house painter, not even an illustrator. She wants to paint masterpieces. We've had three conversations, and I already know that she wants to paint a picture that will hang in the Museum of Modern Art."

"I didn't know that," said Kika.

"Now that they're no longer comprehensible to the general public, fine arts are the easiest to fake," said Massberg. "Take, for instance, the wife of our beloved publisher, take Helen Glass, née Greene. So little is known about what constitutes merit in the visual arts that even Helen Greene thinks she's got something important to say in oil."

"I hadn't heard," said Cross.

"Of course not,' said Massberg. "You never pay her any attention."

"Well, actually I like her quite a bit," said Stuart. "She's a classy woman who married down, and she's never given Herbert anything to complain about."

"If you admire her," said Massberg, "you hide it well."

"Didn't mean to hide it," said Stuart. "I'm restrained. I assumed she'd understand. She's restrained herself."

"Everybody enjoys a little flattery," said Massberg.

"I suppose," said Stuart. "But what are her paintings like?"

"Ghastly," said Massberg.

"Oh," said Stuart. "I'm afraid I'm not terribly surprised."

"What about the nanny?" asked Massberg. "Is she any good?"

"Better be," Cross replied, "otherwise, I'll leave a prestigious job to write my novel and spend all my newly liberated time baking cupcakes for the class picnic and picking Legos out of the bottoms of my bare feet."

"You misunderstood me," said Massberg "I didn't wonder if she could nanny. I wondered if she could paint."

Cross smiled broadly, and then shrugged. "What are the chances?" he asked. "No education. No training. And list for me the great black painters hanging now in the Metropolitan."

"But you think she's a good nanny?" asked Massberg.

"Took the children all of half an hour to fall in love with her," said Stuart.

"Speaking of children," said Kika, "Where are they?"

"I don't have any idea where they are," said Andie.

"Wherever they are," said Stuart, "I'm sure they're perfectly safe. Unless of course they're being sniped," he said, giving Kika a meaningful look.

"Honestly," Kika responded. "You're such an old lady, Stuart. If you took the local paper, you'd calm down. You're acting as if Ossining were the wild, wild West."

"The *New York Times* is my local paper," said Stuart.

"Not anymore," said Kika.

"Who has the energy for two dailies?" asked Stuart.

"I thought you were about to retire," said Kika.

"Pipes is right," said Stuart. "I was being theatrical. I won't quit. I might be fired, though" he said, his face brightening with the prospects of using this scenario to torture his wife and her friends. "I might be forced out. Humiliated. See me in a rocker then, out on the porch, pawing through the *Ossining Citizen Register*."

"Never happen," said Rick Massberg. "You're right at the top of your profession." Rick had brown hair cut as if his mother had put a soup bowl over his head. He was wearing New Balance hiking boots that had never seen a trail, a green flannel shirt and pleated chinos, which seemed designed to accentuate his pear-shaped bottom.

Stuart gave himself points for tolerating his dorky and apparently guileless protégé. "There's something endearing about ambition exposed," he once explained to Andie, "particularly if it's hapless ambition." When sending Massberg out on company business, Stuart often apologized in advance to his contemporaries. "He's a little creepy around the edges, but also brilliant," he'd explain. "The man's read everything."

Despite the edge of condescension, Stuart relished Massberg's company. What secretly delighted the older man was to feign deep humility, and then let his junior contradict him. Which was what he was doing now.

"Pipes is right," said Stuart. "If I leave Acropolis, it probably won't be my decision. I'll be pushed. It'll be a defenestration."

"Now you are overdramatizing," said Rick. "You'll never be fired. You're Herbert Glass's golden boy. He loves you better than either of his own flesh-and-blood sons. Besides which, you've been validated by the world at large. *Publishers Weekly* called you the best line editor in the country. Every time they run an attack on Octopus, they call you up for a quote."

"That's because I'm the only editor in New York who doesn't yet owe his job to the Octopus Corporation," said Stuart.

"There's that," said Massberg, "but you're also a master with a pencil."

" 'A line will take us hours maybe;' " said Stuart.

"'Yet if it does not seem a moment's thought,
Our stitching and unstitching has been naught.'"

"Do you have all of Yeats by memory?" asked Massberg, breaking in.

"Oh no," said Stuart. "Certainly not."

"It was great," said Andie. "We'd get caught in traffic coming down Eleventh Avenue, and he'd recite 'Sailing to Byzantium' for me."

"This is no country for all men," said Stuart, as if to illustrate his wife's point. "Or for line editors either.

"'Better go down upon your marrow-bones,'" he continued, encouraged by his wife's approval.

"'And scrub a kitchen pavement, or break stones.'"

"All right, all right," said Andie.

"Nobody cares about line editors anymore," said Stuart. "Nobody cares about the text at all. We didn't even read the most expensive book we bought last year. We paid two million for a name and a title, for smoke and mirrors."

"That was a bidding war," said Massberg. "There was no time to examine the manuscript. None of the other editors saw it either. And I'll bet you anything *The Red Hot Ticket* earns out. Besides, I'm glad we were able to get the Glass family excited about a new book for the first time in what, twenty-five years? Man can't live by back lists alone. We need a fresh name. We need to show we're players."

"That's where you and I disagree," said Stuart.

"Agree or disagree," said Massberg, "Herbert Glass will never surrender Stuart Cross. You're what people think of when they think Acropolis. Isn't the man who writes those epics about the Civil War heroine going to leave Holt for you? That's what he told Cindy Adams. What is his name? Hammacher Schlemmer?"

"His name is Martin Brookstone, and I wish he would leave Holt, but I'm afraid he's just trying to drive up his price," said Stuart.

"Either way," said Massberg. "You have a reputation."

"Thanks," said Cross, "but you have no idea how fed up I am. Can't do the exact same job for thirty years without burnout."

Rick wagged his head. "You know better," he said. "It won't be the same old job." He moved to his host's side, and awkwardly threw a stubby arm over the taller man's shoulders. "Editor today, tomorrow, Editorial Director," he said, smiling out at a knot of embarrassed listeners. "I bet Herbert Glass sells the apartment within the year and retreats to Blue Hill, Maine, full time. The king is dead. Long live the king," Rick said, stepped away from his colleague, and began to clap. Nobody else joined in.

"So," said Pipes, when the silence had grown embarrassing, "what does anybody think about the nanny and the bathtub?"

The story of Tillie Cove, which had been appearing on the cover of the *New York Post* for two days, had finally gained sufficient authenticity to surface in the B section of the *New York Times* that morning. Cove was an English au pair working on the Upper East Side of Manhattan. She had been charged with manslaughter after allegedly allowing a fourteen-month-old to drown in a bathtub, while she cooed on the phone long distance to a beau in London. That was the *Post* story the first day. The second day, the *Post*'s story was that Mr. and Mrs. Harrison Crown 3rd were eating at Le Bernardin, when their son drowned. An unnamed source revealed that they had shared an order of periwinkles. The entire tragedy, the girl on the telephone, the child perishing in the background, had been recorded by the video security system of the apartment in which it occurred.

"Wasn't there a case like this in Newton, Massachusetts?" asked Kika.

"That's right. Louise Woodward. Back in 1997," said Andie. "The Crown child drowned. Woodward was charged with having shaken a baby to death."

"Louise," said Stuart. "Why does that name ring a bell?"

"It's the name of our new nanny," said Andie.

"Oh," said Stuart, "I knew I'd heard it recently."

"You heard it," said Andie.

"I think Miss Cove will go to jail," said Pipes.

"The camera is a new element," said Stuart. "Which should make it an open-and-shut case."

"Should, but doesn't," said the tax lawyer.

"What you want," said Andie, "is a nanny who will love the children. A good nanny. Like the one Winston Churchill had."

"But not too good," said Kika. "I have a friend whose daughter at Brown won't speak to her biological parents. She spent Christmas vacation in Queens filming the family of her long-time Jamaican nanny. Bitsy Vander has no interest in her actual mother and father. She won a prize for an essay about her nanny titled, 'What Love Means.'"

"And I guess love doesn't mean paying the bills at Brown," said Stuart.

"Nope," said Kika. "Love has nothing to do with paying the bills at Brown."

"The trouble with nannies at all," said Andie, "is that you're damned if you do, and you're damned if you don't. Fall into a truly bad nanny, and you'll lose the children to a grisly death. Fall into a truly marvelous nanny, and you'll just lose them."

CHAPTER 3

"They're with the paragon."

"That's why we picked Louise Washington," said Cross. "Born in the U.S. Educated in England. She's free of troubling ethnicity. Besides which, I don't believe she has a home. We know for a fact that she doesn't have a home phone."

"That's not the reason we picked her," said Andie tartly. "Miss Washington is willing to live in. She'll do light housekeeping and the children's laundry. Her artistic aspirations may be exaggerated—whose artistic aspirations aren't exaggerated in this day and age?—but she draws beautifully. She speaks English and has a driver's license. Her references are superb."

"Is she a looker?" asked Rick.

The host smiled. "She's a fine miniature," he started, but pulled up when Andie put an arm on his shoulder.

"Stuart, dear," she said, clearly exasperated. "Would you please, please put a cork in it?"

"What ever happened to that Scandinavian?" asked Rick.

"Back to Scandinavia," said Stuart.

"And the *jeune fille*?" asked Rick. "Dominique?"

"Back to France," said Stuart.

"Sounds a good system," said Rick.

"Was a good system at the time," said Stuart. "The children are getting older. We want them to have some continuity in their lives. We want a woman who needs us more than we need her."

"Now that you have a professional nanny," said Massberg, "maybe you *can* write that novel."

"Isn't it a little late," said Pipes, "to be starting out on a literary career?"

"There's always time," said Stuart with feeling. "Grant was dying of cancer when he finished his great autobiography. Trollope's mother is another case in point."

"Whose mother?" asked Heather from Bathos.

"Trollope's mother," said Stuart.

"Trollope who?" asked Heather.

"Anthony Trollope," said Stuart. "Anthony Trollope's mother. Anthony Trollope, the well-known English writer," he continued with asperity.

"Oh, yes, of course," said Heather. "He writes for Public Television. I didn't know he had a mother. Or rather, I didn't know his mother wrote."

"Frances Trollope didn't complete her first book until she was fifty," said Stuart loudly, as if the increase in volume would correct the impression that Trollope was a television hack. "When she set down her pen at the age of seventy-six, she'd produced one hundred fourteen volumes."

"Besides which," said Andie, "Stuart has already started. He published a story when he was still at Yale. 'The Last Red Indian' was in *The Best Best Stories of 1956* and just republished in *The Best Best Stories of the Century*. Herbert Glass sent us a bottle of Booker's to celebrate."

"Booker's?" asked Heather.

"It's bourbon," said Stuart.

"I still remember the afternoon I read Stuart's story," said Rick Massberg. "I was pre-law at the time. I was in the Widener Library at Harvard. I read it right through. Then I read it again. I remember thinking, *if an American, who is virtually my contemporary, can create a story this beautiful, and this sad, then I don't want to be in law. I want to be in publishing. I want to hold that man's coat.* That one rainy afternoon spun me around," he said morosely. "I'd almost certainly be a full partner by now."

"Law's loss is literature's gain," said Stuart, "but I wish you wouldn't praise me with such regret."

"True beauty always excites regret," said Rick. "It's a magnificent story. I think I can recite the ending," he said, clearing his throat. "Help me here, Andie," Rick said.

"That's all right," said Stuart.

"You don't have to recite it," said Andie, presenting Rick with a large red hardback with "The Best Best Stories of the Century" engraved on the spine in golden letters. "Page three hundred twelve," she said. Massberg found the place, cleared his throat, and read: " 'He saw them in their thousands, and in their hundreds of thousands. They were in automobiles and cutting the sky in jets. They were afraid.' "

" 'They stank of coffee and urine,' " said Andie.

" 'It is the evening of the Battle of the Little Bighorn,' " Rick read on, " 'and we are the Sioux. We carry lances bowed with scalps still wet. The old men dream dreams. The young man have visions. We are the dead,' " read Massberg. " 'All dead.' "

"My apologies to James Joyce," said Stuart.

"Better than Joyce," said Massberg. "Better than Eliot."

"Come on now," said Stuart.

Massberg shrugged apologetically. "Just my opinion," he said. "I'm entitled to my opinion."

Wallace Stevens had joined the group at this point. "Listen, Stuart," he said. "I just need to say it again: If you ever do want to kick the traces, I'd be honored to handle your work. Honored."

Although he couldn't have explained exactly why, this was beginning to make even Stuart uncomfortable. "If you'll excuse me," he said, "I'd better check on the outside guests." He turned and walked through the kitchen and out the back door. He felt the chill night air on his face, and then he smelled cigarettes. Stuart had grown up in a family of smokers, and despite the triumph of damning statistics, the odor of tobacco burning was still a comfort and a reassurance.

A female form appeared close to his own. "Want one?" Heather asked, her young face a white blur in the darkness. "Remember me? I'm the stupid cunt," she said, fishing the red and white box of Marlboros out of a purse, flipping the top and pointing the package toward Stuart.

"Sorry," said Stuart. "I'd had a bit to drink. And you should know better. Anthony Trollope. You should know who he is."

"And what good would that do me?" Heather asked.

"Isn't knowledge power?" asked Stuart. "Isn't that what your generation believes?"

"Knowledge of Anthony Trollope is not power," said Heather. "This much I know." Then she turned to look at the building they had come out of.

"I love the way Andie furnished the place. She's a great hostess. The guacamole was a treat. And the wine. Though none of it red. Don't you like red wine?"

"I love red wine," said Stuart. "Anything from Bordeaux."

"Your favorite?" Heather asked.

"Lafite-Rothschild."

"My goodness," said Heather.

"I've had it once," Stuart said. "Glass served it to me once. I forget now the occasion. The wine I remember."

"So why wasn't there any?" Heather asked. "I don't mean Lafite-Rothschild. I mean red wine."

"White sofas," said Stuart.

Heather nodded. "Of course," she said. "I keep forgetting that you live here now. It's a wonderful place."

Stuart looked back over his shoulder, nodded, took another drag on the cigarette. "Should hold its value," he said. "We have the largest lawn in the neighborhood. Twice as large as anybody else's."

"Must increase your taxes," said Heather.

"No," said Stuart. "Half of what looks like my lawn actually still belongs to the developer. Couldn't get the easement to build that close to the road."

"Good deal," said Heather.

"I guess so," said Stuart. "Although I still like the city best. I'm going to miss it."

"Really," said Heather. "And what about the city are you going to miss?"

"Late night takeout," said Stuart. "We moved here to feel safe. Andie's still scared."

"Hush now," said Heather, "here comes Cassandra herself."

Andie appeared at the back door, paused, and now was headed to join her husband and the agent.

"Smoking," she said as Stuart and Heather turned to face her.

"Hello," said Heather. "Wonderful party."

"Thanks so much for coming," said Andie and turned to her husband.

"Notice anything?" she asked.

"It's gotten dark," Stuart said. "And very cold. And yes, I'm smoking."

"What time is it?" asked Andie, peering up at Stuart with that famously despairing face of hers.

Stuart glanced at his Swiss Army watch. "It's six fifteen," he said. "Or thereabouts. If there had been trouble," he said, anticipating his wife's question, "the nanny could have called. You didn't tell her to hurry."

"She couldn't have called," said Andie. "Remember the cell phone revolution you started? We all surrendered our phones. We never gave one to Miss Washington. But even you and I had our phones disconnected. We're getting on this new plan you worked out. We just buy the phones. They'll set it all up. No contract to sign. We were supposed to get the phones today, but they hadn't come in."

"Trust me," said Stuart. "We'll get the phones soon. They're nifty little gadgets."

"I'm sure," said Andie, "but in the meantime, there isn't a cell phone in the family."

"Calm down," said Stuart. "Relax. Live in the moment. Remember Lamaze. Breathe deeply. The girls are fine. They're with the paragon."

CHAPTER 4

A Beloved Doctor

The invitation had indicated that the party would be over at seven, but it was nine when Andie came upon Wallace Stevens passed out in the Jacuzzi. Stuart walked-carried the agent downstairs, where he was served coffee. "You should write," the agent kept saying in slurred tones. "Be honored to represhent you. You have the talent." He made the speech to Stuart, to Andie, and then as the agent got into the back of the Lincoln Town Car, Stuart heard Stevens talking to the driver. "Be honored to represhent you," he said, as the car's tires crunched gravel, and it pulled out into the night. Stuart batted his arms against the cold and went back into the house.

Ten found both husband and wife moving through the great room, each with a thirty-gallon green plastic bag, collecting the detritus of social intercourse.

"Let's go through this one more time," said Stuart. "Were the children okay?"

"Yes," said Andie. "The children were okay."

"Who was worried?" asked Stuart.

"I was worried," said Andie.

"Who was right?" asked Stuart.

"We were both right," said Andie. "The new nanny had a flat tire. She needed help. It was a lucky thing that you went out and found her."

"You're missing the larger point," Stuart said, and sat down on a sofa, holding his half-filled garbage bag firmly in one hand.

"Yes," said Andie.

"The point," said Stuart, "*is* that the girls were never in any danger."

"Okay," said Andie. "I'll give you that."

"And while we're at it," said Stuart disconsolately. "Would you remind me why we didn't have this party catered?"

"Two reasons," said Andie. "One, we can't afford it. And then security. We don't want strangers in our house, counting the silverware, ogling the little girls. Remember *Ransom*? The movie opens with a catered party and one of the waitresses has a tattoo on her throat. You glimpse it just under the high white collar. You think, *My God, it's a tattoo*. Then you chastise yourself for narrow-mindedness. She turns out to be working for the kidnappers."

"It was a movie," said Stuart. "Movies are more dramatic than life is. I'm not Mel Gibson. You're not Rene Russo. Nor are we fabulously rich."

"We look rich," said Andie.

"Every nickel is in this house," said Stuart. "The Bank of New York owns the house."

"Criminals don't know about mortgages," said Andie.

Stuart wagged his head sadly. "And what do you know about criminals?" he asked. "Just admit that you were wrong."

"This is silly," said Andie. "You're tired. Plus drunk. Go on up to bed, I'll finish."

So Stuart left his half-filled garbage bag beside the chair and climbed the stairs alone. He paused outside Jane's room to listen as the new nanny—Sugar, or Miss Washington, depending upon your relationship with her—read to his children in a clear and compelling voice:

"He hadn't gone a yard when—Bang!
With open Jaws, a Lion sprang,
And hungrily began to eat
The Boy: beginning at his feet.

"Now, just imagine how it feels
When first your toes and then your heels . . ."

Not exactly soothing, Stuart thought, *but traditional. Which counts for a lot*, he thought. He considered poking his head in, kissing the girls goodnight, but decided against it. He was slightly intimidated by his new employee, and he didn't like his children to see him drunk.

When the master of the house came uncertainly down the stairs at eight that Sunday, he was in jeans and wearing Adidas running shoes without socks. He felt cold air around his ankles. Miss Washington had set both girls up at a table with crayons and construction paper. Louise was in a blue dress and high heels. Over this she wore a hooded sweatshirt, which was ordinarily kept in the broom closet.

"Where are you going?" asked Stuart.

"Church," said the nanny. "I'll be leaving in half an hour, back by ten thirty. Your wife knows about this."

"Fine," said Stuart. "I have no objection. Please pray for my immortal soul," he said, "presuming I have one. What's that quote? Renan. 'Oh God, if there is a God, save my soul, if I have a soul.' "

The nanny smiled wanly.

Stuart turned to his girls.

Ginny, his eldest daughter, the fat one, had a large stain on the front of her white blouse. Stuart supposed it was maple syrup. Jane—also in a hooded sweatshirt—slipped off her chair, ran, and hugged her father around the knees. "Sugar made us pancakes," she said. "Not super pancakes like yours, but pancakes."

"Blueberry pancakes?" asked Stuart.

"Yes," said Jane, "but with the blueberries not broken. They were good," Jane said, rubbing her belly with one hand, "but I like Dad's super pancakes better."

Ginny looked up from her drawing. "Hi Dad," she said. "You know what, though. I like the pancakes better when the blue-berries aren't all mushed."

Stuart nodded dumbly and looked over to Miss Washington, who was working at the sink. Boy, but she was a small woman. The résumé had said five feet, but he'd guess that she was four foot eleven or even four foot ten. "Thank you for making the girls' breakfast," he said.

Miss Washington smiled briefly, and then looked demurely down at her hands.

"Sugar cooked the pancakes, and cleaned up all without hot water," said Ginny.

"Why'd you do that?" asked Stuart, looking over at the nanny. "A special recipe? A challenge?"

"No," Louise told him sweetly. "I didn't use hot water because there is no hot water."

"Oh," said Stuart, "let me look." And then he went to the door to the basement and down into its depths. Once below ground, he switched on the overhead, and put a hand against a pipe coming out of the top of the unit. No heat. He leaned over and hit the restart button on the oil burner. He heard a mechanical rasp and then the growl of ignition. Flames danced behind the Pyrex window. He stood perfectly still. The burner continued to roar healthily. Behind this clamor he could just make out another sound, much lower on the scale, but insistent. He walked across the basement, came to a spot where four pipes were racked together above his head and between the joists. He reached up and touched them. One was cold and he could feel water pulsing.

"I think it'll be okay now," he told the nanny, when he got back to the kitchen. "Give it some time."

Louise smiled and nodded.

"Sugar drew us toys," said Jane. "She drew us the toys we wanted."

"Mine isn't a toy," said Ginny.

"Mine isn't a toy either," said Jane emphatically.

"Show me," said Stuart, and Jane held up a picture of a revolver.

"You want a revolver?"

"I want an equalizer," said Jane.

"Why's that?" said Stuart.

"I just want it," said Jane. "In case somebody's bigger than me."

"She wants to shoot me," said Ginny.

"I do not," said Jane. "I just want it. For self-defense."

"All right," said Stuart, "and you?" he said, looking at his eldest child. Ginny held up a picture of a portable CD player. "I want a personal, portable musical system, so I can listen to Mozart and not my silly little sister."

Stuart nodded. "We'll see," he said. "But you both have to be dreadfully good."

"Do we have to be good before we can go to the zoo?" asked Jane. "Sugar wants to take us to the zoo. She wants to show us the lion. We heard about a lion last night. Now we want to go see one."

" 'And always keep ahold of Nurse,' " quoted Stuart. " 'For fear of finding something worse.' "

"So can we go?" asked Ginny.

"Not today," said Stuart. "Maybe Monday. You have Monday off, I think. Ask your mother. She's not up yet. I'm going out now to get the special Lord's day coffee. Anybody want to come?" he asked with forced cheerfulness.

"On the motorcycle?" asked Jane.

"We've had this conversation," Stuart said. "You know I can't take you on the bike. We can go in the Saab, though, and whoever gets to the car first can sit up front with Daddy."

"No thank you, Daddy dear," said Jane.

"Ginny?" he asked.

His older daughter looked up from her paper and crayons. "Can I have a special Lord's day candy bar?" she asked. "A Sunday Twix?"

"Nope," said Stuart.

"Then I'll stay here," said Ginny.

"Coffee's made," said Miss Washington, pointing to the black Capresso, which was more than half filled.

"Still fresh," she said.

"Andie requires a cappuccino on the weekend," Stuart explained. "Thanks for that, though," he said, shrugging at the coffee pot, as he passed through the kitchen, pausing to put on a Windbreaker and take down his helmet from the top shelf of the closet.

Then he turned to face the new nanny. "I'm sorry we didn't go out for you sooner," he said. "It was a party, you know, and I'm afraid I'd had a bit to drink. There were a lot of cops out there."

Louise nodded and smiled. "The parking lot was full of glass," she said. "Fool children with BB guns. It wouldn't have been a problem," she said, "if the tire iron had any length on it. The bolts must have been tightened pneumatically. I couldn't get the leverage I needed. Ginny was the one who remembered where the pipe was. That's why we had the tire changed when you came. She's a smart one," the nanny said, and switched her eyes to the older girl, twinkled, and switched them back to the girl's father.

"The manufacturers want their vehicles light in order to meet federal standards for gas mileage, so they give us toys instead of real jacks," said Stuart. "I keep a piece of pipe and a rag under the back seat of both cars. I use the pipe for an extension. I should have shown it to you. Glad Ginny remembered."

"You know she tried to tell me about it right away, but I didn't listen," said the nanny. "I don't know if it's because of my wooden ears, or because Ginny isn't used to having anybody hear her. In either case," she said. "We're beyond that now."

Stuart paused and wondered if he should accept this challenge. Although she didn't seem hostile, this bite-size woman was hinting that he, Stuart, did not pay enough attention to his own daughter. He decided to let it go.

"I'm impressed that you got the tire changed at all," he said. "Most women can't change a tire. That should be on your résumé. Which is not to find fault with the résumé you already have," he said.

"I like your friends," said the nanny. "All but the one called Massberg. He gave me the creeps."

"You'll get to like him," said Stuart. "He's really a sweet man."

Outside, Stuart removed the tarp from his motorcycle, inserted the key.

Ben's Extreme Deli had a line, and so Stuart picked up a copy of the *Ossining Citizen Register* to look at while he waited.

The front page above the fold was devoted to the picture of a hunter green Range Rover which stood alone in a parking lot, roped off with yellow crime-scene ribbons held in place by orange highway cones. "Ofay" had been written in black paint on the windshield.

The headline: PEDIATRICIAN SHOT TO DEATH IN OSSINING.

The story: "Law enforcement officials have ruled out suicide in the tragic death Saturday of a Croton pediatrician whose lifeless body was found in the front seat of a 1999 Range Rover in the parking lot of the Hilltop Office complex on Route 9.

"While Samuel French, of 108 Sandhill Road, was apparently killed with the bullets from his own pistol, police report that the pattern of wounds and the absence of powder burns indicate that he was shot from some distance and by another and as yet unnamed individual.

"Town Police Chief Vincent Palumbo told *The Citizen Register*: 'This sort of brutal and apparently random murder is extremely rare in Ossining. Please be assured that we will do everything in our power to bring the killer or killers to justice. Briarcliff and Croton Police have offered to help with the investigation.'"

A second story below the fold and headlined RED VAN SOUGHT IN MURDER reported: "*The Citizen Register* has learned of an accident on the Albany Post Road that might have precipitated the shooting of a Croton pediatrician Saturday. Mrs. George Wooding, a

31

neighbor, told *The Citizen Register* of a collision between a red Ford van and the Range Rover in which the murder victim was found. This took place on the Albany Post Road, just south of the intersection with Scarborough Station Road.

" 'It was the van's fault,' said Mrs. Wooding. 'The van stopped at a green light, and the Range Rover ran into it from behind. The Ford had something about God written on the side. The Range Rover had MD plates. I'm sure of that, because I was so shocked to hear those words and coming from a doctor.

" 'It was dusk,' according to Mrs. Wooding, 'and difficult to see, but it looked as if the driver of the van was black. The man in the Range Rover used the n-word. He had a bumper sticker that read: "I'd rather be sailing." '

"Town Police Chief Vincent Palumbo would not corroborate these details except to say that the driver of a red painter's van was sought for questioning."

Glancing back to the first story, Stuart read on.

"Chief Palumbo also would not speculate on the meaning of the racial slur, which had been written on the windshield of the victim's vehicle in black paint.

" 'The case is wide open,' he said. 'For all we know, that was written by somebody else, after the incident.'

"A pediatrician who had practiced in the county for several years, French was apparently shot to death with a 357 Magnum Colt Python Elite, which he had used in target practice that day at a range in Tarrytown, New York.

"Samuel French, 42, is survived by his wife, Laura, his children, Alexander and Victoria, and his parents, Michael and Sarah French of Palm Beach, Florida. (See Obituary, page 5B.)

" 'Sam believed in giving back,' said Andrew Paton, the pediatrician with whom French shared a practice in offices located in Croton, Ossining, and Tarrytown. 'He contributed generously to local charities. He used to spend his Saturdays teaching sailing to youngsters at the Shattamuck Yacht Club in Ossining.

"'Samuel was a beloved doctor. Just last week he gave a speech on nutrition and education at the Tarrytown Hilton for the annual meeting of the Westchester Chapter of the NAACP.'"

CHAPTER 5

Spend the entire day with your girls.

Back home Stuart found the kitchen empty and tidy in a way it hadn't been empty and tidy since he and Andie had taken possession. The room echoed when he slammed the door. The counters were clear. He put his helmet down on the granite island beside the sink—even the sink was empty. "Hello!" he called. No answer. He hung his Windbreaker over the back of a chair and took the two cups of coffee and a plastic rose out of a brown paper bag. Leaving the bag on the counter, he put the newspaper under one arm, clamped the plastic stem of the plastic rose in his teeth, took a cup in each hand. "Daddy's home," he said, through clenched teeth as he climbed the stairs.

Janey was under the covers with Andie. Ginny was on the floor in the red snarl of her mother's silk dressing gown. She had diamond clips in her ears and was trying to work her feet into a pair of high heels.

"The nanny's gone to church?" asked Stuart, his voice distorted by the rose in his mouth. Andie nodded mutely. He sat on the edge of the bed and put the two brown cardboard cups on the end table, then took the rose out of his mouth, handed this to his wife. "Sorry," he said. "It's an air freshener."

"It's a rose," said Andie. "Thank you, dear."

"You of course are a rose, but were always a rose," said Stuart. Then he leaned over the bed, and they kissed.

"Can we go shopping?" Ginny asked.

Andie pulled out of her husband's embrace to answer her eldest. "You can come with your mother," she said. "Today I'm going to finally get a new VCR."

Stuart straightened, took the top off his drink, and then turned to look at his elder daughter. "If you stand up in those, darling," he told her, "it will end badly. If by some miracle you don't fall over, you'll punch holes in the gown I bought your mother for Christmas."

"Let me try once," said Ginny, but she'd already lost her father's attention. He had drawn the copy of the *Ossining Citizen Register* from under his arm and was spreading it out on the bed for his wife to see. "Explains the police cars," he said.

"Daddy," said Ginny.

"No, Gin," said Stuart, without looking at his daughter. "You can take off the shoes and wear the robe. You can take off the robe and wear the shoes. You can't wear both at the same time."

"My goodness," said Andie, sitting up in bed, taking the lid off her own coffee while she studied the paper.

"Move to the country," said Stuart. "Safe at last."

Andie wagged her dark head impatiently. "Let me finish reading this," she said.

Stuart nodded, drank foam.

The phone rang and Stuart picked it up. "Thanks," he said. "No, it wasn't that much of a mess. Wallace Stevens fell asleep in

35

the bathtub. Yeah, well. We knew he was trouble. Here she is," he said and passed the phone to his wife.

"I saw," said Andie into the mouthpiece. "Stuart bought the *Citizen Register*. That was just down the road. You know everybody don't you?" she said and then paused. "Uh huh," she said, "Uh huh. Makes sense. And they think he was on drugs? Do they have any idea who the shooter was? Uh huh. That's a lot for them to know so soon." Then another long pause, while Andie nodded and sipped her coffee.

"We never let them out alone anyway," she said, finally. "Oh my God. Really? Are you sure?" Then there was another long pause, while Andie listened.

"Yes," she said. "Stuart is small," she said and giggled. "I don't mind. I think all that is overrated." Then she paused again to listen.

"Yes, I don't like to boast, but it is tasty," she said. "You know I went through a dozen avocados. That's the trick, finding avocados that are ripe, but not rotten. Sure you can have the recipe." Another pause.

"No, he's not going to like your present. All right then. I'll tell him."

Her husband was pacing unhappily around the room trying to decipher the conversation from the half of it he could hear.

"I wouldn't take Tommy to that," Andie said. "I know the trailers look innocent enough, but it's actually quite violent." Another pause.

"Now *that's* a decent movie. A much better choice. Yes, Mel Gibson does look good. No, he's not in a kilt this time. Okay then. Let's eat dinner this week. Promise? Chinese?"

Andie hung up the phone, took another pull on her coffee, and looked back at the paper.

"Yes?" said Stuart.

"What?" asked Andie.

"What did Kika say?"

Andie shrugged. "Nothing."

"She must have said something," said Stuart.

Andie sighed. "They had a good time yesterday. Oh, and Kika's subscribed to the *Ossining Citizen Register* for you."

"When you said she knows everybody?" prompted Stuart.

"That's right," said Andie. "Kika knows somebody who knows somebody in the police department. Apparently this guy," she said, pointing at the picture of the Range Rover, "was a bit of a hothead. Got in a fight with a referee at a Little League game a year ago. Lawsuits on both sides. Somebody heard him screaming at a driver he'd run into right outside our window. He had his gun with him, so he was all fired up. And there are allegations that he was taking drugs."

"But he's the one who got killed," said Stuart.

"That's right," said Andie. "Having a gun and screaming at other drivers doesn't mean you have the stomach to use it. He was—after all—a pediatrician."

"And what about me being small?" Stuart asked.

Andie looked blank, as if trying to remember. "You know, that part of the conversation has completely slipped my mind," she said.

Jane poked her head out from under the covers. "What's a pediatrician?" she asked.

"A baby doctor, stupid," said Ginny. "Doctor Armstrong's our pediatrician."

"But I'm not a baby," said Jane.

"Yes, you are," said Ginny, trying uncertainly to get up off the floor, the robe still on, her feet crammed into the toes of her mother's high-heeled shoes.

"No Ginny," said Stuart, as his daughter stepped backward and began to lose her balance. There was a loud, ripping noise.

Stuart didn't look in the direction of the accident. He stood, picked up his cup of coffee and headed out of the room. "I'll be downstairs," he said and was gone.

It was noon before Andie had both girls dressed and ready for "the day's adventure," a trip to Ace Appliance City in Hawthorne to buy a new VCR.

"I'm so pleased to get a chance to be alone with the children," Andie told Stuart. "I'll probably be working late often next week." Louise had been given the keys to the Saab and told not to come back until six thirty P.M. "You have things to do, right?" Andie said, and Louise shrugged. "Always," she said.

"As long as I'm here, she needn't be," Andie explained, when Stuart complained that this wasn't the regularly scheduled day off. "I'll take the children with me to the store. You can work, or go out on the motorcycle, or take a nap for that matter."

Andie and the girls were pulling out of the drive when the phone rang. Stuart picked it up. "It's Warren Justice Bookerman the Third of the *New York Post*," a voice said. "Is Andie Wilde there?" "Yeah, she's here," Stuart said, and called his wife in from the car.

Once Andie had the phone in hand, her husband retreated to his office, and opened the fat brown envelope he'd gotten from Wallace Stevens.

Then Andie was standing in the doorway, knocking tentatively on the frame. Stuart looked up from his reading, annoyed.

"I've got good news, and I've got bad news," Andie said.

"Bad news first this time."

38

"Sir John Gielgud died."

"Oh," said Stuart. "I'm so sorry."

"Now the good news," said Andie.

"Yeah."

"I get to write about him. An appreciation."

Stuart nodded.

"Now the bad news," said Andie.

"Yeah?"

"I have to write the piece now, file it by eight tonight."

"Oh," said Stuart.

"Now the good news," said Andie.

"Yeah?" said Stuart. "What's the good news?"

"You get to spend the entire day with your girls."

CHAPTER 6

"In the Monticello."

When he first stepped through the automatic doors at Ace, Stuart felt his spirits rocket unexpectedly. *Why I didn't I come here sooner?* he thought.

He'd once read an article in a fringe magazine reporting that subliminal messages were piped out to the customers, the sounds masked by the hum of fluorescent lights. If there were such messages, he wondered what they'd be. *New? Now? Free? Win!*

No question but that the atmosphere was highly charged. Ozone seemed to have been pumped into the air. Show tunes were playing in the background. The girls shot out ahead of their father and onto the gleaming floors.

"This is an amazing store," said Stuart, gazing at the burnished aluminum stands stocked with electric toothbrushes, toaster ovens, and heated foot baths. "Looks as if they sell everything."

"Daddy, Daddy," said Jane. "Can I have an equalizer?"

"An equalizer," said Stuart. "What's an equalizer?"

"It's what you get to defend yourself with, if other people are bigger than you are."

"I still don't know what you mean," said Stuart.

"She means a gun," said Ginny. "A pistol. To shoot me with."

"I don't think they're going to have guns here," said Stuart.

"If they do have pistols," said Janey, "will you buy one for me, Daddy?"

"Yes," said Stuart, softening. "If they have pistols, I will certainly buy you the best one they have."

"If they have CD players," asked Ginny, "will you buy me the best they have?"

"No," said Stuart.

"That's not fair," said Ginny.

Stuart looked at his eldest daughter. "Is that the same shirt you ate breakfast in?" he asked. The maple syrup stain had been worked on, but was still clearly visible.

"What does my shirt have to do with it?" asked Ginny.

"I only wish you'd change it," said Stuart. "I don't like it when you look like an unmade bed."

"Does that mean that you won't buy me a CD player?" Ginny said, her voice falling.

"We're here," Stuart said, lowering his own voice, "to buy your mother a VCR. Then home."

The joy having gone out of the expedition, the little party hiked glumly along until it came to an area lined with TV monitors, all switched on, all set to the same golf match, all with the volume off. Putting an arm around the shoulder of each girl, Stuart walked along a wall that had video recorders on three levels, plugged in and set against black fabric, as if they were jewels in a jewelry store. He checked the price tags. One VCR, which was silver, cost $549.99. All the others were black, except for one with fake wood grain and a Sony, which was silver and cost $239.99. Stuart thought Andie would be pleased by the cheaper of the silver VCRs. He left the girls standing together in front of the display and went out on the floor where he found a man, or rather a boy, in a suit. The boy had red hair cut short, acne, and a name tag on his jacket. He seemed to be heading off somewhere and in a terrible hurry.

Stuart stepped in front of the salesman, caught his eye, and put up a hand in the way Indian chiefs used to put up their hands in movies about the wild west.

"Bruce," he said. This was the name on the tag. The boy in the suit looked bewildered.

"Bruce," said Stuart again. "Can you help me?"

The boy nodded, acting as if he'd just been roused from a deep sleep. "Certainly," he said, shaking his head. "Of course I can help. That's what I'm here for."

"Okay," said Stuart, and he took the salesman to the spot where he'd left his two girls.

"Is this a good machine?" he said, pointing at the cheaper silver VCR. "It's a Sony," Stuart said, "and I've had luck with Sonys in the past."

The salesman shrugged. "Whatever you get," he said, "you gotta buy the product insurance."

"I don't want the product insurance," said Stuart. "I want to buy this machine. No insurance. Just tell me what you think of this machine?"

Bruce knelt beside the display, fingered the price tag and then stood back up. "That's a decent unit you've picked out," he said. "And very popular."

"Then we want it," said Stuart nodding.

"Sure," said the salesman.

"Since I have you," said Stuart, "can I ask you some questions?"

"Absolutely," said Bruce, nodding. "That's what I'm here for."

"All right, then," said Stuart. "What does the one I've selected do that the one that costs $169 can't do?"

"That unit," said the salesman, and he pointed, "that unit is a Napoleon, and it's a piece of junk. I don't know why we carry it." He wagged his head sadly. "People buy it, and they're back in here a week later, trying to return it."

"Really?" asked Stuart, excited by the salesman's apparent forthrightness.

Bruce nodded and looked around to make certain they couldn't be overheard. "It shreds the tape," he whispered. "I won't sell it without the policy."

"All right," said Stuart. "I'm convinced. Let's get the silver Sony."

"Just let me check to see if we have the one you want in stock," Bruce said, and walked off to a counter, where he began to work the keyboard on a computer console.

The words of *Guys & Dolls* were being piped out onto the floor: "Luck be a lady tonight. Never get out of my sight. Luck if you've ever been a lady to begin with, luck be a lady tonight."

Stuart put on his reading glasses and went down on one knee to examine the silver VCR, which was on a low shelf in the display.

"It's handsome, don't you think?" he asked the girls.

"Yes," said Ginny. "Can I push the buttons?"

"Not yet," said Stuart. "Wait until we buy our own."

The audio system remained encouraging: "Anyone knows an ant, can't move a rubber tree plant. But he's got high hopes, He's got high hopes."

Now Ginny chimed in. " 'He's got high apple *pie*, in the *sky* hopes.' "

"Having fun?" Stuart asked.

"No," said Ginny.

"And what would make this more enjoyable for you?"

"Shopping for my CD player."

"I want to shop for my pistol," said Janey.

"Look," said Stuart. "It's only going to be a minute now. Then we can look at the movies, if you want. Maybe we can buy a movie you both want to watch on your mother's new VCR.

"You're interested in classical music," he said to Ginny, "we can get *Amadeus*. That's a movie about how the great artist—Mozart—gets betrayed by the envious second-rate artist, Salieri. When you do get your CD player, we're going to get you some Mozart. He's the best."

"Watching a movie would be fun," said Janey.

"Good," said Stuart.

"I don't want to watch a movie with my baby sister," said Ginny. "We have divergerent tastes. I want to listen to my own music. I want to listen to the classics."

"Divergent tastes," said Stuart. "You have divergent tastes."

"I'm not a baby," said Janey.

"Of course you're not a baby, baby," said Stuart, patting his youngest on the head.

"Can't I at least look at the CD players?" asked Ginny.

Stuart put up a hand to silence his daughter. Bruce had turned away from the computer console and was headed back in their direction.

"You want the good news first?" Bruce asked.

"Bad news first," said Stuart.

"I'm afraid we're out of that particular model," Bruce said.

"What's the good news?" asked Stuart.

"We've got one that only costs a hundred dollars more. It's really a much better machine. And simpler to operate."

"But it's black," said Stuart.

"That's right," said the salesman, looking slightly bewildered. "You don't really care about the color, do you?"

"Yes," said Stuart. "I do care about the color. Can we buy the display model?"

The salesman was nodding his head uncertainly. "Let me inquire," he said, spun on his heel and walked off.

Stuart turned to Ginny. "What do you think?" he asked her.

"You want me to be perfectly honest?" Ginny said.

Stuart nodded.

"I think you should buy your daughter a CD player," said Ginny.

Stuart chuckled. "I want to know what you think about VCRs."

"You still want me to be perfectly honest?" asked Ginny again.

"Always," said Stuart.

"I think you're going to get rooked," said Ginny.

"Thanks, dear," said Stuart.

"What does rooked mean?" asked Janey.

"Swindled," said Stuart.

"You're wrong," said Janey, her voice rising, "Daddy is too smart to get swinneled."

"Swindled," corrected Ginny. "Tell her she got it wrong," she said, but her father was turning away from his children to meet Bruce, who was skating across the floor in their direction.

"I've asked stock to look for the box," Bruce said, "but while they're doing that, I want to tell you about a special offer that I'm in a position to make to you today."

"And what's that?" asked Stuart.

"But first of all," Bruce said, "you have to understand that these are delicate pieces of equipment. This technology is brand new. And that the warranty isn't worth the paper it's written on. They only offer a warranty at all so that they can get your name and address."

"There's that," said Stuart.

"And we want satisfied customers," said the boy in the suit.

Stuart nodded.

"Which is why," Bruce said, "we have a special product protection plan. For a nominal fee, we can insure your purchase for up to five years. If anything should go wrong with your equipment—and I mean anything—a licensed technician will come to the house."

"I don't want the insurance," said Stuart. "I told you that."

"And that's cool," said Bruce. "But take a minute to let me tell you how little it costs."

"How much," said Stuart.

"If something went wrong with this machine, and you brought it in to have the problem diagnosed," said Bruce, "they'd charge fifty bucks just to tell you what's wrong. Fixing it would cost even more. Whereas for seventy-nine ninety-nine the unit you buy from me today will be completely protected for three years. If you should sell the VCR before the insurance runs out, the coverage is transferable."

"No," said Stuart. "I want to buy this unit. I'd like a discount, since it is a demo, but I'll pay full price if I need to. I want to buy it now. No insurance."

"All right," said Bruce, wagging his head as if this were the saddest story ever told. "But you're passing up a tremendous deal. I wouldn't be honest if I didn't tell you that you may live to regret your decision."

"Thanks," said Stuart. "But I'll take that chance. Just get me the box."

"All right, I'll check with stock," Bruce said, and headed off.

Five minutes later, he was back. He had the box. He even had the instructions. He didn't have the power cord. Stuart wanted to know if they couldn't remove the power cord from the display. They couldn't. The display power cord was stapled into place.

"I spoke with the manager about your situation," said Bruce. "He told me that you should buy the insurance, and buy the unit. You can take it home, and on Monday you can call the number on your policy. A licensed technician will come to the house with a new power cord. Won't cost you a penny."

"I don't think so," said Stuart. "You know what? Let's buy the one that costs five hundred and forty-nine dollars."

"Okay," said Bruce. "I'll go check on that one," he said, and headed off again.

"Do we need to wait with you?" Ginny asked. "Can't I please take Janey to look at a CD player? Pretty please."

"And a pistol," said Jane, solemnly.

"And where exactly do you want to go?" Stuart asked.

"Up near the registers," said Ginny. "I think the CD players are up near the registers," she said. "And if there are any pistols," she said, giving her little sister a wink, "they'd also probably be near the registers."

"We want to go up near the registers," said Jane.

"All right," said Stuart. "But promise you'll stay together, and up near the registers."

"We promise," said Jane.

47

"Okay," said Stuart, "I'll be coming right along." He walked over to the $549 VCR and began to examine the controls.

Five minutes later, when Bruce had still not appeared, Stuart began to grow anxious about the girls. What was the name of that English woman who turned her back on her infant in a mall and some toughs took the child away and murdered it? He'd read the ghastly story in *The New Yorker*. What was the title of the Ian McEwan novel about the man who lost his daughter at the checkout? *The Child in Time.*

You're being silly, he thought. Both girls had promised to stay near the front of the store. Nobody would try to kidnap Ginny.

Stuart paced uneasily. He looked at his watch. It was eleven forty-five. He looked at his watch again. It was still eleven forty-five. His breathing was shallow. He walked over to the laptops, which were displayed on tables at some distance from the VCRs, but not out of sight. As soon as he got there, though, he was afraid that Bruce would miss him. He went back to the VCR display.

He looked at his watch again. It was eleven forty-seven A.M. He'd collect his children, and *then* look for the salesman. He began to walk toward the front of the store.

Passing through the stereo displays, though, he saw Bruce, speaking intently to a fat, bald man in a blue uniform. Not a postal worker, but an electrician, or plumber, Stuart supposed.

Bruce had the insurance document spread out on the counter. Stuart stepped up behind the salesman and tapped him on the shoulder.

Bruce turned.

"Forget somebody?" Stuart said, but he said it lightly, without letting the anger come into his voice.

Bruce startled, turned to Stuart, and nodded pleasantly. "Be with you in a moment," he said.

Stuart stepped back. The sound system was tootling away. "Up like a rose bud, high on the vine."

"These are delicate instruments," Bruce explained to the man in the uniform. Stuart stood to one side, opening and closing his fists. He could smell the salesman's cloying cologne. The lights were painfully bright, the atmosphere—which had been inviting just minutes ago—seemed hostile now, sterile, and even threatening.

When Bruce finally turned back to face him, Stuart had to breathe deeply to keep the squeak of rage out of his voice. "All right," he told the boy in the suit. "I want the VCR you promised me. I want it now. I also want to speak to your manager."

Bruce blinked, but did not pick up on the implied criticism. "We're in luck," he said. "I found the perfect machine for you. Why don't you bring it to the register, and I'll send the manager up to speak with you."

"It's silver?" asked Stuart.

Bruce nodded. "That's it over there," he said and pointed to a brown box, which was on the floor near a display of fans. "You want me to bring it up front for you?"

"No," said Stuart. "I can do that," and he wondered if this sop was meant to convince him to call off the manager, but apparently not.

"The manager will meet you at the registers," Bruce said.

"I want to find my girls first," Stuart said.

The salesman shrugged. "Do you need to talk to a manager?" he asked.

"Yes," said Stuart.

"Well then you'd better go right up to the register," said Bruce.

"I can't send the manager up to the front of the store, if you're not going to be up there. It's Sunday. He's a busy man."

"Okay," said Stuart, "I'll be there."

"All right then," said Bruce. "Enjoy."

Stuart shouldered the box, walked up to the register, and found himself in line behind the man in the blue uniform. He too had a box on his shoulder. After they'd been standing together for a couple of minutes, the fat man put his box on the floor. Stuart lowered his own box onto the polished floor. They were both standing behind a woman with a shopping cart with a cappuccino machine in it.

Stuart began to scan the room for the girls. For a moment, he couldn't spot them, and he felt the fear tightening at his throat. Then he saw the top of Ginny's head over a rack of movies. *Of course*, he thought, *they're picking out a movie*. The woman with the cappuccino machine moved forward; the man in front of Stuart picked up his box; Stuart picked up his own box; they both moved forward two steps, and then put their boxes down again. The fat, bald man in the blue uniform turned to Stuart, shook his head toward the woman whose cappuccino machine was in a cart. "She's got the right idea," he said.

Stuart nodded. The sound system was sawing away. Stuart couldn't make out the words anymore, but had instead the sensation of drowning in a vat of maple syrup.

"What you got?" Stuart asked the man in front of him.

The fat man sighed. "A VCR. I never know what to buy," he said. "I picked this one out for the brand, it's a Sony. And for looks. It's silver."

Then he peered down at Stuart's box.

"I can see you made the smart decision," he said. "You got the cheap one. I probably should have done the same. You got the Napoleon. But look," he said, tapping the box. "The Napoleon comes in silver. I hadn't known that."

"I got the Napoleon?" said Stuart, and he looked down at his box, astonished. "The salesman told me this was a rotten unit. I tried to get the one you have. They told me they were out of them. But you bought yours after I'd tried to get mine."

The fat man shrugged good-naturedly. "Maybe he found it, after he was done with you? I imagine the stock room is a mess."

"Wait a minute," said Stuart. "Did you buy the insurance?"

The fat man nodded. "It's a delicate piece of equipment," he said. "The technology is all new."

"That little shit," said Stuart, involuntarily, and saw distaste in the face of the man in uniform. But he was angry.

The insignificant betrayal seemed to have hit a vital organ. His spirits plummeted. *Ginny was right*, he thought, *I am being swinneled.* This reminded him of the girls. "Look," he said to the fat man, "would you do me a gigantic favor?"

"Sure," said his new friend, although he seemed surprised, if not dismayed by the urgent tone. "I'm sure they all work, more or less," he said.

"If the manager comes up here," said Stuart, without explaining, "would you tell him I'll be right back?"

"Okay," said the fat man. "You want me to hold your spot in line?"

"That won't be necessary," said Stuart, and he started off toward the place where he'd last seen his daughter's hair. There it was again, mouse brown. He saw it over the racks, in the area where movies were sold. He was breathing heavily by the time he reached the section, and came around a corner expecting his eldest daughter. The hair didn't belong to his daughter, though. It didn't even belong to a girl. He'd spotted a boy of about fourteen in chinos and a T-shirt which had "God Sucks!" written across the torso in red letters. Stuart pivoted and headed back toward the middle of the room. Just then he saw Bruce, skating across the floor at a diagonal. Stuart waved Bruce down. "I'm going to have your ass," he said.

Bruce did something inside his mouth with his tongue and nodded.

"First," said Stuart, "I need to know where the CD players are."

"Are you interested in a CD player?" Bruce asked.

"I just want to know where they are?" said Stuart.

"Wait a minute, and I'll go with you," said Bruce.

"I don't want to wait a minute," said Stuart. "I don't want to go there with you. I want to know where the CD players are. And that's all I want."

"All right," said Bruce, and shrugged. "Have it your way. Sally's off today, so there's nobody over there to help you. The CD players are all in locked cases," he explained patiently, and as if Stuart were a slow learner. Then he leaned back and pointed to a location way at the other end of the store. "Over behind the refrigerators," he said.

Stuart hurried off across the room, scanning as he went. He didn't see Ginny. He didn't see Janey either.

Nor were the girls in the CD section. Nobody was in the CD section. Stuart turned and walked quickly back toward the front of the store. *I only left them for five minutes*, he was telling Andie in his mind. *It wasn't even five minutes. They promised me they'd stay together.*

The sound system was burbling away, "I'm just a girl who can't say no, I'm in a terrible fix . . ."

Stuart wondered if the children were in the bathroom. The restrooms were near the front of the store. He broke into a jog. Several shoppers looked up at him, and then turned away embarrassed.

The men's room appeared to be empty. The door to one of the stalls was locked.

Stuart walked to the stall, dropped on his knees and looked under the partition. Didn't look like anybody had a little girl there. Looked like a man whose chinos and boxers were down around his running shoes. Smelled like a man whose chinos and boxers were down around his running shoes. There was a loud farting sound.

Stuart crawled backward noisily.

"Heah, what are you doing out there?" the man said.

Stuart stood up, walked quickly out into the hall. He knocked on the door to the women's room. No answer. "Knock, knock," he said, opened the door and walked inside. Both stalls were closed. Again Stuart dropped to his knees. He crawled toward the stalls, but quietly this time. He saw one pair of taupe panty hose over high heels. One pair of tube socks over work boots.

He crawled backward quietly, stood, pivoted. *I made it*, he thought, but when he opened the door, he found himself looking right into the face of his real estate agent, Joy Gainsborough-Orsini. A blonde in her late thirties, Joy blushed easily; her cheeks were now bright red. "I love the neighborhood," Stuart said, trying to draw attention away from his appearance in the women's toilet. The bluff worked, or at least Joy Gainsborough-Orsini didn't scream. *So we did pay too much for the house*, he thought, *else she'd call the police.*

The family—it had been a family, hadn't it?—had come to the store to buy a VCR. So Stuart jogged off in the direction of the

VCRs. He was halfway there, scanning the room, when he thought he saw a familiar form in the area that displayed exercise equipment. He veered off to the right. Yes, it was Ginny. Up on an exercise bicycle. He sprinted.

"Are you all right? Baby, are you all right?" he said, catching his breath, putting a hand on his daughter's forearm.

Ginny nodded, but kept peddling. "I've gone twenty-seven calories so far," she told her father. "How many calories in Twix?"

Stuart smiled and took a deep breath.

"I'd guess there are about three hundred calories in a Twix," he said. "Sure am glad to see you, though. But where's your sister?"

"She didn't want to exercise," said Ginny. "Jane doesn't care about her figure. She went to look for pistols."

"You were supposed to watch her," said Stuart.

"That's all right," said Ginny. "She's with a nice man."

"With a man?" he said.

"A man in a raincoat," said Ginny. "A nice stranger in a raincoat with a beard. He gave us candy. Mints. He took her behind the stoves to see if they had any guns there."

"Stoves," said Stuart. "Where are the stoves?"

"Way back in the back room," said Ginny, still pumping away. "Did you know the CD players are all locked up?"

"Yes," said Stuart. "I know. You stay right here. Promise you'll stay right here." He began to trot off in the direction of the appliances. He'd gone about fifty feet when he saw Janey, holding the hand of a man with a beard in a raincoat.

Stuart stopped running and walked toward them, clenching and unclenching his fists, trying to slow his breathing.

The man looked up and caught Stuart's eye. Then he looked down at Jane.

"Is that your dad?" he asked.

"Yes," said Janey. "That's him."

"Well, well," said the man. "So we didn't lose him after all." Then he put out his hand. "George Wooding," he said. "Your little girl was very worried about you," he said. "I was just taking her up to the front desk, and we were going to have them call for you on the PA."

"Thank you," said Stuart.

"I recognized your daughters from the development," Wooding continued. "I was telling her, she should come over some day, for Alice's homemade fudge. You bought Tara?"

"Yes," said Stuart.

"We're right next door," Wooding said. "In the Monticello."

CHAPTER 7

"Nannies come and go."

Tearing across the platform at the Scarborough station that Monday morning, Andie snapped the stiletto heel of her right shoe and pitched forward onto the cement. Dropping her briefcase as she went down, she threw out both hands so that her wrists and palms took the brunt. Rolling to her side, she looked up to see a man in a blue uniform standing with one foot on the platform, one on the train. He had a poker face. Was that concern he was trying to conceal, or mirth? Andie wondered, rising awkwardly to her feet. "All aboard," the conductor said. Andie peeled off the shoes, grabbed her briefcase, and sprinted the remaining distance, jumping into the car in her stocking feet.

Bemused men and women looked up from cups of coffee and around folded newspapers. There was a smattering of applause. Still standing just inside the door, Andie colored slightly. Then she blew the dark bangs out of her eyes, nodded briefly in acknowledgment, and found a seat next to a fat man in a dark suit, white shirt, and red necktie. He smelled of perspiration and lime shaving cream. The bell rang, metal doors squealed shut, and the 8:24 lurched noisily toward Grand Central Terminal.

"Better deal with that," the fat man said, pointing at Andie's bloody hands. "You'll ruin your clothes." Then he tucked his canvas book bag up against the window, rested his head on this makeshift pillow, and began to snore.

Andie raised one hand uncertainly, and the stone-faced conductor appeared. He was a short man with raven-black hair combed into a pronounced DA and an eagle tattoo on his monstrous right biceps. When he saw the blood, he whistled, vanished, and reappeared with paper towels and a first aid kit. Together they stanched the bleeding and applied two large Band-Aids. The conductor then presented his injured passenger with a three-page form. A glance revealed that this document, if signed, would absolve the railroad of any responsibilities in the fall. "It's up to you," the conductor said. "It's just that if I don't give it out, then *I* lose *my* job."

Andie nodded in acknowledgment, accepted the papers. "You've done your duty," she said, smiling wanly.

"I *am* going to insist that you check in with our medical officer at the terminal," the conductor said, lowering his voice to add to his authority. "Directions to his location are on the form."

"Of course," said Andie. "I'm okay for now," she added, holding up her wrists to show the two neat bandages. "You've been very kind."

"You look a little like a suicide attempt," the conductor said, grinning, but Andie didn't laugh, so he bowed once and backed away. "Don't forget to stop in at the medical office," he said. "It's free."

Andie nodded.

"The ticket isn't," he continued.

"Oh, sorry," said Andie. She pulled a lose twenty from her suit

57

pocket and paid $11.50 for a round-trip. "I had two weeks off. I let my monthly expire," she explained. She nudged her seatmate, who produced his monthly commutation ticket from a breast pocket, displayed it, and returned it to his pocket, without ever opening his eyes. Andie wondered if he could see through his lashes—the fat man had beautiful eyelashes—or if the movement—so frequently practiced—could be enacted blind.

Above the sound of the train, she could hear passengers coughing and clearing their throats. She smelled soap and coffee. *Boy do I miss my girls*, she thought, and when she inhaled, she had the pain in her lungs she'd experienced as a child after a long day swimming in the river near Vandalia. Yes, she had grown up to swim in that river. Outside of the tragedy that had taken place there, and the months of depression that followed, she couldn't recall having felt this wretched. She couldn't recall having felt this incomplete since she'd first started dating Stuart, and had had to be away from him.

She'd phone Kika when she got back to the apartment. "I'm blue," she'd say.

"I know," said Kika. "You miss your movie star."

Stuart wasn't actually all that handsome, but then movie stars weren't necessarily handsome either. Models were handsome.

Movie stars had a quality even more subtle and difficult to define. Movie stars, like Stuart Cross, had substance. Stuart exuded a vitality, a gravity, that made his life look genuine and dramatic in this world of props.

He used to tantalize Andie by taking other women to book parties. She'd have a movie to cover, of course—which is why she couldn't go to the party herself—but stepping out of the crowd and onto the city streets, she would be swept with a vertiginous sense of loss, which at first she couldn't identify. *It's Stuart*, she'd think, after a moment, *I miss him. I love him.* Walking back to her own apartment, she'd fluctuate between jealousy and the great satisfaction of knowing that her need was simple. If life was the problem, then Stuart Cross was the solution.

Now, as the train picked up speed, she felt that same aching hollowness, but it wasn't for Stuart anymore. Now it was for the children, children she was paying somebody else to be with.

The nanny had been on the job for a day and a half and during that day and a half she—Andie—had hardly seen the girls. First, the party, and then an appreciation of John Gielgud. She'd given up her Sunday without fully realizing that she wouldn't see Jane and Ginny on Monday either.

Was there any way out of this? Andie played back the conversation she'd had with Fowler after his assistant got her on the phone: "I hate to bother you at home." He said, "Just say the word, and I'll give the assignment to Susan Logan . . ."

Today's screening wasn't until ten, so if she dashed—skipping the medical officer, of course—there might be time to drop the heels off at a shoe-repair stand, buy fresh stockings (the knees were shredded) and also shoes. Nikes? Flip-flops? New heels?

Plan in place, Andie put the briefcase in her lap. This had taken the fall harder than its owner had. The cordovan leather was badly scored; the brass trim on one corner had buckled and burst two miniature screws.

Andie snapped both clever latches, removed the *New York Times* and also the press package for that morning's movie: *Where the Money Is.* She closed the case, kept it on her lap, though, as a desk. She tore the manila envelope and withdrew an eight-by-ten-inch photo of a stripper with cash stuffed in her G-string and a large black revolver pointing out at the viewer.

The fat man's snoring stopped. Not daring to look to the right or to the left, Andie slid the picture back out of sight, shifted in her seat, and opened her copy of the *New York Times*.

There was a brief item on the murdered Croton pediatrician. Apparently French was not the innocent he had at first appeared to be. There had been a dispute with the AMA. He'd been in and out of a drug rehabilitation facility in Connecticut.

Tillie Cove was on the front page of the B section. The nanny's lawyer, a man named Robert Allyn, had called a press conference. Allyn expressed his own and his client's "deepest sorrow. While Miss Cove shares the agony Mr. and Mrs. Crown must feel now," he continued, "she does not acknowledge culpability. My client had been specifically instructed to bathe the child, and the receptacle she was clearly meant to use was in no way suitable for the task. This tragedy could have been averted if the Crowns had cleaned their own infant, or if my young and inexperienced client—virtually a child herself—had been given a safety tub. The American Academy of Pediatricians specifically enjoins parents not to bathe children in adult tubs."

Allyn was pictured holding up a blue plastic newborn-to-toddler bather, which he'd purchased for $12.95 and brought to the press conference. He also handed out catalog copy on the Crown Jacuzzi. The Acme Maelstrom was seven and a half feet long, two and a half feet deep and had jets run by a nine-horsepower electric engine.

"Nannies come and go," said Allyn, "but parents—not mercenary substitutes—however caring, however professional—are ultimately responsible for the safety of their own children."

CHAPTER 8

"The children are very proud of you both."

Andie put down the paper, wiggled her toes. Nothing broken. In her freshly battered monogrammed leather briefcase—a gift from Stuart—she carried a small Filofax, which held change, credit cards, and some cash. She also had a steno pad, two Bic pens, and Louise Washington's résumé. This came in a clear binder, and Andie withdrew it now. The first page was a picture of the nanny in cuffed chinos, boat shoes, and a blue button-down dress shirt. The young woman was sitting on a stone wall near a great old apple tree in what might have been New Hampshire or Vermont.

"It could be a Gap ad," Stuart had said, the first time he and Andie went through the document together.

Centered on the second page, the résumé listed the new employee's basic statistics:

Age: 37
Height: 5′
Weight: 97 lbs.
Interests: Portrait painting

Reading:

Anything written about Vincent van Gogh, or Francisco Goya. Anything written by G. K. Chesterton or C. S. Lewis.

The third page was titled "Mission Statement" and featured a single paragraph set in some odd type.

"The safety of those in her care is the nanny's first and overriding responsibility. Miss Washington will provide a psychological environment in which the child(ren) feel secure and are safe. Properly nourished, and hydrated, her charges need never be bored. Building on this sense of well-being, the nanny will help the child(ren) with age-appropriate academic skills: reading, penmanship, and basic mathematics. Since she is an artist by profession, she will also teach the child(ren) how to draw. All of her charges will learn the fundamentals of composition."

Andie thought the typographical cleverness was excessive. It was always the mark of a desperate freelancer to rely too much on such tricks, she mused. But still, she found the thoroughness and confidence of the document deeply reassuring.

The last page was titled "References."

"In order to save time and trouble," the résumé continued, "I've taken down representative statements from several of my former employers."

The first testimonial was from Helen B. Lovely, of 408 Happy Ending Lane in Bethesda, Maryland.

"Miss Washington nurtured Ashley and Jessica for four crucial years from 1992 to 1996. We had moved to Washington from Manhattan so that my husband, Dr. Lawrence Binderman, an oncologist, could join a growing practice in Bethesda. I had come on as a full partner with the D.C. law firm of Bible and Minces. We adore our children. At that phase in our lives, however, Dr. Binder-

man and I were forced to acknowledge that the professional ob-
ligations we faced were going to make it unlikely that we could give
the girls as much quality time as we both felt they required.

"Louise is a gem. She's a talented woman (ask to see her painting
of Trafalgar Square) whose life was an expression of our values and
tastes. She did just what I would have done, had I the time. She
took her charges to every museum on the Mall, performed light
housekeeping, helped with the driving, and washed and ironed the
girls' clothes. In the evenings and on rainy days, they played board
games. The TV was rarely switched on. Starting with *Madeline* and
Hillaire Belloc, the nanny read out loud to the girls most every
evening and on many afternoons. The books she chose included
Kipling's *Just So Stories* and the complete works of A. A. Milne.
(Yes, yes, we were forced to interfere here briefly, making it clear
that while we admired Kipling as a writer, his political positions are
both dated and of course racist.) Once a week each girl would
memorize a poem."

"The complete works of A. A. Milne, for *children*," said Stuart,
who had been reading over Andie's shoulder the first time she went
through the résumé. "Milne also wrote for adults."

Andie had looked back at her husband and scowled.

"All right, all right," said Stuart, putting a hand on his wife's arm.
"This woman is perfect. She'll scour the nappies."

"Jane has been toilet trained for three years," Andie said. "There
never were any nappies." (This was a sore point, since she had
recently taken a test in *Cosmo* titled, "Rate the Mate." Andie
realized now that she should not have given Stuart points for
recognizing the brand names of paper diapers.) "Besides which,
nappies are thrown away nowadays," she said with asperity. "If
you'd ever changed one, you'd know that."

Mary Poppins Inc. had sent the Crosses three other prospects on the day they met Louise. The first was an immensely cheerful woman named Dolly from Trinidad. "She would have been my choice, if it weren't for the walker," said Stuart, who had stayed home from the office to be present for the interviews. Outside of the walker, Dolly seemed to be in robust health, but she was seventy-six years old. The second applicant, a stocky woman of indeterminate age, was dropped off by a brother or cousin, who drove a cab out of nearby Hawthorne, New York. The language barrier had made it impossible to determine when or if the cousin or brother was coming back. The candidate spoke no English and had one prominent stainless-steel tooth. After fifteen minutes in which Stuart tried, unsuccessfully, to determine if Natasha was indeed her name or only a name they both admired, the job applicant was moved into the kitchen. Andie brewed tea, and presented her guest with a steaming mug and a freshly opened bag of Pepperidge Farm Mint Milanos. Natasha, if that was her name, downed the scalding tea in three thirsty gulps, fished out a single cookie, and then put the nearly full bag into her vast, black handbook. When the girls were herded in to see her, the candidate nodded politely to each child, drew a chair up to the television, turned it on, and switched through the channels until she found *The Young and the Restless*. Then she sat down to watch, her handbag clutched in her lap.

She was still in the kitchen when Lisa appeared. Lisa was a twenty-two-year-old NYU dropout, who wanted to "like, see if I'm into children. I mean, not just the idea, the reality. You know, the way they smell and all. I mean, with the population the way it is, you have to figure these things out. And I'd rather, like, get to know with your children, rather than having my own."

Lisa paused at this point and noted the absolute silence of her two listeners.

"Oops," she said, slapping a hand to her mouth, "did I say something wrong?"

"No," said Andie. "Of course not. Candor is a pressure we can bear."

Slight but toothsome, Lisa had shoulder-length chestnut hair and a pert little chin, which she waved about endearingly. "They like told me at Mary Poppins that you're a famous editor," she told Stuart. "Are you really? They, like, said you knew Samuel Beckett."

Stuart looked uncomfortable. "I don't think there are any famous editors anymore," he said. "Not since Scott Berg made a hero of Maxwell Perkins."

Lisa moved close to her prospective employer, fixed him with her green eyes, dilated her pupils. "But if there were famous editors anymore, you'd be one of them?"

"Maybe," said Stuart. "But editors aren't famous. Robert Gottlieb and Michael Korda are at the top of the field. If I have value, it's just in having been around for a long time."

"But you edit great books," Lisa said. "I, like, love books. I mean, that's why I went to college. Duh. Does this like really sound stupid? I always act stupid around smart people."

Stuart would have hired Lisa in a heartbeat, but Andie hissed at him to "forget it," and ushered the young woman back out to the canary yellow Ford Mustang convertible she'd arrived in.

"Do I, like, have the job?" Lisa asked bewildered, when Andie opened the door of the car for her. "We'll phone the agency," said Andie.

"Do you have any more questions?" asked Lisa.

"None," said Andie, smiled and wagged her head. "We learned everything we need to know."

"Do you suppose Mr. Cross has any questions?" Lisa asked.

Like do you give head, Andie thought, but didn't say. "You go on home now," she said. "We'll be in touch."

When Stuart heard a knock several minutes later, he assumed it was Lisa, coming back for the purple scarf she'd left in the front hall. When he opened the door, though, it wasn't Lisa. The woman standing on the front step was so short that, for a moment, he thought it might be a student selling Girl Scout cookies. He looked over her shoulder for the adult driver and chaperone. Then he saw crow's-feet, the lines around the stranger's mouth. The eyes were unusually bright, the face was mobile and intelligent, in the way some children's faces are, but clearly marred by life. Weathered.

"Louise Washington," the stranger had said, and then given him a small, cold hand. "What a striking house," she continued, as Stuart struggled to bring together his contradictory impressions. "I had no idea you could find open country so close to the city."

The girl? Woman? Was she black? She had dark skin and an English accent, the sort of accent that once came out of the public schools.

The nanny was in tight jeans, cinched around her miniature waist with a simple and slightly worn leather belt. Above this, she wore a blue oxford shirt. Her face was a vertical oval, and the ovals of her eyes were horizontal, which with prominent cheekbones gave a slightly Oriental impression. Stuart smelled soap. Her hair was pulled back through a thick rubber band and then went on in a braid. She carried an Eddie Bauer backpack. This was blue and trimmed with brown leather. The initials LW were stitched into the back. Under her left arm, she had a large sketch pad. The visual

66

impression was very much that of an eighth grader, perhaps returning from a field trip to a museum.

"Please come inside," said Stuart, and then hearing Andie in the foyer, he made a sweeping gesture from the guest to his wife.

"Andie," he said. "This is Louise Washington."

The women shook hands. "I was telling your husband," said Louise, "how much I admire your house."

"Oh, thank you. And how can I help you?" she said, assuming, as her husband had, that this was a visiting child. "Are we neighbors?"

"The job," said Louise.

"Which job?" asked Andie.

"Miss Washington is a nanny," Stuart explained.

"Oh," said Andie, blushing. "I'm so sorry . . . It's not as if I were gigantic myself."

"No problem," said Louise, and rolled her eyes knowingly. "It doesn't help that I carry a backpack and a sketch pad. I was proofed just last week."

Andie cocked her head. "But you have a beautiful voice," she said. "I can't place it."

The nanny shrugged self-deprecatingly. "I studied in London for a year," she said. "I guess it stuck."

Avoiding Natasha in the kitchen, Andie and Stuart led the job candidate into the great room. The prospective nanny looked around. "This *is* grand," she said, but she said it without a trace of judgment, envy, or reproach, as if they were all on a house tour together.

Miss Washington waited until Andie and Stuart had both been seated before taking her place at the end of one of two facing sofas. She put her sketch pad down beside her.

Stuart noticed drawings of tombstones on the top sheet. He pointed to these. "I have to ask," he said.

Louise looked down at the drawing indicated, looked back up, and smiled sweetly. "Oh," she said. "I came here an hour early so that I could spend time up in the Sparta Burying Grounds. You know they are diagonally across the road from you? There are headstones from the late eighteenth century. And look," she said, and turned to the fourth page in the book. This was a picture of a brick wall with headstones set into it, and a roughened section where a stone had been knocked out. A plaque read: "This stone was pierced by a cannon shot fired by the British sloop of war *Vulture*."

"Where's that from?" asked Andie.

"The Sparta Burying Grounds," said Louise. "Right across the road."

"I had no idea," said Stuart. "I thought this was a good neighborhood."

"No," said the nanny, and laughed softly. "There's been a lot of fighting on this ground. Indian wars. Revolutionary War. Zoning wars."

"I assumed this had been forest," said Stuart. "Then farms. Then development."

Louise shook her head. "There were farms, but then estates before development. The brick wall across the street is from the estate of Frank Vanderlip, president of the First National City Bank," she said. "The school you see at the second break in the wall going south is the one he built for his children and grand-children to attend. The Ionic columns you see at the first break in the wall were taken from the front of the bank at 55 Wall Street."

"You from around here?" asked Stuart. "How do you know all this?"

Louise shrugged almost apologetically. "I read."

"You're so gifted," said Andie. "And informed. What makes you think you want to be a nanny?"

"I don't know," said Louise. "I suppose it runs in the family. My mother was a nanny. I love children. My paintings are only now beginning to sell."

Stuart gave Andie a knowing glance, as if to say, "Isn't everybody an artist nowadays?" and Andie rolled her eyes, so that he could see them, but the nanny could not.

Louise reached into her backpack and withdrew a résumé, which was bound in plastic, with a clear cover. This she handed to Andie.

"Remind me," she said, "how old are your girls?"

"Six and nine," said Stuart.

Louise smiled warmly, as if remembering something delicious she had eaten. She said nothing.

"I love the way they smell," sighed Andie. "It breaks my heart that I can't spend more time with them myself, but we're all so busy. We both work in the city. Too busy to breathe."

"Oh," said Louise. "I'm so sorry."

"You know the poem?" asked Stuart, but then continued, without waiting to be answered: "A poor life this, if full of care, / We have no time to stand and stare."

"Oh Stuart," said Andie, and then looked an apology at the nanny.

"No, no," said Louise. "Don't apologize."

"We do feel harried," said Andie. "Also conflicted."

Louise smiled knowingly. "It's hardest on the women," she said. "I know how you must love your girls. I can be flexible. I can always be told to vanish."

"I'm so glad," said Andie. "I'm often in the city, but sometimes a screening will fall through, and when that happens, I'd love to be able to take over."

"Of course," said Louise. She paused and looked at her hands.

"Do you have any questions for us?" said Andie.

"Well," said Louise. "Since you've brought up the city, I want to ask about museums. You don't object to museums, do you?"

"No," said Andie. "Of course not. What prompts that question?"

Miss Washington shrugged. "I know this sounds old-fashioned, but I despise the popular culture," she said. "Living this close, I like to take the children to the city, whenever it's convenient. We start with the Museum of Natural History," she said, and smiled almost apologetically. "Just to break down the resistance. I show them the whale and the mammalian dioramas, let them eat pieces of chicken cut in the shape of dinosaurs. Then we move across Central Park to the Metropolitan."

"I approve entirely," said Andie, "providing the girls get their schoolwork done. Ginny's in the fourth grade at Hackley, and they have masses of homework."

The bell rang. Stuart rose and got the door. It was the cab-driving relative of the job applicant who was still in the kitchen watching TV. This engendered a mime show, which looked as if it might never end. Then Louise came in out of the great room, spoke briefly to the cab driver in a language Stuart couldn't identify. The cab driver embraced Louise—she came up to his sternum. He collected Natasha, if that was her name, and the two backed, bowing and smiling, out the door.

Without explaining what had happened, the prospective nanny turned to Stuart and asked, "Would it be all right if I spoke with the girls?" Stuart nodded dumbly.

Both children were still in the kitchen. Ginny was now watching the TV with keen interest. Andie switched the set off.

"Oh Mom," whined Ginny. "That woman in the hospital bed is pregnant with Keith's baby. Keith's an internationally celebrated brain surgeon. The baby may be born with Klinefelter's syndrome. Who's Klinefelter? He doesn't even know she's pregnant. She's dying of pancreatic cancer. Where's my pancreas?" she asked, pulling up her blouse and examining her ample midriff.

"Tuck your shirt in," said Andie. "I don't know where the pancreas is exactly. We can look it up later. In the meantime, there's somebody I'd like you both to meet." She turned to the nanny, who had followed her into the kitchen. "This is Miss Washington."

"You girls can call me Sugar," said the nanny, coming around the parents to shake hands with each child in turn. Jane shook hands solemnly, and then moved to one side, making way for her elder sister.

Ginny was almost as tall as the visitor. They shook hands, and then Ginny said, "Are you a pipsqueak?"

Stuart heard himself gasp.

"No," said Louise, evenly. "I'm small, but not insignificant." She looked Ginny right in the eye and smiled, and there was a lot in that look—resignation, humor, but also a quiet authority. Stuart expected Ginny to explode, but she did not. The big girl and the small woman seemed to understand each other.

The moment passed, and Jane produced the puzzle she had recently mastered. Miss Washington squatted and observed, but didn't interfere, as the younger Cross child put together the two-hundred-piece painting of a sailboat regatta set against an advancing thunderstorm.

"That's brilliant," Louise said, when the last piece was in place. "Absolutely brilliant!" Jane beamed.

Ginny had retreated to the kitchen table and had been reading catalogs, looking up from time to time as if to check on the stranger's progress with her sister. Louise stood up now, caught Ginny's eye. "You're way too old for puzzles. Do you like to draw?"

Ginny nodded. Miss Washington opened her backpack, removed a box of crayons, and then tore two pages out of her sketchbook.

"But I'm no good," Ginny said. "Mrs. Gleason says I don't take enough time with my drawings."

"Can you keep a secret?" asked the nanny.

Ginny nodded mutely.

"You promise you won't tell your art teacher this?"

Ginny nodded again.

"I bet your art teacher has it exactly wrong," said Louise. "I bet she has an absolute genius for getting it wrong. Your problem is that you take too much time. You can't be afraid of mistakes. We all make mistakes."

Ginny smiled despite herself.

Then Louise Washington removed her black Casio G-Shock, strapped it to Ginny's wrist, and found the stopwatch mode. "Let's each take five minutes," she said. "Let's each take three-hundred seconds and draw a bear. I'll go first. You time me."

Once this deal had been struck, the nanny looked back over her shoulder, caught Andie's eye. "Would it be all right if the girls and I had some time alone?" she asked.

"Certainly," said Andie. "Of course." She and Stuart backed out of the kitchen.

There was some awkwardness at first as to what exactly the

parents were supposed to do. "I'll look at the Wallace Stevens manuscript," said Stuart. "I'll set up in the great room for now."

"I'm going outside," said Andie. "Walk our pristine acre. See if I can figure out about landscaping. I'd like to make it seem as if this house was always here. Or at least I'd like to dispel the impression that it just landed here from Mars on the day before yesterday."

Fifteen minutes later the phone rang. Stuart picked up. "George Hamilton Carter, from the *New York Post*," he was told. "Is Andie Wilde available?"

Stuart cupped the phone's mouthpiece, walked to the door, and opened it. "Andie," yelled. "Telephone. It's your bread and butter."

Andie bustled into the house, went upstairs, and took the call on the bedroom extension.

Stuart settle back into the sofa, read the first two pages of a manuscript, and fell into a light doze.

Snapping back into consciousness, he wasn't certain how long he'd been asleep, and so got up and walked toward the kitchen. He was halfway there when he heard the sound of his elder daughter laughing. He wondered if the nanny wasn't paying attention. He rarely heard Ginny laugh this freely, except when she was pinching her baby sister.

But the nanny was paying attention. She was standing right beside Ginny, whose face was wreathed with smiles.

"Look Dad," Ginny said, "I drew a bear." She held up a sheet of sketch paper.

"Why a bear?" Stuart asked. "Although that's good," he said, looking more closely. "It's very good. Did Miss Washington help you?"

"No," said Louise curtly. "I didn't help."

73

By this time Janey had her arms around her father's knees. "Louise promised to teach me how to draw too," she said. "But next time. She has to go home now."

"Oh," said Stuart, looking at the nanny. "Do you need a ride?"

Louise checked the Casio, gently removing it from Ginny's wrist. "No," she said, putting the watch back on. "If I leave in the next ten minutes, I can catch the local."

"I'd be happy to give you a ride to the station," said Stuart.

"I'd so much rather walk," said Louise. "But thank you for the kind offer," she said and smiled to cover the excessive civility. "And thank you for giving me a chance to meet two such exceptional girls," she said, catching each child's eyes in turn, and twinkling.

"Can't Sugar stay for dinner tonight?" asked Ginny.

"Sugar?" asked Stuart.

"They call me Sugar," said Louise. "I asked them to."

"Sugar," said Stuart, trying the word out in his mouth.

"You can call me Miss Washington," Louise said.

"Well, Miss Washington," said Stuart. "Can you stay for dinner? Turkey burgers and fresh asparagus broiled with olive oil and sea salt? I'd give you a ride home afterward."

"No," said Louise.

"Honest," said Stuart. "I'd be pleased to give you a ride."

"No," said Louise again, "I'd better catch this train. My pager number is on the résumé. Please call if you have any questions." She grabbed her sketch pad, slipped on her backpack, and walked to the door.

"Let me get Andie off the phone," said Stuart.

"Please don't interrupt Mrs. Cross," said Louise, backing out the door. "The girls told me what she does. A film critic. And you're an editor. The children are very proud of you both."

74

CHAPTER 9

"Dagger to my heart."

The immediate difficulty had been in contacting the paragon. Miss Washington's beeper number was on the résumé, but no home phone was listed. Ten minutes after the winning nanny left the house, Andie dialed the beeper, left the Cross phone number, and hit the pound key. "I hope I did that right," she said, and dialed the number again, repeated her number, and pressed the star key.

"The woman just this instant boarded the train," Stuart said. "She'll call when she reaches home. I bet we hear from her within the hour. She loved the house. We didn't even show her the maid's quarters."

Miss Washington hadn't phoned, though, not that evening. Nor had she contacted her potential employers on Saturday or Sunday. Lisa phoned once to ask if "you, like, have any questions." And once to ask, "If you've, like, seen a purple scarf anywhere. My brother gave it to me."

Andie had answered the second call and put the scarf in the mailbox. Natasha's cousin also phoned. Dolly phoned. Andie's frantic call to the Mary Poppins Agency in White Plains produced this recording: "Thank you for patronizing Mary Poppins Inc.,

Westchester's prestige child-care provider. If we take care of the children, we take care of the future. If you are calling because you would like your résumé listed, and to set up a screening interview, press one. If you are phoning because you seek our assistance in locating a child-care professional, press two."

Andie pressed two and got this message: "Thank you for calling Mary Poppins Inc., Westchester's prestige child-care provider. Our offices are open from eight A.M. until five P.M. Monday through Friday. If you care to leave a message, please do so after the beep. If you want to send a fax . . ."

When Stuart reached a live person at the agency on Monday at eight fifteen A.M., it turned out that the only number Mary Poppins had for Miss Washington was the pager number, the same one that the Cross family had tried repeatedly without success.

It wasn't until after six on Monday evening that the nanny broke silence. "This is a courtesy call," she told Andie, who had been serving the children dinner when she answered the phone. "I've been offered a job in Scarsdale."

"And what job is that?" asked Andie.

Miss Washington sighed. "Ambrose," she said. "A little boy. Not as darling as your girls, but his parents seem eager to have me. There's room in the attic to store my paintings. Two days off— they'll determine which days—use of a BMW, and five hundred dollars a week. That's after taxes."

"But you'd live rent free with us," said Andie. "Stuart and I were kicking ourselves after you left for forgetting to show you the maid's quarters. You'd have your own entrance and powder room."

"This is very kind of you, Ms. Cross," countered Louise, "but Dr. and Mrs. Willingham are giving me the apartment above their garage."

The girls were seated expectantly at the kitchen table, each with some broccoli, some cauliflower, but not yet any macaroni and cheese. Now Andie returned the pot of macaroni to the stove, and fell into a chair herself.

"I want my macaroni," said Ginny. "Maca maca maca roni. I'm hungry. I'm famrished."

Andie cupped the phone's mouthpiece with one hand. "Eat your broccoli first," she hissed. "Famished. Famished is a word. Famrished is not."

"I hate broccoli," said Ginny. "It makes me toot."

Andie cupped the phone's mouthpiece a second time. "That's a vile word to use at the table," she said to Ginny. "When I was your age, I would have had my mouth washed out with soap for using such a word."

"Toot," said Ginny. "Toot isn't a bad word," but she'd already lost her mother's attention. Andie was purring into the phone: "We have a new Volvo wagon with four-wheel drive—and a Saab convertible," she said, and paused.

No sound from the other end of the line. "Are you there?" she asked. "The girls love you."

"And I like them," said Louise, "but . . ."

"Six hundred dollars," said Andie. "Please."

"Now I feel mercenary," said Louise. "I do like your girls. But the Willinghams are terribly generous. They had also agreed to give me an hour and a half off every Sunday to go to an early service."

"We'll let you go to church," said Andie. "Is there anything else?"

"Well," said Louise. "I have a closet full of paintings. Will there be a place where I can store them while I work for you?"

"We can't give you a closet," said Andie. "But our basement is dry and virtually empty. You can have as much space there as you need."

"You sure you're comfortable giving up the space?" asked Louise.

"I'm sure," said Andie. "I want you. Having met you, I couldn't bear to have anybody else. The girls want you."

"Do they really?" asked the nanny. "That's important."

"Yes," said Andie. "They talked about you all weekend. Do we have a deal?"

"Well, I should call the Willinghams."

Andie stood, and began to serve the girls their macaroni and cheese. "I won't be part of a bidding war," she said. "Of course you should call these other people, but either you accept our offer now, or it's withdrawn."

There was a long pause on the other end of the line.

"That's six hundred dollars after taxes. You'll have Social Security."

"All right," said Louise. "I like your family."

"Good," said Andie. "Today is Monday. When can you begin? Tomorrow?"

This, too, was greeted with silence.

"Wednesday then," said Andie. "Can you move in by Wednesday?"

"You know I'd love to," Louise had said. "But this is very sudden. I need time. I must have at least two weeks."

"Were these other people prepared to wait two weeks?" Andie asked.

"Of course," said Louise. "You want me to live in? They wanted me to live in. I need the time to close up . . . my other life."

"Okay," said Andie. "It's a done deal. I'll have your room all set up by Tuesday. You can move in earlier if you like, but we'll expect you on the seventeenth. That's Saturday. It's also Saint Patrick's Day. We're planning a party. You can help."

"Noon on the seventeenth," said Louise. "I'll wear the green. I'm staying with my brother. Now let me give you his phone number."

When it wasn't raining Stuart walked the half mile up from the station, so he was surprised to see the black Saab with its top down nosing toward him as he came off the Scarborough platform at six forty-seven P.M. that Monday. Both girls were strapped in back. Andie was driving.

"A little chilly, isn't it, to have the top down?" Stuart asked, having lowered himself into the passenger seat and given his wife a peck on the cheek.

"Jane sisted," Andie said.

Stuart leaned into the back of the car and looked down into the eyes of his younger daughter.

"Is that right?" he asked.

Jane nodded gravely. "I sisted," she said.

"Any word about the paragon?" asked Stuart, slipping back into his seat and turning to face his wife.

"I've got good news and bad news."

"It's been a long day. I want the good news first."

"We've got her."

"Bad news?" asked Stuart quizzically.

"Six hundred dollars a week," Andie said. "After taxes. She won't start until Saint Patrick's Day."

"Let's hire Lisa instead," said Stuart. "I bet we could have her for three hundred dollars."

"You want a ditz watching the girls? They'll grow up to be ditzes too."

"What's a ditz?" asked Ginny from the back seat. Neither parent acknowledged the question.

"We could go back to Mary Poppins," said Stuart. "Get more names."

"No," said Andie. "I want her. The girls want her."

"Mommy's sisting," said Jane from the back seat.

"That's right," said Andie. "I'm sisting. I'll take two weeks off starting right now. I've got a month's vacation coming. The girls will be in school. I can finish setting up the house. Spend the extra time with them. The nanny will come on the weekend before the beginning of spring break. During the break, she can take them to the Metropolitan."

Stuart fastened his seat belt, and then sighed. "So you're taking on an unplanned-for expense, and also endangering your job? Two with one blow. Do you have any idea how much six hundred dollars after taxes might cost?"

Andie shrugged helplessly. "It's for the girls," she said. "It's an investment in their future. These years are crucial. It's this nanny or no nanny at all. Trust me."

"And what about Susan Logan?"

"I've been writing four reviews a week; Susan Logan has been writing one review a week. And criticizing the work I do. This will give her a chance to fail."

"What if she's great?" said Cross. "What if she rises to the occasion? What if Bobby Fowler adores her?"

"I'm betting against it," said Andie. "If Fowler adores her, he can have her flat-chested self."

"And what would you do then?" asked Stuart.

"I'd stop going to the movies. I'd live in the real world," Andie said, gunning the engine as she made the left up Scarborough Station Road.

"Remember what Ginny said, when you brought Jane home from the hospital?" said Stuart.

"How could I forget?" said Andie.

But Stuart repeated the line anyway: " 'Now that she has a good girl to take care of, is Mommy going to stay home with us?' "

"Dagger to my heart," said Andie.

CHAPTER 10

"Buy an aquarium."

Susan Logan savaged the two highest-budget movies released during her tenure as top critic. Each one got half a star. This might have established Logan as a maverick. Pauline Kael consistently panned the most popular films during her brilliant tenure at the *New Yorker*. But Susan Logan took the perilous additional step of predicting noisily that the movies in question would be box-office poison. Both films were outrageously successful.

"She's conflated aesthetics and commerce," said Stuart, "and got it backward. Anything that sells is good, because the people have spoken. We all agree on that. Anything that doesn't sell is bad. Those are the first two axioms of contemporary philosophy. But she's developed a third rule: anything that's bad won't sell. The woman's a simpleton, or else willfully naïve."

And so the job had been there when Andie came back to it—along with the promotion. Now she was at the top of the heap. Not the most distinguished heap, perhaps, but Andie was young.

Weighted with authority and shod in new white Nike cross trainers ($69.95), she arrived at the screening room just five minutes early that Monday morning. The pale-faced publicist seemed unusually eager to please; this was often a very bad sign. The young woman quizzed Andie about the girls and oohed sympathetically when she saw the Band-Aids.

"Fell trying to catch the train," Andie said. "It's nothing." And she took another copy of the press kit. She noticed an insulated foam cooler with ice and six six-ounce plastic bottles of Poland Spring. There were also three small white paper bags of popcorn. *Wallace Stevens would be pleased,* Andie thought, but declined the refreshments and let the publicist show her into the elegant screening room. Once inside, Andie made out the dark and slouching forms of several other critics. Each critic was alone and sitting alone. This too was a bad sign.

Nobody said hello. Film critics were not a convivial lot. *If I had a heart attack here,* Andie had wondered on more than one occasion, *would anybody notice? Would anybody care?* She could easily imagine the lights coming up and her colleagues—were they colleagues?—holding notebooks and coats, picking their way around her body and out into the light.

Andie flipped past the now-familiar picture. The synopsis was unclear, although apparently this was an epic. Oscar bait.

It seemed the protagonist was a Depression-era stripper who went to church and robbed banks. Or maybe she dreamed that she robbed banks. Or maybe she dreamed that she went to church.

When the lights went down, the film itself did little to clear up the confusion. The camera would cut from dollar bills being stuffed into a G-string to dollar bills being stuffed into a collection plate to dollar bills being stuffed into a canvas sack.

The stripper seemed to have been raped as a child by a man in a frock coat who might have been a fatherly priest, or her father the priest.

83

The narrative was highly digressive and worked, when it worked at all, as a sort of pastiche, a collage of earlier movies.

Sitting in a reclining chair made of blond wood and lined with black leather, Andie was bored and so found herself daydreaming. Sometimes the daydreams were from her actual life, sometimes they had been provided by Hollywood. She couldn't always tell the difference.

Psychologists called this Reagan's syndrome, after the actor who had been so successful in the role of fortieth President of the United States. Andie had Reagan's syndrome bad. When she saw—and this often happened—three movies in a day, the fabricated images forced their way into her interior life. She would dream from movies at night, and then remember them as if they were her own past.

The psychological valve, which in healthy civilians separates the active world from the world of the spectator, had been over-whelmed. And just as a poorly functioning epiglottis will let chunks of undigested food down into the lungs, Andie's overwhelmed conscious mind let great undigested chunks of fictional experience down into her memory.

She was not insane. She made the necessary distinctions when it was necessary to make them, but if questioned suddenly, she was not always absolutely certain what had happened to Andie Wilde, and what had happened to Katharine Hepburn, Julia Roberts, or Henry Fonda. Was she sad because her younger sister had drowned outside of Vandalia, Ohio, or because Debra Winger had died of breast cancer in *Terms of Endearment*?

Did she think true love was doomed because of her recent experience with a distracted and ambitious husband, or because Robert Redford hadn't stayed with Barbra Streisand in *The Way We Were*?

Memory responds to drama and the movies—of course—were far more dramatic than was the life in which they were recalled.

The tendency to give greater value to the imaginary than to the actual was heightened by strangers and even intimates who were infinitely more apt to ask about movies than about her husband or children or herself.

When Andie was a child, the Wildes had lived in a development that bordered a working farm, and so she had been given the pony she begged for on her eighth birthday. When she fell off and sprained an ankle, her father sold the animal, and this over her bitter and impassioned protests.

Recalling the single week she had spent with the somewhat grandly named Bucephalus, the films she played in her mind were cobbled together out of scenes from *Gone With the Wind*, *Black Beauty*, *National Velvet*, and *The Black Stallion*.

Because movies are frightening, Andie was often frightened. The phone never rang at night without exciting the certainty of tragic news. She couldn't descend a set of basement stairs without imagining her own brutal slaying, nor could she swim in the ocean without hearing the John Williams score and sensing the approach of an enormous shark.

When she came to a crossroads, pulled out into the intersection, she would inevitably visualize an unseen vehicle striking the car from her blind side. She'd blink, wait for the impact, and then go on.

Andie was not alone. America had become a nation of hysterics. History's fattest, safest, and most sedentary people lived imaginary lives of overpowering romance and breathtaking drama.

They died by the thousands of obesity and heart disease, but wouldn't mount a bicycle without a helmet and a water bottle.

Where the Money Is had been written and directed by one of the young auteurs who had a much deeper association with film than with life. Therefore, the reference points in his bewildering narrative were taken from other movies.

Because the story line was so weak, it functioned for Andie as a memory aide like a wampum belt or rosary beads, sending her off into one reverie after another.

The camera came in on the hands of a small girl twisting together in anxiety. The music grew ominous. The camera pulled back, and over the shoulder of the young girl. Andie saw the rapist father, closed her eyes and imagined instead a child in diapers, climbing on a rock ledge at the verge of a body of water. For a moment, Andie wondered—now what movie am I recalling that from?

Nobody had blamed her. "Nobody ever blamed me," she'd told her psychiatrist. "My parents blamed themselves."

Where the Money Is, which might have bored a civilian to tears, left the critic feeling wrung out and full of fresh anxiety about her children. Her precious younger daughter, Janey, had been named after the sister who drowned.

Careful to compose her face so as to give the publicist no clue as to her judgment of the film, Andie accepted a bottle of water. Sipping this, she walked ten blocks to 44, the restaurant across from the Algonquin, the place where she was scheduled to have lunch with her boss. Asking for Robert Fowler, she was given a sheet of the restaurant's creamy notepaper with his name on it and a telephone number, his office number. Then she was led to an alcove and presented with a house phone.

Andie had spent so many hours in darkened auditoriums that she had come instinctively to expect that life would follow the narrative needs of a feature film. Why show a woman making a telephone call if she is not going to receive a pivotal piece of information?

Ear to the receiver, the critic imagined horrific scenarios: Had Fowler changed his mind? Would he fire her? Had he been shot by a jealous husband? Diagnosed with Stage 4 colon cancer? Had he slipped in the tub?

Fowler's assistant, a bearded playwright named David Kantor, did sound concerned. "Ms. Wilde, that you?"

"Yes," said Andie.

"I don't know how to put this," said David.

"Put what?"

"I don't want to offend you."

"Let me help you then," said Andie. "Have I been stood up for lunch?"

"All right," said David. "Here goes: Bob had completely forgotten about his school conference which is way out in Montclair and which is this afternoon."

"Yes," said Andie.

"You know the trouble Maximus has been having ever since the third grade?" David continued, picking up momentum as he went along. "Bob was going to send Lily to the conference, but she was called to Washington for the congressional hearings. We tried to phone you at home, but you'd already left. Your cell seems to be disconnected. Bob made me promise to apologize."

"No apologies necessary," said Andie.

"If you want to eat lunch alone," David said, "or with anybody else, you should do so, and we'll pick up the tab. The cancellation is not a veiled criticism. Do you hear me?"

"I hear you," said Andie.

"Bob told me to tell you we love you. 'Tell her we love her.' Those were his exact words. We're so glad you've taken the job. It's thumbs-up all around."

After the momentary stab of disappointment, Andie was surprised to find that she was relieved. *I'll take an early train,* she thought, *give the paragon the rest of the day off, and take the girls to the toy store.*

"You know what," she said to David. "I think I'll go right home. I had planned to come in and set up my office, but I can do all that tomorrow. When Bob's there."

"That sounds sensible," said David. "We need you tomorrow. Bob has some business, and he was hoping that afterward the two of you could take Maximus to the new Disney movie. The remake of *Oedipus Rex.* What's it called?

"*Happily, Happily Ever After,*" said Andie. "Tell Fowler I'll be at his service tomorrow. But if it's really all right, I think I'll take the rest of today off. I miss the girls."

Andie caught a cab to the terminal, bought a copy of the *New York Post* and spent ten long minutes waiting while a man in a gabardine suit finished his call. She remembered how Stuart had mused that now that everybody with money has a cell phone, the public phones have been neglected. *So why, knowing that,* she thought angrily, *is he leaving me without a cell?*

"I know, Pumpkin," the man in gabardine was crooning, "I'm not surprised that you feel tired and hopeless in the mornings. The death of a child is something you never really get over. Doctor Ross told us as much. Give the pills time to work. And don't forget that I'm going through it too. We still have each other. And the boys. You have to think of the boys."

When Andie finally got her turn in the booth, the mouthpiece was warm and moist. She took a handful of quarters from the zippered pouch in her Filofax, returned the Filofax to the briefcase. She put the change in the left pocket of her suit jacket and took a deep breath, inhaled the sweet cologne of the man with the dead child, and dialed her own number. "Thank you for riding the MTA," she was told by a recorded voice. "Fifty cents please for the first three minutes." Andie thrust her hand into her jacket and somehow managed to get the coins out of her pocket and into the slot. "Thank you for using AT&T," said James Earl Jones in a voice Andie had once admired, but now detested.

The first ring seemed to come from a great distance. Andie clamped the earpiece so tightly against her head that it hurt. Her home phone rang again, still faintly, and she heard her own voice, cheerful, welcoming: "So sorry. Not available this instant. Please leave a message, and we'll get back to you as soon as is humanly possible."

Andie punched in the family code—50–23—Stuart's age and her own, when they'd been married. She heard what sounded like a computer, talking down its digital nose at her. "There are eighteen messages. Press one to play back all messages. Press two for other functions."

Andie pressed "two."

"Press one to play back new messages," said the computer, "press two for other functions."

Andie pressed "one." "You have one new message," the machine said, and then she heard a deep melodious voice: "Hey, Sugar, you there? If you're there, pick up." There was an expectant pause, and then the voice again, still confident: "Did a drive-by Saturday. Boy, I sure can see why you went for it. The good life. Some house. I guess everybody's got to serve his own time. Even ofay. Don't forget where you came from, though. You know where to reach me. Bye-bye." "End of final message," said the answering machine.

Andie dropped the receiver. Then she picked it up, and broke the connection. She stood still staring blankly. When her eyes swam back into the focus, she saw that "Hiya Cutie" had been written in crimson nail polish across the machine's armored chrome coin box.

Andie felt a tap on her shoulder. It was a teenage boy with a square head, jet black hair cut short, and a silver ring in his left eyebrow. "Excuse me, ma'am," he said. "Are you done?"

"No," said Andie, her voice breaking. "I'm not done." She pivoted back into the cubicle, picked up the receiver a second time, dialed her number a second time. Again she was thanked for riding the MTA. James Earl Jones congratulated her movingly a second time for using AT&T. A third recorded voice asked her to insert two quarters. "Fifty cents please, for three minutes." This she did.

Again she heard her own voice, cheerful, enthusiastic. "So sorry. Not available this instant . . ." She punched in the code. "Press one to play back all messages," she was told again by the machine. "Press two for another function." She pressed "two" and was told, "Press one to play back new messages. Press two for another function." She pressed "one." The computer seemed almost to pause pityingly. "No new messages," it told her.

"Shit," she said aloud, and started to dial again, careful not to look back over her shoulder, sensing the aggrieved presence of the young man with the ring in his eyebrow. This time she selected "All message playback," and had to keep inserting quarters while she listened to nineteen messages: "It's Steve Solon. Yes, I want to go to your party. I need directions . . . This is Bell Plumbing. Will anybody be home on Thursday? Hiya honey. This is Kika. You there? There have been reports of a kidnapping in Briarcliff. They think it's a child custody case, but I'd keep my eyes on those precious girls. At least for the next day or two. Give me a call." And sixteen other messages before she got again to the rich, deep voice with just the touch of swagger:

"Hey, Sugar, you there? If you're there, pick up." There was an expectant pause, and then the voice again, still confident: "Did a drive-by Saturday. Boy, I sure can see why you went for it. The good life. Some house. I guess everybody's got to serve his own time. Even ofay. Don't forget where you came from, though. You know where to reach me. Bye-bye."

Andie stuffed more quarters into the phone and dialed Stuart's office. His secretary picked up.

"Althea?"

"Yes."

"This is Andie. Is Stuart there?"

"I'm sorry, but he's out to lunch."

"At the Pen & Ink?"

"I don't know. I seem to recall him saying something about avoiding company hangouts."

"Okay," said Andie, "I'll try the Pen & Ink. If he calls in, tell him we need to talk. I should be home by two P.M. Tell him I'll be home by two P.M. Have you got that? Tell him I'm leaving the city. I'll be home by two P.M. Maybe two thirty."

"Is something the matter?" asked Althea, her voice gone syrupy in response to the obvious panic, reminding Andie that this woman had never liked her.

"I don't think so," said Andie.

She hung up, forced more coins into the slot, and dialed the number of the Pen & Ink from memory.

"So sorry, madam," she was told. "Mr. Cross is not dining with us today."

Andie hung up and looked at her watch. This was going to be the second dash for a train in one day. This time, though, she was wearing the proper shoes.

She managed to board the 12:55 for Scarborough without falling down, and found a seat. The journey up the river, which had served generations of commuters as a spatial Valium, didn't quell Andie's growing anxiety. The Croton veterinarian was on page three of the Post. VIOLENT DEATH STALKS THE SUBURBS. This story was fast losing its simplicity and its appeal. French was a baby doctor, but also an unusually difficult man, not the ideal victim. At the time of his death, he was defending against two malpractice suits, and was also involved in legal disputes with neighbors on both sides of his Croton property. Apparently he liked to "plink"—his word—in the backyard with his .357 Magnum pistol.

Andie read the story headlined, BRIARCLIFF MOTHER SUSPECTS KIDNAPPING! A seven-year-old girl had last been seen Friday getting on the school bus. The single mother had given police the description of her ex-husband, a German national.

The Cove story was on the cover and exhaustive. It included the high school snapshot of Terry (short for Tertiary, short for Harrison Crown 3rd)—Andover class of '85. Shelley Crown (née Winters) was shown on a horse. There was a picture of the entrance to the Crown apartment building on East End Avenue, with a doorman holding up his hand in a vain attempt to block the lens. None of the Crown contingent would speak for the record.

The nanny's friends, on the other hand, were a loquacious group, coming forward to say that: "All Tilly ever wanted was to take care of children. That was her dream."

A sidebar chronicled other nanny tragedies, including death by fire, shakings, drownings, and kidnappings. Even Andie was astonished by the purple horrors her newspaper could summon by quoting from its own morgue. Text on the Lindbergh child was choice. The infant body count was so high that the very survival of the species seemed at risk.

An editorial, which was flagged on the front page, took Cove's side. Andie tried to avoid the three cubicles from which this twice-weekly feature was generated. Andie had earned the enmity of the immensely fat, immensely famous Pamela Chesterfield Arnold, when—on her first day in the office—she had filled the awkward pause following introductions by saying, "Congratulations! When are you due?"

The woman was known to stay in the office 24–7 and worked a brace of ambitious young assistants almost to death. Arnold was the paper's most celebrated writer. Her awkward prose tapped directly into the venal and unforgiving thoughts that her readers—amateur haters—were too decent to allow into consciousness.

In a column titled "Spoiled Babies Watching Babies," the *Post* opinion-maker hit out at the Crowns. "Parents committed to an eighty-hour workweek mustn't have children," she wrote. "If they absolutely need something to love, then let them buy an aquarium."

CHAPTER 11

"I want a friend."

The Saab came to a screeching halt in front of the garage mahal. Andie jumped out, leaving the car door opened, ran up to the kitchen, and tried the knob. In the same instant, she determined that the door was locked and also realized that she'd forgotten her house keys.

"Hello," she called in a voice that squeaked with tension. And then louder, "Hello." No response. She stood still, waiting for her breathing to subside. Above the roar of the pulse in her ears, she could hear the artillery of heavy traffic on the Albany Post Road.

Kika has keys, she thought. *What if the children are hurt inside while I'm driving to Kika's house?*

Andie flashed on all the actors she'd ever seen breaking into locked houses. Where were her black leather gloves, then? Where was her diamond glass cutter, her rubber suction cup?

She walked back to the Saab, took out the rag that Stuart had put with the jack and the length of iron pipe. She wrapped the rag around her right hand, returned to the kitchen door, made a fist and struck the pane of glass above the knob. Nothing. She threw her weight into the second blow. This time the pane cracked, but didn't break. Andie heard a faint beeping from inside and then the whoop, whoop of the burglar-alarm siren. She struck the window a third time. It didn't break.

Panicked now by the siren of her burglar-alarm system, she stepped back to the drive and snatched up one of the whitewashed stones that bordered the asphalt. She ran to the kitchen door and banged the window with the rock. The pane shattered. Andie dropped the rock, reached through the broken window, and opened the door. Withdrawing her wrist, she caught it on a shard of glass that had been left jutting out of the frame.

Once inside, she went to the control panel, punched in the correct numbers. The siren whooped twice and was still. Andie could smell lemon-scented ammonia.

That's right, she thought, *it's Monday. Rosa comes on Monday. Rosa's the only one who ever sets the alarm.*

Andie stood still and listened for the voices of her children. Nothing. She could hear a tap dripping. No, it wasn't a tap. What she heard was the sound of her own blood dripping onto the kitchen tile. She plucked a dish towel off the hanger near the sink and, using her teeth, she tied a bow around the newly injured wrist. The phone rang. She jumped. She walked to the wall unit and picked up.

"Maximum Security," said a voice.

"I'm here," said Andie. "I'd locked myself out. I was in a hurry. Did you get any other alarms from this house today?"

"Code please," said the voice.

"It's me," said Andie, breathlessly.

"Code please," said the voice, suddenly stern.

"Oh," said Andie. "What is it? Give me a hint."

Silence on the other end of the line.

"I've got it," said Andie: "The Last Red Indian."

"Mrs. Cross?" asked the voice, which now swelled with sympathy.

"Yes."

"Are you okay?"

"Fine," said Andie.

"Mother's maiden name?" said the voice.

"O'Conner," said Andie.

"Last four digits of your Social Security number?"

"Oh come on," said Andie. "You're supposed to be on my side."

"Last four digits of your Social Security number?" repeated the voice.

"Four, three, oh seven," said Andie.

"Okay, then," said the voice.

"Have you had any other alarms from this house?" asked Andie again.

"No ma'am," said the voice.

"Are you certain?" asked Andie.

"Are you sure you're okay?" asked the voice.

"I'm okay," said Andie.

"If you're not really okay," said the voice, "say, 'I'm okay,' again now."

"Fine," said Andie, "I'm fine, and thank you for doing your job." She put down the phone, and looked around at the empty kitchen.

"Hello," she called out. "Miss Washington? Ginny? Jane? Anybody home?" She stopped to listen, but all she could hear was her own labored breathing. "HELLO!" she screamed, her voice cracking to reach full volume. Still nothing.

96

Then she noticed that the answering machine's red light was blinking wildly. *Memory's full*, she thought.

She climbed the stairs to the second floor, and came up onto the landing half expecting to find the dead and mutilated bodies of her children. She recalled the dead girls in *The Shining*. No bodies. No signs of struggle. She went into the room the children slept in. Both beds were neatly made. *Miss Washington*, she thought. *Rosa won't make beds.* Instead of being pleased by this uncharacteristic tidiness, Andie experienced a great wave of remorse. There was a stuffed bear on Ginny's pillow. But this was not Ginny's favorite animal. Andie's eldest daughter had formed an intense, if improbable, attachment to a stuffed alligator originally named Alvin, but re-named Hamlet by his young mistress. The family had been on a driving trip to the Florida Keys at the time. Janey was in a Snuggli, and Ginny was very needy, still reeling from the birth of her perfect sibling. So Stuart paid an outrageous $49.99 for the toy, although he urged his daughter to keep the name. "I like Hamlet," Ginny insisted. "Isn't that your favorite play?"

"It's not really an appropriate name for an alligator, though. There aren't a lot of alligators in Denmark. Alvin Alligator works as an alliteration."

Remembering this, Andie took the bear off the pillow, and replaced it with the alligator.

"I don't want an alliteration," Ginny had explained, solemnly. "I didn't want a little sister either," she said, pausing to watch both parents flinch. "I want a friend."

CHAPTER 12

"My girls! My baby girls!"

.

"I wonder what Mrs. Type A is so frantic about," said George Wooding, who had had the good luck to be seated in the breakfast nook of the Monticello for Andie's dramatic homecoming.

"First, she breaks a window. Now she's in and out of Tara like a prairie dog," the retired IBM engineer told his wife, who was working at the sink. "I told you I'd met the husband Sunday in the appliance store. He'd lost the children." Wooding chuckled appreciatively.

Alice came to her husband's side, put a hand on his shoulder, and they both watched as Andie popped out of the kitchen door, paused, and popped back inside again.

"An Armani suit and white sneakers," said Alice. "Do you suppose that's how all the big film critics dress?"

Andie had been driven back inside by the thought that the answering machine was full, and that she might be out in the yard when Stuart phoned. She pressed a button. Nothing. She pressed the button again. "Erasing all messages," the machine said.

"Shit," said Andie, aloud. Uncertain where to go next, she walked back out the kitchen door and turned left, circling the house. It was a bright day, unseasonably warm. The Saab was parked where she'd left it. Andie closed the car door. She peered in through the garage window. The Volvo was gone.

"Ginny," she called in a tremulous voice. "Jane, are you outside? Miss Washington?" She wondered if any neighbors were home to enjoy her desperation.

Back in the kitchen, she phoned Stuart's office. "Sorry," said Althea, her tone gone throaty now with condescension, "Mr. Cross will be so upset to know that you couldn't reach him. I'll have him call the moment he comes back from lunch."

"When would that be?" asked Andie, remembering that her husband's secretary had gone to film school at NYU.

"I don't really expect him for an hour yet," said Althea.

"You don't know if he took the car?" Andie asked.

"I thought he always walked to the station," said Althea. "He tells me he always walks."

"Not always," said Andie angrily, and then modified her tone. "Most of the time," she said, and then her voice trailed off.

"The moment he comes in," said Althea, "I'll have him call. Is there anything I can do? Can I tell your husband what this is about?"

"Just have him call," said Andie.

Next she dialed Kika's number from memory, but Kika didn't pick up, and because her husband, Thomas, worked at home, the phone menu network was tiresome and extensive. Andie hung up without leaving a message.

She went back out to the Saab, retrieved her battered briefcase, brought it into the kitchen and removed the résumé. This she now spread on the glittering stone surface of her granite-topped island, turning to the page of references. Using a bowl of apples to keep the binding splayed, she dialed the Lovely household in Bethesda, Maryland.

The phone rang once, and then she got a recorded message: "Sorry," it said, "but the number you have reached is no longer in service. Thank you for using AT&T."

Andie rechecked the number and dialed again.

The phone was answered on the fourth ring.

"Ms. Lovely?" asked Andie.

"No."

"May I speak with Helen Lovely, or Doctor Binderman?" Andie asked.

"No," said the voice.

"Is this the Lovely residence?" asked Andie.

"No home," said the voice. "Doctor no home."

"Do you know when they'll be back?" asked Andie. "Either of them?"

"Late," said the voice. "Doctor tell me late."

"All right, then." said Andie. "Do you have a pencil?" After she'd dictated a message, she hung up, and phoned the second number she could find. This time she got the voice of an exquisitely spoiled little girl: "If you have business with Samantha," the child trilled, "or with her Daddy, Paul, or with her Mommy, Martha, then you should leave a message . . ." In the background, Andie could hear a man whispering harshly: "After the beep. Say 'after the beep'." "After the beep," piped Samantha, and hung up.

The phone beeped. Andie took a deep breath and began: "I'm calling because you're listed as one of the references for a nanny we now employ named Louise Washington. Could you possibly call me back?" Then she left the home number, and then also that of her office phone.

When she tried the third reference, Andie was connected to a corporation. "Thank you for calling The Leading Edge," she was told. "Your business is very important to us. Due to the unexpectedly enthusiastic response to our last catalog . . ." Andie hung up. She looked around the kitchen, as if searching for inspiration. She tapped her fingernails on the granite counter. Then it came to her.

"When we buy our own house," Stuart had said, "We're going to have a cabinet devoted entirely to keys. A locked cabinet devoted entirely to keys. Just like the one at your family place on Lake George. I've always wanted to re-create it."

Now Andie went to the kitchen table, opened the drawer, and found a set of house keys. These she took to the broom closet and used them to unlock the cabinet they'd hired a carpenter to install. From inside she took out the duplicate for the maid's quarters. She left the house keys dangling from the cabinet lock.

She reached down into the basket of supplies kept in a bucket below the key cabinet by the cleaning lady. She removed a pair of bright yellow rubber gloves. When she untied the kitchen towel with which she'd bound her wrist, her most recent wound reopened, and she could feel blood pooling in the fingers of her glove.

"This will be your sanctuary," she'd told Louise on Saturday. "You can do what you want in here," she'd volunteered eagerly. "You can read Karl Marx, if you want. Drink the cooking sherry. As long as you do your job, we won't pry or intrude. That's a promise."

Now she tried the door of her new nanny's private domain, found it locked, and used the key.

The apartment was astonishingly neat. An easel was propped

against one wall, a box of paints below it. Carefully, so as not to leave evidence of the violation, Andie felt under the pillow. Nothing. Then she checked the surfaces of the bedside table and the dresser. Nothing to excite alarm. There was a large scrapbook on the dresser. This seemed to have newspaper articles in it about Louise's painting. On another occasion, Andie would have taken the time to examine the book with care, but not now. Her children were in peril.

She began to go through the dresser. In one drawer she saw jeans. In another, panties with representations of ice cream cones on them. She plumped the pile, and felt a hard object underneath. She removed the panties, uncovering a knife. It was a bone-handled switchblade. Weren't these illegal in the United States?

Another drawer held tube socks. Reaching in among these, she came upon a second hard object and withdrew what appeared at first to be a .45 caliber automatic. When she looked closely, though, Andie could see that it was actually much smaller than the gun it was designed to represent. It was tiny. Squinting her eyes, she pointed the barrel up at the ceiling and pulled the trigger. The toy clicked, and a flame appeared at the end of the barrel. Making a mental note to question Louise about smoking, Andie returned the lighter to its hiding place.

The desk they'd surrendered to the maid was the same one Andie had worked on herself in the apartment in Chelsea. This had a single, center drawer. She yanked it open: pencils, paper clips. The drawer had been cunningly constructed, so that if pulled almost all the way open, it stuck, appearing to reveal all its contents. If a secret metal flange was thumbed, the drawer came all the way out of the desk, revealing a second, smaller compartment. Andie thumbed the metal flange and removed the drawer from its housing. This was the secret compartment she herself had used to store her passport, the title of the Saab, and three recent letters from a poet whose work and person she particularly admired. Apparently Louise had discovered the secret of the drawer, and Andie found a sheaf of letters held together with a pink rubber band, just like the ones Louise used to hold the hair out of her face. Andie took the letters in both hands. The return address was a town in upstate New York, but had a long number after it with letters.

It's a prison, Andie thought. *This woman is getting letters from prison.*

She sat on the edge of the bed, wondering if she could read the letters, and then get them back in order and in place. She'd have to take off the gloves first.

Before committing to this, she removed the rubber band and folded back the top of the first letter.

"Dearest Sugar," she read. " 'Stone walls do not a prison make, nor iron bars a cage.' But they'll do in a pinch. I miss you."

The doorbell rang. Andie jumped, as if discovered. Heart racing, she folded back the top letter, replaced the rubber band, returned the bundle to its compartment, put the drawer back into the desk, surveyed the room for signs of intrusion. The dresser drawer that held the cigarette lighter concealed among tube socks hadn't closed completely. She pulled it out and tried to jam it closed. It wouldn't go. *The lighter is taking too much space now*, Andie thought. She tried once more to close the drawer, then removed two pairs of tube socks, put one in each suit pocket. Finally, the drawer closed. The doorbell rang again. Andie inhaled deeply, looked around. Then she walked quickly out of the maid's room and locked the door behind her. The bell rang a third time and lingered.

Andie went to the broom closet, put the key back in the cabinet, closed the cabinet, locked the cabinet, putting the house keys in the pocket of her suit jacket. She yanked off the gloves, and now both wrists began to bleed freely. She closed the door to the broom closet. The doorbell rang again and then again.

Andie walked to the island, pulled out the concealed trash bin, tossed the gloves into the new white liner, which Rosa must have put in place. She patted her pockets, found the tube socks, and dropped them into the trash as well. She took a piece of paper towel for each wrist and went to the front door, holding her hands together so as to provide a compress for the wounds she had reopened by removing the gloves. Once at the door, she peered out through the glass peephole that Stuart had insisted the builder install. "So you won't be raped," he told Andie. "Or at least you won't be raped by anybody but me."

The peephole held a wide-angle lens, which distorted. Andie saw two people. Mailmen? No. They were police. *Oh, God*, she thought.

The police were apparently unaware of her presence. One was a short, stocky man. The other was a slight woman with long, snarly red hair. They were both bareheaded, holding their hats. Both had grim expressions on their faces. Was this boredom, or were they bringing dreadful news?

The woman was chewing gum, wagging her head as she spoke. The words were muffled, but Andie could hear them clearly enough through the hollow front door. "I've been at work a week now, and I've already seen more action than I did in six months in the Bronx," she said. "We've got murder, kidnapping."

"Bullshit," the man said. "I don't know where you were in the Bronx, but we don't usually have any trouble out here."

"And this is supposed to be where people move to raise their children," the woman continued. "That's a good one," and she laughed mirthlessly.

Andie began to fumble furiously with the lock. When she got the door open, the man turned to face her. "Police," he said, holding up his badge. "Officer Marks. Is this the Cross residence?"

"Yes," said Andie. "I'm his wife."

The policeman looked down at his notes.

"So you're Ms. Wilde?" he said.

Andie nodded.

"Officer Pigniole," said the woman with snarly red hair. "Can we come inside? We need to talk."

"Officer who?" asked Andie.

"Pigniole," said the woman "Pronounced like the nut."

"What's this about?" asked Andie.

The redhead turned to her colleague. "I don't know, John," she said. "What do we tell her?"

What was the movie? Andie thought. Saving Private Ryan. *The solemn messengers in uniform. Mrs. Ryan coming out of the kitchen, coming to the door. The dead children.*

"There was a lot of blood," Officer Marks told his wife that evening. "I could smell it even before I looked down at her hands."

Andie had felt her legs go out from under her, just as Mrs. Ryan's legs had done. Slowly, as if shot through the lungs, Andie had sat back awkwardly on the floor. "My girls!" she said. "My baby girls!"

CHAPTER 13

To See the Lion

The wooden desk, which Stuart compulsively left bare on Friday evenings, was marred this Monday morning with a single pink message: "Please call Herbert Glass at your earliest possible convenience." Without removing his jacket, he dialed the number.

"Oh, Stuart, you just missed him," said Glass's secretary, Sophie. "He came in briefly this morning, and he's already headed out of town."

"I'm sorry," said Stuart.

"Don't be sorry," said Sophie. "It's nine A.M. I know what he wants."

"Am I going to hear a joke?" asked Stuart. Glass was notorious within the company for starting every public meeting, every meal with a joke. Sometimes they were funny. Sometimes they were not funny. They were always long.

"I suppose you *will* hear a joke," said Sophie, and she didn't chuckle. "Mr. Glass wants to eat lunch with you tomorrow, Tuesday. If you could possibly meet him at one P.M. In the Grill Room at the Four Seasons."

"One P.M. at the Four Seasons," Stuart repeated, and he thought he managed to keep the surge of hope from distorting his voice.

"Right," said Sophie. "He knows it's your favorite restaurant. It's where he always takes you for your birthday. It *is* your favorite restaurant?"

"Close enough," said Stuart.

"Can I tell him you'll be there?" asked Sophie.

"I'll be there," said Stuart, "and thanks." He put the phone down, hung his jacket in his office closet, and took in his surroundings with satisfaction. From behind his outsized desk the editor of Acropolis books looked down on the lion statues outside the Fifth Avenue entrance to the New York Public Library. The office—which had been designed and furnished for Herbert Glass, who never occupied it—had a floor to ceiling credenza and a chesterfield sofa. "You're the third lion," Massberg told him. Stuart smiled now, savoring the recollection.

The sofa, the view, the rich carpet still gave the editor a vague thrill. The smell of wood polish reminded him of church and beyond that of the assemblies he'd attended and dozed through as a child.

Now he closed his door, and without sitting, he called Steven Solon at Random House.

"Missed you at our party," he said, settling into his chair at last.

"It killed me not to come," said the other man. "Wallace Stevens reported that it was a great bash."

"Boy did he ever get drunk," said Stuart. "What did he tell you?"

"He said that Andie was gorgeous, you were wise, the food spectacular. Especially the guacamole."

"So why didn't you come?" asked Stuart.

"You know how ex-wives can be?" said Solon. "I was going to see my son Saturday night or I wasn't going to see him at all this week."

"I understand," said Stuart. "But here's the deal. I'm meeting with Herbert Glass tomorrow. I think he's going to offer me the job."

"Which job is that?" asked Solon.

"The big job."

There was a silence on the other end of the line.

"Are you there?" asked Stuart.

"Sure, I'm here," said Solon.

"Why the silence?" asked Stuart.

"I don't know," said Solon, "I suppose I was taken aback. What job exactly do you think he's going to offer you?"

"Editorial Director," said Stuart.

"In all but name you already *are* the acting Editorial Director," said Solon. "Have been for some time. Glass is completely occupied with real estate. He doesn't interfere at all anymore, does he?"

"Rarely," said Stuart.

There was a pause, and then Solon went on. "You don't have any indication that he is going to start interfering in editorial matters now?" he asked.

"No," said Stuart.

"Okay," said Solon, although he didn't sound pleased.

There was a long silence, which Stuart finally broke. "You know I've never campaigned for the position," he said. "I'm not connected. Massberg lunches out more than I do. I sit in my office and edit text."

"Yes," said Solon. "There's that. But you're good at it."

"I want this job," said Stuart. "I can taste it."

"Of course you want it," said Solon. "Andie just got promoted, you think you should be promoted too. You've been working toward this for most of your adult life."

"I'm afraid I haven't been very politic about it, though. I mean I send the Glass family marmalade at Christmas, but that's about it."

"Marmalade?" asked Solon.

"Excellent marmalade," said Stuart. "From Fortnum & Mason. Still, I'm not sure that's enough. Also I do have something of a negative reputation."

"What do you mean by that?" asked Solon.

"Whenever Octopus buys another publishing house, the people at *Publishers Weekly* and even at the *New York Times*, they call me up. I'm the voice of outrage."

"You have a high profile," said Solon. "That's a plus."

"Yes," said Stuart, "but I've also infuriated the corporation that now handles a third of the book business in this town."

"Don't worry," said Solon. "There's only one person you need to please. That's Herbert Glass. And he adores you. He has two biological sons, but you're his favorite."

"In any case," said Stuart. "Here's the plan. Editorial Directors need vision. I can't just promise more of the same. I want a larger acquisitions budget, of course. More importantly, I need to hire you as editor. I want you in my old post the moment it becomes my old post. You're five years younger than I am. When I retire, you get my place. By then we will have made Acropolis into the leading house."

"Whoa!" said Solon. "I don't know about this."

"What don't you know? I assumed you'd be flattered."

"I am flattered, but I like it here. I'm one of many. I'm a face in

109

the crowd. I destroyed my marriage working the hours you do. Now I catch the five twenty-four. I sleep peacefully at night."

"But remember how much fun we had in the old days?" said Stuart. "Then we were one of many. Now we'd be alone in the field. Since the Glass family bought the firm back from Pretty Kitty, Inc., we've become the largest substantial, privately held publisher in New York. We can do what we want. We can do what we think is right."

Solon didn't say anything.

"Hello," said Stuart. "Are you there?"

"Here's the problem," said Solon. "I don't believe you can afford me."

"We can afford you," said Stuart. "We just paid two million dollars for a book I despise. We can't afford not to have you."

"I still don't know," said Solon. "I like Random House. I'm a Random House sort of guy."

"How about lunch?" asked Stuart.

"Lunch?"

"Are you free for lunch today?"

"I have a dentist appointment."

"Does it hurt?"

"Does what hurt?"

"Do you have an exposed nerve?"

"No."

"All right, then, meet me for lunch."

"The Pen & Ink?"

"Not today. Let's go where nobody else from Acropolis ever goes."

When Stuart came back from his meal that afternoon, it was almost three. Althea followed him into his office.

"Want to hear a joke?" he asked her.

"Not really," said Althea.

"Take a minute," said Stuart. "I just heard it from Solon."

Althea didn't say anything, so Stuart charged ahead. "It's about a guy who decides to be a screenwriter. He's got a house in Malibu and one day . . ."

"Is this going to take a long time?" asked Althea.

"Moderately long," said Stuart. "But this would-be screenwriter, he's never written anything. Never felt the need . . ."

Althea was looking at her hands.

Stuart swallowed. "You don't like it?" he asked. "You've already heard it?"

Althea shook her head. "I had other things on my mind."

"Did Glass phone?"

Althea shook her head.

"Martin Brookstone? Did he phone?"

"No," said Althea, closing the door behind them both. "It's Andie," she said. Stuart blanched.

"Andie's been trying to reach you since about noon. Getting more and more anxious each time she called. I tried to calm her down. I would have had her phone you, but I didn't know where you were. Something about the girls."

"The girls?" asked Stuart, immediately regretting all three glasses of wine.

Althea put a hand on her boss's shoulder. "Then the police phoned. They were at your house."

"The police? Why?"

"They wouldn't tell me why."

"Did they leave a number?"

"It's your number. Your house. Do you want me to place the call?"

"No," said Stuart. "I'd better call now, though. And I need some coffee." Althea backed out of the office and closed the door. This time Stuart did take off his coat, and hung it up, before sitting down at his desk and dialing his home.

The phone was picked up on the second ring. "Cross residence," said a female voice, but one he didn't recognize.

"Hello," said Stuart, uncertainly. "Who is this?"

"This is Officer Pigniole. How can I be of assistance?"

"Officer who?" asked Stuart.

"Pigniole," said the woman, "Pronounced just like the nut."

"Is everything all right?" Stuart asked. "Are the girls all right?"

"Excuse me," said Officer Pigniole, "but I didn't get your name."

"Stuart, Stuart Cross. You're at my house. Are the girls okay?"

"I'm glad you brought that up, Mr. Cross," said the woman on the other end of the line. "Your wife is very concerned about her children."

"Why's that?" asked Stuart.

"Well, apparently Mrs. Cross came home from work, and they weren't here. Or that's what she told us. We let her try to phone her husband."

"That's me," said Stuart.

"We let her phone her husband," repeated the policewoman, as if annoyed by the interruption. "She couldn't reach him."

"I was at lunch," said Stuart.

"You were at lunch at two thirty?" asked the policewoman.

"Yes," said Stuart angrily. "It was a business lunch."

"Oh, I see," said Officer Pigniole. "In any case, your wife told us that you had recently employed a new, black child-care worker. And that you didn't know her very well."

"Now, now," said Stuart. "You're getting way ahead of yourself."

"You didn't just start with a new African-American child-care worker?"

"We did, but she has excellent references."

"The woman is gone. The children are gone. We have had to restrain your wife. You know she had given herself some nasty wounds?"

"You had to restrain her?"

"Yes, we had to restrain her. This was while *you* were at lunch. She might have killed herself."

"All right," said Stuart. "Is Andie there? Can I speak with her?"

"I don't think that would be advisable," said Officer Pigniole.

"Why ever not?"

"I hope you don't mind my asking," said Officer Pigniole, "but we need to know this. Has Mrs. Cross ever tried to take her own life before?"

"No," said Stuart. "I need to speak to my wife. Is she there?"

"Yes," said Officer Pigniole, reluctantly. "She's here."

"Is she hurt?" Stuart asked, his voice rising with concern.

"No, she's not hurt. Or not badly."

"All right then," said Stuart. "Let me speak with her."

"We'd rather not disturb Mrs. Cross right now. We've called a doctor, and your wife has been sedated. She was very upset."

"I thought she was all right," said Stuart.

"She *is* all right," said Officer Pigniole. "You're not listening. Your wife is fine. Upset. She's upset. About the children."

"Look," said Stuart. "Could you please let me please speak with my wife?"

The police officer didn't say anything.

"I want to speak with my wife now," said Stuart.

"I'd rather you didn't," said Officer Pigniole. "She's resting. Did you know how depressed she was?"

"She wasn't depressed this morning," said Stuart. "She just got a promotion, for Christ's sake."

"Doctor Bangs gave very strict instructions," Pigniole said, and then Stuart could hear Andie in the background sounding petulant and weepy. "It's my telephone," he heard her say. "It's my house. My telephone. My husband. Mine, mine, mine."

Then she came on the line. "Stuart, is that you?" she said.

"Yes, it's me."

"Oh, Stuart," she said, and began to weep. "You come right home. Will you *please* come right home?"

"Absolutely," said Stuart. "I'm catching the next train. Are you all right?" he asked.

"I'm fine," said Andie.

"You sure?"

"I'm sure."

"Why are the police there?"

"I don't know," said Andie. "They came and rang the doorbell. I thought it was about the children. So then they started looking for the children." She lowered her voice, and he could hear her cupping the speaker of the phone with one hand. "This horrid woman thinks I murdered the girls," she whispered. "I guess it was all the blood. I tried to convince them that it was my blood. Then they called a doctor in, and he gave me a shot."

"What about the girls?" asked Stuart.

"They're not here," said Andie.

"Is that why you're so upset?" asked Stuart.

"Yes," said Andie, her voice cracking. "That *is* why I'm so upset. I get home. No children. No nanny. No note."

"They weren't supposed to be there," said Stuart.

"So where are they?" asked Andie. "Do you know where they are?

"They're fine," said Stuart. "Miss Washington took them to the Bronx Zoo. Remember they read that Belloc poem about the lion? 'And always keep a-hold of Nurse / For fear of finding something worse.' Miss Washington took them to the Bronx Zoo. To see the lion."

CHAPTER 14

"Who the children belong to."

Despite, or—perhaps because of—his wife's hysteria, Stuart did not leave Manhattan immediately. After draining the putrid cup that Althea had delivered—"I knew you wouldn't want me to make a fresh pot this late in the day," she explained—he went out of the building for sixteen ounces of black coffee and a package of Marlboros, stopping on the street to smoke a cigarette for the second time that week, and also the second time in ten years. He could feel the blood rushing down into his toes, and then a great burst of determination. *I'll handle it*, he thought. Back at his desk, he composed a fabulously opaque rejection to a writer he suspected might be a friend of the Glass family, phoned Heather at Bathos to ask about Martin Brookstone. He got her voice mail. "You've reached Heather Senson at the Bathos Literary Agency. I'm either away from my desk, or on another call. Please leave a message, and I'll get back to you as soon as possible."

"It's me," he told the machine. "Stuart. Stuart Cross. I need to know about Martin Brookstone. If I could possibly hear before tomorrow. You can call me at home." Briefcase finally packed, he was heading out of the office, when Rick Massberg waved Stuart into his own modest cubicle.

"You okay?" the younger man asked.

"Sure," said Stuart. "Fine."

"You look, I don't know . . ." said the younger man, "rattled. Anything the matter?"

"Fine," said Stuart, "everything is fine."

"Anything I can do?" Massberg asked.

"No," said Stuart, "but thanks."

"Anything going on?" asked Massberg.

"No," said Stuart, "or not for sure."

"When it is for sure, you'll tell me?" asked Massberg.

Stuart nodded, and as he nodded it occurred to him that Massberg might expect to be Editor-in-Chief, might be offended when Solon was brought on board to be above him. "Whatever happens," he told his junior in a slightly drunken non sequitur, "whatever happens, I still want you here. Whatever happens, I very much want you here."

Once in the elevator, the false bottom fell out of his spirits. Whatever fire had been lit by wine and nicotine went suddenly out. A wet log in there, steaming, but not smoking. He cupped a hand over his mouth, and blew out into it, smelling the Merlot and tobacco on his breath. *I'm going to be very late*, he thought, *and I never should have said that to Massberg. Now he thinks I'm a broken down old drunk.* Stuart looked at his watch. It was five thirty-five P.M.

Out on the street, he ran for a block, but finally gave up, because of the heavy pedestrian traffic. By the time he reached Grand Central, he'd missed the 5:47.

With twenty minutes to kill before the next train, he went back outside for another smoke. On the sidewalk, he noticed a man with

117

a turban selling discounted toys from a folding table. Among these was a replica of a .38 caliber revolver. This was made of plastic, and designed to spray water instead of lead. The gun cost three dollars. Stuart bought it and still had time to pick up the *New York Post* before mounting the 6:07, finding a seat just before the bells rang and the doors closed.

An editorial bordered in crimson and titled: "Don't Mollycoddle Criminals!" was jumped from the front page. Written by Thomas Paine (not that Thomas Paine), the piece began by quoting an ancient who had once been a photographer from the *New York Star*. The man remembered how he had used to scramble to get the first picture of the suspect in a notorious crime. "Those shots were worth a lot," he said, "because once in custody, the defendants were so badly beaten by the police." The man charged with the Lindbergh kidnapping, for instance, had been almost unrecognizable after questioning. "Justice was swift," wrote Paine.

At this point, the lights went out, the heat stopped, but the train kept moving, rocking uneasily on its rails. Metal grated against metal, and the train came to a full stop. Stuart folded his newspaper, closed his eyes, and tried to breathe deeply. Five minutes later, the train began to move again, the lights flickered, and came back on.

"While I will not condone violence against the untried," Paine continued, "it sickens me to think of the high life often lived behind bars."

There followed bullets with examples of high life lived behind bars.

Stuart thought he recognized two of the four examples as having been cribbed from Nicholas Pileggi's 1985 bestseller *Wiseguy: Life in a Mafia Family*.

"The criminals live like aristocrats," Paine wrote, "while the true aristocrats, the men and women in blue, are paid like postal clerks and treated like the help."

Leafing through to look up his horoscope, Stuart was surprised to see an appreciation of Sir John Gielgud. It was not as prominent as Andie's had been nor as long. It was tag-lined—Susan Logan.

By the time his train came up out of the Park Avenue tunnel, the color had gone out of the sky, and Stuart was fast asleep. He dreamed uneasily of himself in prison, eating steak, and drinking glass after glass of Mouton Rothschild.

"No more for me now," he murmured, when he felt the conductor shaking his shoulder. "Time to wake up," he heard, and opened his eyes to see a vaguely familiar figure with the exploded veins in his nose of a present or former drunk. "Scarborough's next," the man said.

Stuart thanked the conductor, put the *Post* in his briefcase, rose, and stood between cars until the train stopped. The outside air braced him and sodium lights cast the station parking lot in sharp and unforgiving contrasts. Bowed down by a terrible lassitude, Stuart climbed Scarborough Station Road on foot and in the dark.

Cresting the hill, he was cheered by the imposing bulk of his new house. The missing nanny met him at the door. Her hair was pulled back by a rubber band, and she was wearing jeans and a dark blue fleece with "Patagonia" in white letters above her heart and zippers at the wrists.

Stuart stood for a moment, uncertainly, at the threshold. Louise stepped forward and took both his hands in hers.

"Police gone?" he asked.

Louise nodded. "I'm so, so sorry," she said, leading her employer inside and then backing into the kitchen. "I feel dreadful about this. I shouldn't have gone without leaving a note."

"That's right," said Stuart. "But who would have guessed that Andie was going to come home? Next time," he said, and wagged a finger, "leave that note."

Both girls were at the table. Jane had been drawing, and looked up now, her delicate brow still furrowed with concentration. Ginny was searching around in her mouth with a finger. She had been leafing through the Neiman Marcus catalog. Stuart could smell gingerbread.

"I hope you weren't concerned," Louise said. "Here they are. Safe as houses. Your wife's in bed. But I promised to send you up the instant you came in."

Jane climbed down from her chair, ran, and threw her arms around her father's waist. "We saw the lion," she said, and then recited her favorite lines from the poem: " 'The Lion made a sudden stop, / He let the Dainty Morsel drop.' What's a morsel, Daddy? Am I a morsel?"

"You certainly are a morsel, baby," Stuart said, picking up his younger daughter and squeezing her against his chest.

"How was the lion?" he asked, revolving slowly, with the child in his arms.

"Sleeping," said Jane.

Ginny looked up from her catalog, but did not leave her place at the table. "Hi, Dad," she said. "Why's Mom sick?"

"Your mom's okay," said Stuart. "I'm just going up to see her. How was the zoo?"

"The nanny wouldn't buy me a hot dog," said Ginny. "She wouldn't buy me ice cream. I was dizzy."

"I'm sorry if you had a bad time," said Stuart, leaning forward and trying to put Jane down.

"Hold me up," said Janey.

"I'd love to," said Stuart, "but Daddy's tired. Another time," he said, but his daughter only held him tighter, kissing him on the cheek.

"I'm sorry, baby, but you have to get down now."

"All right, then," said Janey, and let herself slip until she was standing on tiptoes.

Gently but decisively, Stuart untangled himself from her arms.

"We didn't have a bad time," said Ginny, who pretended not to notice her little sister's antics. "We had fun. I was hungry, though."

Still holding one hand on the top of Janey's head, Stuart stepped around the table and kissed his older daughter on the lips; she did not meet his eye.

"Janey misses you and Mom," Ginny explained. "She's not very mature."

Stuart hung his coat over a chair, put his briefcase on the kitchen table, opened it, and withdrew the plastic water pistol.

"Oh, Daddy," said Janey jumping up and down. "Goody, goody."

Ginny had her eyes glued to the catalog.

Stuart turned to Louise. "Is Andie asleep?" he asked.

Louise nodded. "She's been medicated. But I promised. She wouldn't go to bed until I swore that you'd go up there and wake her the instant you came in."

So Stuart made the climb to the master-bedroom-suite-to-die-for. He could see his wife's black hair spread on the white pillow. He sat on the edge of the mattress. The movement was enough to wake Andie, who turned over. Her face was puffed, her eyes rimmed with red. She was wearing the silk blouse in which she'd started off to work that morning. This had a silver pin in the likeness of a dolphin still fastened above the right breast. When

Stuart hugged Andie, she threw her arms around his neck, and he felt the rasp of bandages. Holding his wife in his arms, he took down her right wrist and saw the gauze and tape that had been put in place by Doctor Bangs.

"How'd this happen?" he asked.

"Long story," said Andie.

"You didn't actually try to kill yourself?" Stuart asked. Andie shook her head.

"The police told me you tried to kill yourself," he said.

Andie nodded. "You've been drinking," she said. "And smoking cigarettes."

"That's right," he said.

"What time is it?" asked Andie.

"I don't know exactly," said Stuart. "It's after seven."

"When did you leave the office?"

"As soon as I could. Then the train got stuck in the tunnel."

"Is that why you're so late?"

"Well, actually," said Stuart, "it looks as if the other shoe is finally going to drop. It looks as if I'm going to get the promotion. But you're the one who had the adventure today. What the hell happened here?"

"Blow by blow?" asked Andie.

"Blow by blow," said Stuart.

"All right, then," said Andie, sitting up in bed, and shaking the hair out of her eyes. "But you're going to have to make me a pot of tea. Prince of Wales. It's in the cupboard above the Cuisinart."

Stuart nodded, and then the phone rang. He picked it up. "Hello," he said. "Yes, she's here." Andie was shaking her head violently. "This is her husband, Stuart Cross. Can I take a message? Hello then, Mrs. Lovely, and thank you for calling us back. Miss

Washington did work for you? Yes, she's here now. And you liked her?"

Stuart put his hand over the phone and turned to Andie. "Mrs. Lovely says that Miss Washington was the best nanny she ever ever had."

Stuart listened and nodded. "Yes, that's what we wanted to know," he said. "Complaints? No, we don't have any complaints. Just checking. Being careful. Thanks again for calling. This means a lot to us." Then he hung up, looked at Andie, and shrugged.

"She wasn't there when I called, of course," said Andie. "Nobody was there. Nobody was here either. You couldn't be reached. Nor did I have any idea where the girls had gone. The paragon might have left a note."

"Or I might have left a note," said Stuart. "Who would have guessed that a note was needed? You haven't been home from work early since Janey was born. That's more than six years. Not once."

"I feel differently now," said Andie. "I missed the girls. I'd been with them every day for two weeks."

Stuart nodded.

Andie propped herself up in bed. "I'm terrified that I'll look back on those two weeks as the last good time I ever had."

"But you love movies."

"It's a fabulous job and all, but I had the best fun ever staying home with the girls. I don't know if you even noticed, but I baked cookies every day."

"Not exactly what Ginny needed most in the world," said Stuart.

Andie sighed. "They were oatmeal cookies. We only ever had them for the after-school snack and once for dessert."

"I remember," said Stuart, softening.

"I loved Saturdays the best. I'd make them breakfast. You'd be asleep. I'd just sit at the kitchen counter. I'd make a list of chores. Then I'd read the paper. I'd just sit. Do nothing. Think nothing. Hearing them moving around in the house."

"The Zen of unemployment," said Stuart.

Andie nodded.

"You're forgetting the mortgage," Stuart said.

"I love the house," said Andie, "but I love my daughters more."

"That's why we hired Miss Washington," said Stuart. "You can have your cake and eat it too."

"I'm not so sure," said Andie. "But my head is full of cobwebs. Get me that tea. You and I need to have a private planning session."

"About what?" asked Stuart.

"It's about Miss Washington. We need to talk about the new nanny. We need to talk about who these children belong to."

CHAPTER 15

"The job is yours."

"Where'd you go this time?" Andie asked, when her husband reappeared half an hour later with a tray. Stuart pushed a pile of magazines to the floor and put his burden on a bedside table.

"Just look at this," he said, and pointed. There was a pot of tea, a butter plate with three neatly sliced wedges of lemon, a tiny pitcher of honey, a bottle of Heineken, an empty glass engraved with the likeness of a stag, and two plates, each with a chicken sandwich, a slice of pickle, and three Pringles. There were also two dessert dishes, each with a square of gingerbread topped with whipped cream. "Louise made up the meal," he explained. "The girls baked gingerbread this afternoon. Apparently the police ate most of it, but these two pieces survived."

"What were you doing while the tray was being prepared?" asked Andie.

"Calling the office," said Stuart, "I checked my voice mail." He picked up half of his sandwich and held it out for examination. "The bread is toasted. She got that toaster oven to work again. The woman's a genius. She even cut off the crusts."

Andie's face did not indicate enthusiasm for any of this.

Stuart sat on the edge of the bed. He poured Andie a cup of tea, added lemon, and a dollop of honey. He poured Heineken into the glass.

The phone rang. Stuart picked it up. Put his hand over the mouthpiece. "It's Kika," he said.

Andie shook her head. "Tell her I'll call tomorrow," she said.

Stuart took his hand off the mouthpiece and spoke into it. "Can Andie call you tomorrow?" he asked.

"I just want her new guacamole recipe," said Kika.

Stuart put his hand back over the mouthpiece.

"She just wants your new guacamole recipe," he said.

Andie nodded. "Tell Kika I'll leave the recipe in the kitchen. Right on the phone table. She can come get it anytime."

Stuart relayed this information, put down the receiver, and picked up his beer.

"Where'd you get that glass?" asked Andie. "That's from my uncle's country house. We never use those glasses."

"I guess Louise picked it out," said Stuart. "It is designed for beer. I like it."

Andie took a sip of tea. "I wish she'd ask me before she goes into the cupboards."

"You were asleep," said Stuart.

"Okay," said Andie. "First things first. Can you stay home tomorrow?"

"No," said Stuart.

"Can't you read manuscripts at home?" asked Andie. "Isn't that what you do, read manuscripts? Can't you—for one day—read them at home? Rick Massberg is always saying you could work at home three days out of the week."

Stuart put down his glass of beer and stood.

"Point one," he said. "Rick Massberg is not my boss. Point two, Glass wants to meet me for lunch tomorrow. I think he's going to offer me the Editorial Directorship."

Andie pulled herself to a more upright position. "You hate fish," she said. "He'll make you eat Dover sole."

"I've eaten a lot worse than Dover sole in my career," said Stuart. "Besides which, I don't have to eat the sole. I'll order the steak this time. Surprise the old man."

"In that case, I'm going to need to quit my fabulous new job," said Andie. "Somebody has to be at home," she said.

"Now you're sounding genuinely crazy," said Stuart. "We went over this. I thought you loved this job. You just got it. Why quit?"

"Because I love my family more."

"Exactly," said Stuart. "That's why we hired the world's costliest and most highly recommended child-care professional. The jewel in the crown of Mary Poppins."

"You mean the paragon?" asked Andie.

"I mean the woman who baked the gingerbread, made the sandwiches, took the girls to the zoo."

Andie put down her tea and crossed her arms. "Point one," she said. "I wanted to be the woman who takes the girls to the zoo. She gets no credit for that. Point two, I don't trust her."

"You're upset," said Stuart. "You've had a hell of a day." He sat back down, picked up his sandwich, and took another bite. "Boy but this is good," he said, wagging his head with appreciation.

"You weren't with me today," said Andie.

Stuart nodded, still chewing. "I know that," he said. "Must have been a nightmare. But it's over now. And really, nothing's wrong. Nothing ever was wrong. Here," he said, and passed Andie half of her sandwich. "Try it."

Andie took a tiny bite of sandwich.

"Isn't that tasty?" asked Stuart. "I think she made the mayonnaise. This woman is magic with the girls. I've never seen them so happy and involved. And this is vacation. On vacation they usually lie around in front of the TV like a couple of landed fish. Last weekend they read a poem about a lion. Today they went to the zoo and saw the lion."

Andie chewed and swallowed. "Two things you don't know about. When I called here from the city there was a message on the machine for her."

"So?" said Stuart. "She lives here."

"I think it was from a black man. Something about ofay and how she should remember where she comes from."

"So she has black friends," said Stuart chewing happily. "What did you expect?"

"You wouldn't take this so lightly if you'd heard the message," said Andie.

"All right," said Stuart. "I'll go right downstairs after dinner and play the message."

"You can't," said Andie. "I erased it when I came home. I was in a panic and the machine was full. Trust me, though. If you'd heard the voice, you'd be on my side about this."

"I am on your side," said Stuart.

"Get up and close the door," said Andie. "In case she's listening."

"Can you hear how you sound?" asked Stuart. "You've got to try to calm down."

"Get up and close the door," said Andie.

Reluctantly, Stuart put his sandwich on its plate, stood up, and closed the door. Then he came back and sat again on the edge of the bed, but this time he didn't sit near his wife.

"Listen," said Andie. "I called home from the city. Heard this message about how we are the ofays and live in this monstrous house. I tried to call you right away, but you weren't there. So I took the train home, read all the coverage of the Tillie Cove case in my own paper."

Stuart snorted. "I think it splendid that the *New York Post* values you so highly," he said. "But you mustn't take their news coverage seriously. The Cove case is a tragedy. Our case is not a tragedy. Lots of children who don't die have nannies. Other children die without nannies."

"You didn't hear that message," said Andie.

"No," said Stuart. "I didn't."

"I went through her room," said Andie. "I found a bunch of letters. Written to her. Letters that seemed to be from prison."

Stuart sighed wearily. "Are you quite certain they were written from prison?"

"I think they were," said Andie. "I was in a hurry. But each envelope had a long number on it with letters. I think they were written by a prisoner."

"According to Henry Louis Gates," said Stuart, "a young black man's chances of going to jail are one hundred times as high as are his chances of going to college. You can't be astonished that a black woman might have acquaintances in jail. I bet Louise also has friends in college."

"These were love letters," said Andie.

Stuart stood, walked to the door, walked back to the bed. "What if she does know somebody in prison. In the late 1960s, I had friends behind bars."

"I bet this guy isn't there for an antiwar protest," said Andie.

"You don't have any idea why he's in prison," said Stuart.

"The letters were hidden," said Andie. "In that space behind the drawer in that desk I used to work at."

"What space?" Stuart asked.

"Never mind," said Andie.

"Besides," said Stuart, "we gave her that desk to use. Didn't you promise that her private quarters would be sacrosanct?"

"Thank God I did check," said Andie. "You know what else I found?"

"What else did you find?"

"I found a switchblade and a gun."

"You found a gun?" asked Stuart. Now she had his attention.

"Well, actually," said Andie, "it's a cigarette lighter."

"A cigarette lighter?" asked Stuart.

"Yes," said Andie, "but it's designed to look like a gun."

"Like a .45?" asked Stuart. "Only miniaturized?"

"That's right," said Andie.

"I used to have one of those," said Stuart.

"Couldn't somebody use a gun like that to rob a bank?" Andie asked.

"No," said Stuart. "That's why it's miniaturized. It doesn't look anything like a real gun. Hold that up at a bank, and they'd laugh at you. Now the pistol I bought Janey today in the city, that could actually be mistaken for a real gun. Only it has this orange plastic stopper on the end where the squirting nozzle is."

"You bought Janey a pistol?" asked Andie.

"I bought her a squirt gun," said Stuart. "Take it easy. I'm beginning to think I should pour a bucket of water over you."

Andie began to weep. "I knew you wouldn't understand," she said. "I had a terrible day. I was completely helpless. I think the girls are in danger." The weeping turned into sobbing.

Stuart put down his sandwich and took his wife into his arms for the second time that evening. "You've always thought the girls were in danger," he said, raising his voice so that it could still be heard over his wife's sobbing and also working to keep any impatience out of the tone.

"All right," said Stuart. "But understand about this lunch. Glass wants to meet me at the Four Seasons. He celebrated his seventy-second birthday a month ago. The Glasses aren't the Rockefellers. They don't live forever. Herbert's father died at sixty-nine. Herbert keeps up with the real estate, but he's paid very little attention to the publishing house for the last couple of years. I think he's going to make me Editorial Director. This is not a lunch I want to miss."

"All I'm asking," said Andie, "is that you call his office in the morning, and see if the lunch can't be postponed. What time does Sophie get in?"

"Eight."

"Call at eight ten then. Say it's a family emergency. Ask if he can eat lunch with you Wednesday instead of Tuesday."

Stuart didn't respond.

"Please do that," said Andie. "For me."

Stuart stood up again. "I hate this," he said.

"If Herbert Glass is planning to make you Editorial Director, he's not going to change his mind because you postpone lunch for one day," said Andie. "How long have you worked there? Twenty-five years?"

"Twenty-seven years in May, and I'd hate to flush my professional life down the toilet because you're hysterical about the fact that our black nanny has black friends."

"I'd stay home myself," said Andie, "but I quit work today at noon. I must go to the office tomorrow. I have a review to write,

131

and I also have a two P.M. movie I can't miss. It's the new Disney animation. You know how devoted Fowler is to his son? He wants to bring Maximus to the screening."

"Jesus," said Stuart. "If I don't get this job because your boss wants to see cartoons . . ."

"Listen," said Andie. "If you take off tomorrow, then I'll take Wednesday."

"I don't think any of this is necessary," said Stuart.

Andie reached out and took her husband's left wrist in her right hand. "Don't worry," she said. "The job is yours."

CHAPTER 16

"Serve the children for lunch."

When the drug Doctor Bangs had given her wore off that night at about three A.M., Andie woke up and turned on her reading light. She made a racket flipping through *Variety*. This woke Stuart, who turned on his light as well. They sat side by side in bed reading, but not speaking. It was after four A.M. when Andie switched off her light and turned her back to her husband. Stuart waited five minutes then turned off his own light, placed his back against his wife's. He lay in the dark. He imagined his phone call with Sophie. "Oh, Stuart," she would tell him, her voice swelling with an affection she had never shown him in the waking world. "I hate to do this, but I really have to insist. Mr. Glass—as you well know—is the least demanding of employers, but he must see you tomorrow."

"All right," said Stuart in the dream, "I'll tell Andie that you insist." Then he drifted off to sleep.

When Stuart woke up, he could tell how late it was by the way the sun poured into the room. He'd slept through the alarm.

"Oh, shit," he said, when he had picked up his watch and confirmed that it was after seven. He nudged Andie, who leaped out of bed.

Andie was in the bathroom suite with the door closed almost immediately, so Stuart put on his robe and went to the bath off the guest room.

There he shaved and took a quick shower—he hadn't entirely abandoned the idea of going into the city. If he sensed at all that there was going to be a problem at work, he'd go at Andie again. By eight oh five A.M. he was clean, back in his bedroom, and on the phone with his boss's office. Sophie took his proposal with astonishing equanimity. "Of course I'll check with Mr. Glass," she said, "but I can't imagine a problem. You're right to put your family first. This is still, after all, a family business."

"Do please stress that this family situation is important," said Stuart. "I couldn't bear to seem cavalier about my responsibilities."

Sophie laughed merrily. "How long have you worked for us now, Mr. Cross?" she asked.

"I'm not certain," Stuart lied. "More than twenty years," he said, as if guessing.

"That's right," said Sophie. "I've been here for eighteen of those years, and you've never been delinquent. But look, I'll call Mr. Glass the moment I get off the phone with you. If there's a problem, I'll call you right back. If not, then the lunch is postponed until tomorrow. Same time, same place, but tomorrow. Okay?"

"What if you can't reach him?" Stuart asked.

"I can reach him."

"What if you can't?"

"If I can't reach him, then I'll call you," said Sophie. "How's that?"

"I'd be grateful," said Stuart.

"Okay, then," said Sophie. "If you don't hear from me in ten minutes, then you stay home today, take care of your little family. Tomorrow you meet Mr. Glass for lunch."

"All right," said Stuart. "Many thanks."

The moment he hung up, he wished he'd asked Sophie to call him either way. It would be embarrassing to call again. He turned from the phone to see Andie come out of the bathroom with her body wrapped in one large white towel, and her hair wrapped in another. She disappeared into the walk-in closet.

"Notice anything?" he asked.

"Not particularly," she said, her voice muffled by the closet wall.

"It's almost eight thirty A.M. Jane isn't in bed with us. Ginny isn't trying on your jewelry and high heels."

"That's right," said Andie. "I miss them."

"Well, I don't," said Stuart. "I bet they're dressed already. And fed," he said. "Drawing or memorizing poetry."

"Or else she drugged them, and they're still asleep," said Andie, coming out of the closet now in black lace panties and a matching bra.

"Did you have any luck with the office?" she asked.

"Yes," said Stuart.

"And?" asked Andie.

"And I can take the day off," said Stuart.

"Good," said Andie, "I thought so." She came over to Stuart and pecked him on the cheek.

"My hero," she said. "Remember what Norman Vincent Peale said. The graveyard is full of indispensable people."

"Yeah," said Stuart. "It's also full of dispensable people."

He put a hand on his wife's shoulder.

"Ouch," said Andie, pulling away. "You're freezing."

"Cold hands, warm heart," he said.

135

"Brrr," said Andie, retreating into the bathroom.

Stuart sat on the edge of the bed. He could hear the hair dryer starting up.

"So when will you be home?" he asked.

Andie shut off the hair dryer. "Probably not until after seven P.M.," she said, and started the dryer again.

"I didn't like the way Sophie sounded," Stuart said. The hair dryer kept going.

"I don't like the way Sophie sounded," he said again, this time projecting his voice so that it could not be ignored, even over the roar of the dryer.

The hair dryer stopped. "What did you say?" asked Andie.

"I didn't like the way Sophie sounded," Stuart said.

"She's never much liked you," Andie said and started the hair dryer again.

"I suppose," said Stuart. "So today I'm stuck alone."

"What?" asked Andie, but this time she kept the dryer going.

"I said I'm stuck alone with these horrid manuscripts," shouted Stuart. "I'll miss you."

Andie turned off the hair dryer again.

"You're stuck alone with manuscripts and your beloved children," she said.

"And my beloved children," Stuart said, but without enthusiasm.

"Why not move into the room we put aside as an office for you?" Andie asked. "They're going to give me a new laptop at work, so you can use my old PowerBook. I'll transfer my files later. It works beautifully. WordPerfect is installed."

"I'd rather buy a new computer."

"Buy a new computer then," said Andie. "Order it or drive right out to CompUSA in White Plains."

"I could do that," said Stuart.

"Might as well," said Andie. "Our budget's already in ruins. Between this house and this nanny."

"You had to have them both," said Stuart.

"That's right," said. Andie. "Which is not the same as being able to afford them."

"I won't buy a new computer," said Stuart.

"You can buy a new computer," said Andie. "But if you go anywhere in the car, I want you to take the children. Both children."

"Even when I go to RadioShack and pick up the phones?"

"Even when you go to RadioShack and pick up the phones."

"That means I can't do anything on the motorcycle?"

"Exactly right," said Andie, and she turned the hair dryer back on.

Stuart went to his dresser, removed a pair of worn khakis and a T-shirt that read THE OSSINING CITIZEN REGISTER: IT'S HOW YOU KNOW. Kika had given it to him. "As a hint," she'd said.

He pulled on the pants, the shirt, and a pair of tube socks; then he went downstairs. Louise had the girls at the kitchen table. She was showing them a book.

"We're each picking out a poem to learn this week," Louise explained. "We've all had breakfast. Can I make something for you?"

"I'm going to boil Andie an egg," Stuart said. Louise got up from her place at the table. "No, no," she said. "Please let me make your wife her egg. I don't think she likes me, and I want to change that."

"Of course she likes you," said Stuart. "She twisted my arm to get us to hire you."

"That was before," said Louise.

"She loves you," said Stuart.

Louise wagged her head sadly. "Not anymore. Which is why I should make the egg. Three minutes? Does she want the toast dry?"

"Three minutes," said Stuart. "I always put out butter with the toast. That way she can make up her own mind."

"It's done," said Louise. "Sit down now and read the *New York Times*. Let me get you a cup of coffee. You like it black?"

"Black as sin," said Stuart and nodded. "If you bring me a second mug of coffee, I will carry it up to Andie. She could drink it while she puts on her makeup."

"How does your wife take her coffee?" asked Louise.

"Black," said Stuart.

"Let me send Ginny upstairs then with a mug," said Louise. "Doesn't Ginny enjoy helping her mother pick out jewelry?"

"That's right," said Stuart.

"Come here, beautiful," said Louise, and Ginny hopped down off her chair and walked over to the island to receive the mug of coffee. "Would you like to take this up to your mother?" asked Louise.

"Okay," said Ginny.

"Aren't you afraid she'll spill?" asked Stuart.

"Oh, Dad," said Ginny.

"No," said Louise. "I'm not afraid she'll spill. She's got nerves of steel, your daughter. Isn't that right, beautiful?" she said and switched her eyes to the girl.

"Nerves of steel," said Ginny, and started up the stairs.

"You need me today?" asked Louise.

"Yes," said Stuart. "Why do you ask?"

"It's Tuesday," said Louise.

"Tuesday?" asked Stuart.

"My day off," said Louise.

"Your day off," said Stuart, and his face fell.

"That's all right," said Louise. "I had no plans. I'll stay."

"Would you?" asked Stuart.

"Of course," said the nanny. "And since I'm here, why don't you let me make you an omelet?"

"Ginny and I shared an omelet," said Jane. "An egg-white omelet."

Stuart turned to his younger daughter and smiled.

"Did you enjoy it?" he asked.

Janey nodded prettily. "Sugar says that most people who have a weight problem skip breakfast. Does Ginny have a weight problem, Daddy?"

"No," said Ginny, who'd come back down the stairs unobserved. "I have a sister problem."

"No eggs for me this morning, thanks," said Stuart.

"When I was straightening out the kitchen cabinet, I found Scottish oatmeal," said Louise. "Would you like a bowl of Scottish oatmeal?"

"Oatmeal sounds thrilling," said Stuart. "I'd love a bowl of oatmeal."

"With raisins?" asked Louise. "I saw organic raisins in the cupboard."

"With raisins," said Stuart. "Free-range raisins."

When Andie finally came downstairs with Ginny in tow, she was in a terrible rush. "It's eight twenty-four," she announced. "I absolutely must catch the eight thirty-six." Stuart noticed that his wife was wearing a thin band of gold at her throat; Ginny was wearing a string of pearls, which she'd looped three times around her neck.

He rose and swept an arm at the place that had been set at the table for his wife.

"Breakfast," he said. "Miss Washington made you breakfast."

"I can't," said Andie. "Thank you, though," she said, and looked at the nanny.

"It was nothing," said Louise.

"And thanks also for working today," said Andie.

"No problem," said Louise. "I like to be needed."

"Now drink your juice," said Stuart.

Obediently, Andie drained the juice glass, kissed both girls on the forehead and started out the door. Stuart grabbed a piece of toast, wrapped it in a paper napkin, pausing to put on his boat shoes. He then followed his wife out of the house. He stood, hunched against the cold, while Andie got in the car, started the engine, and lowered the window.

"I've got to go," said Andie. "Parking is going to be murderous. I'd like to avoid any sprinting this morning."

"Want me to drive you?" asked Stuart.

"No thanks. I can make it. I like knowing the car will be there."

"Okay," said Stuart.

"Look," said Andie, "If *she* gets a phone call, I want you to listen in."

"I will not," said Stuart.

"You don't need to be obvious," Andie said. "Pick up the phone, and then if it's for her, and you're noticed, you can excuse yourself."

"You're acting the absolute nut," said Stuart.

"Humor me," said Andie.

"All right," said Stuart, "I promise. Here," he said, and passed his wife the piece of toast. "You can eat this on the train. The girls had an omelet for breakfast. An egg-white omelet. She's making me a bowl of that oatmeal the Hassmans gave us for New Year's."

"All right," said Andie. "I can see you're hooked. Watch her, though. Please, please watch her. Make sure the paragon doesn't serve you the children for lunch."

CHAPTER 17

Petty and Vindictive

Stepping back into the warm kitchen and kicking off his boat shoes, Stuart felt his spirits sag. He enjoyed the office. He liked Herbert Glass, looked forward to seeing his boss. He enjoyed the Four Seasons.

"Sit with us, Daddy," said Jane. "We're drawing and reading poems. You can sit with us and read the newspaper."

"Okay," said Stuart, looking up and into the face of his youngest, "I'll do that, but you've got to promise not to interrupt."

"We promise," said Jane. "We're both so glad to have you home," she said.

"Thanks," said Stuart. Ginny was also seated at the table. She had a book of Blake's poetry beside her, but was actually looking at the picture of the disk player that Louise had drawn for her. She had a pencil and was doodling around the edges of the sheet of paper. She did not look up, nor did she second Jane's enthusiasm for her father's presence. She was still wearing the pearls, but now she had them looped twice around her neck, which made the string loose enough so that she could put part of it in her mouth.

That's two thousand dollars my eldest daughter is teething on, Stuart thought, but kept the observation to himself.

He looked at the *Times,* drank his coffee, and finished his oatmeal. Trouble in the Middle East. He wondered idly if they'd ever thanked the Hassmans for the oatmeal. He could see the handsome tin out where Louise had placed it. Apparently the people who made the oatmeal were oatmealers to the queen.

Stomach full, he climbed the stairs, took his wife's laptop to the room designated as his office, sat disconsolately in his chair, plugged in the laptop. Turned it on. Opened a file. Titled the file "Novel" and saved it. Now his spirits plummeted. *Low blood sugar,* he thought. *I should have had protein for breakfast.* He stood, walked back to the bedroom to-die-for. He made the bed and lay on his back on the spread. *I should call somebody at work,* he thought. *Just see what's going on.*

Then he heard the muffled ring of the doorbell. He looked up at the ceiling. There seemed to be a slight discoloration. *A leak?*

"Mr. Cross?" It was Louise, calling to him from the foot of the stairs.

"Mr. Cross," she said again. "You have visitors."

"Visitors?" he called back, sitting up in bed.

"The police," said Louise.

"What's it about?" asked Stuart, alarmed. Now he was on his feet and heading toward the top of the stairs.

"They say it's a routine investigation," said Louise. "Shall I let them in?"

"Yes, of course," said Stuart, "I'll be right down." He returned to the bedroom, shucked off his T-shirt, put on a white dress shirt, dark socks, and a pair of cordovan loafers. He checked his face in the mirror, ran a brush through his hair, went downstairs, and turned into the great room.

A short, stout young man with a mug of coffee—Louise must have distributed beverages—had settled deeply into one of the two sofas that flanked the large-screen TV. The mug the policeman was using had "The World's Greatest Dad!" emblazoned on the side in red print. Janey had given it to Stuart the year before on Father's Day.

A woman with snarly red hair was in one of the armchairs. She too had coffee. Hers was in mug on which a blurred photo of Ginny holding the infant Janey had been printed. Her black police shoes were on the ottoman that came with the armchair.

Stuart walked first to the man, took his hand, and shook it.

"John Marks," the officer said, from deep in the sofa. He didn't get up, nor did he smile.

"Cross," said Stuart. "Stuart Cross. Pleased to meet you."

"Officer Pigniole," the woman said, holding out a limp hand for her host to shake. She also did not rise.

"Haven't you and I spoken?" Stuart asked

"Yes," said Pigniole. "Yesterday. You phoned here from the city. Is your wife feeling better today? I assume she's upstairs in bed."

"Well," said Stuart. "Actually not. I mean she is feeling better, but she's not upstairs. She's in the city. She's at work."

Officer Marks released a loud whistle of disbelief. "You're kidding," he said.

"No," said Stuart. "I'm not kidding. She's at work."

"After yesterday?" asked Marks. "She still went off and left the kids alone?" He turned to the woman with the snarly red hair. "Piggy," he said. "Do you believe this?"

The woman's eyes darkened, but she said nothing.

"Well *I'm* here," said Stuart.

"Sure," said Marks. "I see that, but you weren't here yesterday. Your wife thought her daughters were dead. That's what she told me. She said she could sense the danger they were in. She told me it couldn't be a simple mix-up. She said she was psychic."

"She is psychic," said Stuart. "Or has seemed to be."

"Well," said Marks. "She was wrong about her children. Yesterday she was in despair. She tried to kill herself. And today she's gone right off to work. Talk about a short attention span."

Stuart inhaled sharply. He thought of telling the assembled peace officers that Andie was an important film critic. He exhaled. He said nothing.

"Days like this," said Marks, "I thank the Lord we have enough money so that Barbara can stay home with our kids."

"There's one thing you seem to be forgetting," said Stuart. "There was nothing wrong yesterday. The girls were with their nanny at all times. The girls were at the zoo."

Marks smiled condescendingly. "You couldn't have convinced Mrs. Cross of that yesterday," he said. "She wanted us to call in the FBI. She threatened to have me fired, when I wouldn't do it. She wanted roadblocks, helicopters. Lucky we didn't listen to her. She might have cost the county a bundle."

Stuart took a seat, feeling the rage boil up inside. He drew another deep breath. "All right," he said. "Enough about yesterday. I'm sorry it happened. But now it's over. And furthermore, I can't imagine that you've driven out here today to relive yesterday. You must have other business."

"You're right," said Marks. "We're here about the murder."

"Murder?" asked Stuart.

"Yeah," said Marks. "A pediatrician was murdered not far from here, and we have a witness who tells us she saw the car he was driving. Apparently the doctor got in an accident, a fender bender right outside your window. This would have been Saturday evening. Saint Patrick's Day."

Stuart stood and walked to the Gothic windows at the end of the room. "Right out there?" he asked.

Officer Marks rose, joined his host.

"That's right," he said. "You can see where somebody drove right onto the grass. Is that your lawn?"

Stuart looked at the torn sod, the exposed red mud and felt violated, as if the property were an extension of his person. "Yes and no," he said.

"Our witness," said Marks, failing to take up on the distinction, "our witness reported that the doctor's car rear-ended a van right out here just at dusk on Saint Patrick's Day. In fact we've gathered up some busted glass from the sides of the road. Looks like you're going to have to call the gardener in to fix up your nice big lawn."

"Who is the witness?" Stuart asked. Snarly hair spoke up from behind them. "I don't think it would be appropriate for us to divulge that information at this time," she said.

Stuart nodded, turned to Marks. "You think the accident is related to the murder?"

Marks shrugged, keeping his face a blank. "Don't put words in my mouth," he said. "We're following standard police procedure. We're gathering information. Which is why we're here. We wondered if anybody in the house might have seen the accident."

"We were having a party. We heard the sirens. We saw the police cars," said Stuart. "A bunch of us looked out the window. If anybody had been aware of the earlier accident, I think they would have mentioned it."

Louise appeared now at the door to the great room. "Why not move into the kitchen?" she said. "I've sent the girls upstairs with their books. We've got fresh coffee for everybody, and I'm taking orders for cinnamon toast."

When the party rose to move to the kitchen, Stuart saw how small his tormentors were, how the woman's shoulders were rounded with worry or illness. The man, still in his twenties, had already begun to lose his hair and his chin.

Resettled in the kitchen, Louise brought her employer a fresh mug of coffee. Stuart started the conversation again, this time on a more conciliatory note.

"I do want to thank you both for yesterday," he said. "I don't mean to seem ungrateful."

Marks nodded. Pigniole acted as if she hadn't heard. Louise gave Officer Pigniole a plate with two pieces of cinnamon toast on it, neatly quartered.

"Despite the house," Stuart said, and waved his arm to indicate the size of the kitchen, "I didn't come from this. I know that policemen have a difficult and sometimes dangerous job. I also appreciate the sensitivity with which you handled"—he caught himself before saying *subdued*—"my wife."

This was greeted with silence. "I know Andie can be difficult," he said. "She's terrified that something will happen to the children. She had a younger sister who died when she, herself, was only seven."

Louise reappeared and served toast to the men.

Marks drew the back of his hand across his mouth. He picked up a section of toast, tasted it. "Good," he said.

147

"I just wanted you to know where we were coming from," said Stuart.

Neither officer spoke.

"And I also understand," said Stuart, "that you are the thin blue line. The reputation of the local police departments is part of what brought us here," he lied.

"There's not much we can do anymore," Marks said, through his toast. "Most of the time our hands are tied."

Stuart was nodding "My wife's newspaper is always making that point. They had a headline yesterday. 'Don't Mollycoddle Criminals.' "

"The *New York Post*," said Marks. "Your wife works for the *New York Post*?"

"Yup," said Stuart noncommittally.

Marks put down his toast, got up from his seat, reached across the kitchen table, and gave Stuart a buttery hand. Stuart took the hand and shook it.

Marks sat back down, took another piece of toast. Then he took a sip of coffee. "Great paper," he continued, chewing as he spoke, so that Stuart could see the toast inside his mouth. "I read the column you're referring to," he said, still chewing, and broadcasting crumbs onto the dark wood of the kitchen table. "Boy was it on target. That's what we end up doing half the time," he said, "mollycoddling criminals. First we apprehend them, then the lawyers show up," he said, and swallowed at last. "Then the perps get mollycoddled. Sometimes the criminals get mollycoddled right back onto the street."

Stuart took another piece of toast. *Silence*, he thought, *is often taken for affirmation.*

Marks nodded mutely, as if accepting Stuart's assent. Pigniole had moved the sections of toast around on her plate, but hadn't yet taken a bite.

"The criminals can come out on top," said Stuart. "They become famous. Look at Jack Henry Abbott. We even had an editor in our publishing house who turned out to be a violent criminal. And then they published three books about him and produced his execrable plays. Noel Hammersmith. Maybe you remember him."

"No," said Marks.

"He's just one example," said Stuart.

"Wait a minute," said Marks. "Was he on TV?"

"He was on TV a lot," said Stuart. "Even now they dust him off sometimes, give an interview. It happens when they're on the case of another serial killer."

"That's right," said Marks. "I saw him."

"That's right," said Stuart. "He was—by his own admission—happier in prison than he had ever been on the outside. And you guys can't even let them confess if they want to, until you've read them their Miranda rights. What's ironical is that the guy they named the rights after was a recidivist. Finally died in a bar fight."

"I hadn't heard that," said Marks. "Not that I'm surprised."

"I think so," said Stuart. "In any case, I know how difficult and thankless your job might seem. And I appreciate what you're doing."

"Now we've got to get back to business," Marks said, taking out a small black notebook and a pencil.

Did Stuart know the doctor who had been killed? No. Did Andie know him? Stuart didn't think so.

Officer Pigniole went out to the police car for a legal pad. She needed the names and addresses of everybody who had come to the party. Stuart had to go upstairs and get his address book.

149

Louise had been upstairs with the children, but had come down at regular intervals to refill coffee cups. When it got to be noon, Stuart excused himself and followed the nanny back upstairs, "to check the kids," he told the police, but when he and Louise reached the landing, he stopped her, whispered in her ear. "Do not under any circumstances offer these people lunch," he whispered. "Do not."

"I was just going to ask the girls if they were hungry," said Louise.

"Do not touch or mention food, until the police are out of the house," said Stuart. "Not a word."

Stuart then returned to the kitchen, and was surprised how boldly Marks worked food into the interrogation.

"The incident in question would have been a long time after lunch," he said, "closer to the dinner hour."

Stuart nodded mutely.

"This is some kitchen you've got," said Marks. "Are you a chef?"

"No," said Stuart.

"But the nanny can cook?" asked Marks.

"That's not what she's hired for," said Stuart.

"I liked the gingerbread," said Marks. "Didn't you like the gingerbread?" he said, pointing what might once have been a fine chin at his silent colleague.

Office Pigniole didn't answer.

"Nothing in the oven?" Marks queried, and made snorting noises.

"No," said Stuart. "But thanks for asking. I'd like to have a boy, but two children are really all we can afford."

"Your girls are upstairs," Marks said. "Aren't they going to have lunch?"

"I don't know," said Stuart. "They're girls, you know," he said. "Eat like birds."

Marks nodded again.

"Something else I can help you with?" asked Stuart.

And Marks took his best shot. "I hate to eat at restaurants. What I really like is home cooking."

"You like bread pudding?" Stuart asked.

The policeman liked bread pudding.

"And a burger?"

"Sounds perfect," said Marks.

"Well," said Stuart, getting up from the table. "Then you are in luck. There's a diner just up the road. Listed as one of the best in America. Can't get in there on Sunday, but today should be no problem. Burgers are delicious. Bread pudding has won awards."

And so the police duo ultimately left the Cross residence at about twelve thirty P.M.

When Marks finally surrendered the notion of a free lunch, Stuart softened. They were so small, and so pitiful, so weighted down with equipment. When they got up to leave, he noticed that the woman seemed to have a limp.

But he held fast. He had work to do. A phone call to make, and if that failed he had a book to write. He waited until both officers were in the car. He waited while they sat in the car, apparently talking on the radio. He waited until the car had pulled out of the drive. Then he walked to the bottom of the stairs and called for the nanny and his children: "Ally Ally Incomefree. Ally Ally Income-free."

Louise and the girls came down the stairs.

"Daddy," Janey asked, "are we in trouble?"

"No trouble, dear," said Stuart.

"Did they read you your rights?" Ginny asked.

"No," said Stuart.

"Well then, we're all okay," said Ginny. "Nothing you told them will be admissible in court."

"Thanks," said Stuart. "You're going to make a terrific lawyer."

"Did you like the police?" asked Janey.

"No," said Stuart. "Not really."

Louise smiled faintly. "I've seen worse," she said.

"I suppose," said Stuart.

"Can I make lunch now?" Louise asked.

"Yes, you can."

"Burgers?" asked Louise.

"Perfect," said Stuart.

"Show Daddy what you drew," said Janey.

"You drew something?" asked Stuart.

"Sketched," said Louise. "I'm always sketching."

"Show Daddy," said Janey.

So Louise went back upstairs and returned with her sketchbook. She put it on the kitchen table. The scene seemed to be framed with the window of Janey's bedroom. First the curtains, then the panes of glass, and outside the police car. The sketch was black and white, but Stuart could still see what had been done. The drawn woman standing beside the police car was Officer Pigniole. She had the uniform, the look of grievance, the mixture of defeat and defiance in her posture and in the lineaments of her face. She looked—if anything—more like Officer Pigniole than Officer Pigniole looked like herself. Except for one thing. The police-woman standing beside the car in the picture had black skin.

"When did you draw this?" Stuart asked.

"While I was watching the children."

"Are you always drawing?" Stuart asked.

"Almost always," said Louise.

"Can I show you something?" asked Stuart.

"Of course," said Louise.

Stuart went upstairs and then returned with a paperback copy of W. Somerset Maugham's *The Moon and Sixpence*.

"Painting and writing are similar," Stuart explained. "This book is about a painter, but I've always felt its truths could also be applied to writing." He pointed out the passage where the forty-year-old former stockbroker, Charles Strickland, is hunted down in Paris by the narrator, a writer who has been sent as an emissary of the man's abandoned wife. Everybody had assumed that Strickland ran off with a woman, but it turned out he simply wanted to paint.

The narrator questions his quarry closely. Here Stuart read aloud from the book.

" 'Supposing you're never anything more than third-rate, do you think it will have been worth while to give up everything? After all, in any other walk in life it doesn't matter if you're not very good; you can get along quite comfortably if you're just adequate; but it's different with an artist.'

" 'You're a blasted fool,' " he [Strickland] said.

" 'I don't see why, unless it's folly to say the obvious.'

" 'I tell you I've got to paint. I can't help myself. When a man falls into the water it doesn't matter how he swims, well or badly: he's got to get out or else he'll drown.' "

Louise listened politely. "Actually," she said, "I have read the book."

"Oh," said Stuart, trying to hide his dismay. "Don't you like the quote?" he asked.

"I do, but it wasn't my favorite quote in the book."

"And what was?" Stuart asked.

Louise leafed through the paperback, found her place and read out loud in her turn: "'It is not true that suffering ennobles the character,'" she read, without looking up. "'Happiness does that sometimes but suffering for the most part makes men petty and vindictive.'"

CHAPTER 18

"More people worry than work."

Burgers eaten, dishes washed—by Louise—the Cross party made its second attempt in three days to tech up. They got in the Volvo, drove to RadioShack in Chilmark. Stuart was embarrassed and also saddened to discover that he could not decipher the prompts on his new cell phone without first putting on his bifocals.

The selling feature of his plan was that he didn't sign a contract, wasn't committed to any service. Because of this theoretical freedom, the phones were more expensive than he had somehow supposed, costing $230 apiece. In the end, he decided to get two—one for himself and one for Andie—instead of three. The nanny could borrow a phone when it was necessary. And if a phone came out soon with a larger, more easily decipherable screen, he would buy it for himself, pass one of the other two onto the sharp-eyed Louise.

"Everything in this country is designed for young people," he told the nanny. "I'm a dinosaur."

"Young white people," said Louise. "Young white people with money."

★   ★   ★

When they got back to the house, Stuart shepherded the girls and the nanny to the kitchen door, and then walked around the property. The back corner of the lawn was marshy. This was odd, because he couldn't remember the last time it had rained.

Stuart went back inside, up to his new office, turned on the laptop. Opened the file titled "Novel." Looked at it for a minute or so. Then he phoned Rick Massberg at the office.

"What's going on?" he asked, trying very hard to sound casual.

"Nothing much," said Rick. "How come you're not here?"

"Family emergency," Stuart said.

"But everything's okay?" asked Rick. "Nobody sick? Nobody hurt?"

"Nobody sick," said Stuart. "Nobody hurt."

"Everything hunky-dory?" asked Rick.

"You *are* a wordsmith," said Stuart. "That's it exactly. Everything's hunky-dory. What about at the office?"

"Nothing," said Massberg.

"Details," said Stuart. "I want details."

"Let's see," said Massberg. "Althea's wearing a new sweater. Dark blue? Purple? I'm not certain. Shows off her figure. Matches her eye shadow. Very becoming."

"Any rumors?" asked Stuart. "Glass in evidence?"

"Let's see," said Massberg. "No sign of Herbert Glass. No rumors that I've been let in on."

"There must be something going on," said Stuart.

"Well," said Massberg, "the coffee wagon just came through. That what you're looking for? No crumb buns left. That's your headline then: CRUMB BUN SHORTAGE."

"All right, all right," said Stuart. "Call, though, if anything comes up. I'll be home. Keep me in the loop."

He hung up and phoned Stephen Solon. Solon didn't pick up, so Stuart left a message: "Hey, Steve. Great to see you yesterday. Been doing any thinking? I'm home today. Give me a call."

Then he phoned Heather at the Bathos Literary Agency. "I haven't heard yet from Martin Brookstone. It would mean an enormous amount if I could tell my publisher that he's moving to Acropolis. Is that still on?"

"Of course it's on," said Heather. "But you can't tell anybody yet. Martin needs time to break the news to his editor at Doubleday. They've been together for fifteen years now. He promised he'd call me tomorrow. If he doesn't, I'll call him."

Then Stuart phoned Althea. She took down his new cell number, but he thought she sounded distant.

"Anything the matter?" he asked.

"I don't know," said Althea. "Rick Massberg is acting like the cat that ate the canary."

"What do you mean?"

"When the coffee wagon came by at ten this morning, he had two crumb buns. Then he didn't go out for lunch. Or I don't think he did. I only went out for forty-five minutes, and he was there when I left, there when I came back. He's not a man to miss a feeding."

"What was he doing when you went out?" asked Stuart.

"Talking," said Althea. "On the phone."

"He's a good talker," said Stuart.

"One other thing," said Althea. "Soon as he got in today, he asked me if you were off. I said I thought you were coming to work. I said you always come to work. So then he said he thought you weren't coming in today. He'd already called Sophie and found that you were staying home. This was news to me."

"Sorry," said Stuart. "I was so fixated on making sure Glass wasn't offended that I didn't think of telling you. I don't ever take days off. I don't know how to do it."

"Is everything okay?" asked Althea.

"Yeah," said Stuart. "Everything's fine. It was just Andie being hysterical."

"That's what I figured," said Althea. "She really had the wind up yesterday."

"It's about the new nanny," said Stuart. "I think the new nanny is great, but she *is* brand new. An unknown quantity. In any case, I'm staying home today. There's no real reason for this, except to keep Andie sane."

"I figured," said Althea. "What I haven't figured out yet is what's got Rick Massberg so tickled."

"I suppose I'll learn tomorrow," said Stuart. "I'll be in tomorrow early."

"Good," said Althea. "Put the fat monkey back in his cage."

"Thanks," said Stuart. He hung up and called Massberg again.

"Hey Rick," he said, trying hard to keep the tension out of his voice. "What's happening?"

"Since you called last?" asked Massberg, a note of incredulity creeping into his voice.

"Today," said Stuart. "What's going on today?"

"Nothing," said Massberg.

"Nothing I should know about?"

"Nothing you should know about," said Massberg. "I suppose we're all hoping that Glass is going to give you that promotion soon." There was a pause and the younger man started up again: "How long have you been working here?"

"Thirty years now," said Stuart, exaggerating only slightly.

"Anything ever happen?"

"Sure," said Stuart, "things happened."

"And if you weren't here for one day?" asked Massberg. "They wouldn't have happened?"

"Sometimes," said Stuart.

"Give me one example," said Massberg. "That's all I'm asking for. One single example. Over thirty years."

"Three years ago," said Stuart. "We had you in for an interview. You know what Glass said afterward?"

"I've heard," said Massberg, and there was defeat in his tone, also fatigue.

But Stuart would not be stopped. "Herbert Glass said 'Over my dead body.' He said, 'You can hire that cocky son of a bitch, but it'll be over my dead body.'"

"I know," said Massberg. "I've heard the story."

"And I said," continued Stuart, having surrendered completely to the gravitational pull of this office favorite, "I said, 'Let's give him three weeks. If in three weeks, you don't love Rick Massberg, then I'll quit too.'"

"And in three weeks," said Massberg, sounding very tired of all this. "In three weeks, we'd won him over."

"No," said Stuart. "Credit where credit is due. In three weeks, *you'd* won him over. Completely. But the fact remains that if I hadn't been at work that day three years ago, you never would have been given the chance."

"It was that essay I wrote, wasn't it?" said Massberg.

"Might have been," said Stuart. "What was the title again?"

"Do I have to say?" said Massberg.

"Yup," said Stuart.

"It was titled 'Is Anti-Semitism Legitimate?' That wasn't my title. The editors provided the title."

"I bet," said Stuart. "But that was a coup, being so prominently published, when you were still so young. You wrote that an unhealthy percentage of New York publishing was controlled by Jews."

"I couldn't turn down that assignment," said Massberg. "You're a writer. You understand."

There was a long silence. Then Stuart started up again. "This is the man who got you your job speaking. Is there anything the man who got your job needs to know today?"

"You need to know how to calm down," said Massberg.

"All right," said Stuart. "If you're telling me to calm down, then I can calm down."

"You know what Robert Frost said about worry?" asked Massberg.

"No," said Stuart. "I don't know what Robert Frost said about worry."

"Frost said that 'The reason why worry kills more people than work is that more people worry than work.'"

CHAPTER 19

"Thank God you didn't go into medicine"

Andie rolled over Wednesday morning, felt something tickling her nose, and grabbed it. "Hey," said Stuart, rearing back and pulling the necktie free. He turned and walked into the bathroom-to-die-for, switched on the dressing-room lights. "Now you've wrinkled it," he said. "I'm going to have to put on a new one." Crossing the bedroom as he unfastened the tie, he vanished into the closet, reappearing with a second necktie: this one was red with tiny wheelbarrows.

"What?" mumbled Andie, still bewildered, still half asleep.

"So much depends on a red necktie," Stuart said, "covered with wheelbarrows." He went into the bathroom, shut the door, switched on a light.

"What time is it?" asked Andie, when he came back out into the bedroom. "It's still dark."

"Shush," said Stuart. "You go back to sleep now, Baby. Miss Washington's going to drive me to an early train."

"How early?" asked Andie.

"Early," said Stuart.

"What time?"

"Just six," he said. "I couldn't sleep." Then—holding his necktie back and to one side—he leaned over and kissed his wife on the cheek.

"You know I had a dream," said Andie, sitting up now in bed. "I dreamed that Susan Logan took the children to the zoo, and fed them to the lion."

"Interesting," said Stuart, "but I don't think it's the children that Susan Logan has her eyes on."

The 6:03 A.M. out of Scarborough was half empty. Stuart sat near the doors, where the seats faced each other, and he could cross his legs. He spread out the newspaper. *Yes, IBM is performing wonderfully,* he told the imaginary Herbert Glass. *They have a brand. So do we. Look at Tiffany. Look at Mercedes. Over the short term, prestige can be expensive. Over the long term, it's enormously profitable.*

Out of the train and with the *Times* tucked under his arm, his briefcase swinging at his side, Stuart felt a great sea of confidence welling up inside. *Glass adores me,* he thought. *All I have to do is smile a lot and say thank you. I may not be psychic, but I couldn't be this wrong.* The early morning streets were wreathed with steam escaping from manhole covers. He smelled bacon frying. He stopped at a delicatessen and bought a large cup of black coffee.

Settled at his post, Stuart turned his chair around and admired the spines of the books he'd published in the last five years. They hadn't all been commercial successes, but neither had they been shameful in any way.

"If a bad book sells a thousand copies," he once told an interviewer from *Publishers Weekly,* "that's bad. If it sells a hundred thousand copies, that's worse. People forget that *Mein Kampf* was a popular book. Octopus would have published *Mein Kampf* in a heartbeat. I like to think I would have turned it down. Governmental censorship is dangerous. Intelligence and taste needn't be."

At eight oh five, Stuart took the elevator to Glass's real estate office, which was on the eleventh floor. Sophie had just come in and was removing her coat.

"Am I still on for lunch?" he asked, standing in the hall.

Sophie seemed not to have heard him. She hung up her raincoat, took a brown paper bag out of her handbag, and put it into the center drawer of her desk. She sat at her desk. Just as Stuart had determined that he would need to speak again, Sophie brought her flinty, blue eyes up, and focused them on his own.

"A little early to be thinking about lunch," she said.

"It's not really about the food," said Stuart.

"As far as I know, lunch is still on," Sophie said.

"Look," said Stuart. "I'm stepping out for half an hour to get something for my daughter. If anyone comes or calls, will you tell them I'll be back before nine?"

Sophie nodded.

"Can you answer my extension?"

Sophie nodded again.

Stuart went back out into the city, walked two blocks and stopped in at Nobody Beats the Wiz. He picked out the disk player that most closely resembled the one in his daughter's drawing. This cost $124.99. He let the salesman convince him to buy a pair of "invisible" earphones. "Very popular with the kids," the salesman said. The earphones went deep into the ear. "Don't look closely," the salesman explained, "and you'll miss the wires entirely. Looks like the music is in your head."

"This is for my daughter," said Stuart.

"How old?" asked the salesman.

"Nine," said Stuart.

"She'll love them," the salesman said. "And what about the insurance?" he asked. "Kids these days. And this is a delicate piece of equipment."

"No insurance," said Stuart, and took the bill and his American Express card to the register where he was shocked to discover that the earphones—an afterthought—had added $67 to the cost. *She might really like them, though,* he thought and signed. Then he went back to the office.

When Althea arrived at nine fifteen A.M.—her workday was supposed to begin at eight thirty—she set up noisily at her desk, which was in the public space outside her boss's office. Then she came back into his elegant quarters and closed the door.

Stuart stood and gave her the plastic bag with the CD player in it. "Don't let me forget this," he said.

Althea nodded. "So what's going on?" she asked.

"No idea," he said. "I have a lunch with Glass at one P.M. I came in early today hoping to catch up on some work and then speak with Massberg."

"Well, that's not going to happen," said Althea. "Massberg's taken the morning off."

"What?"

"He told me yesterday late. Said he's got a physical. He'll be in after lunch."

"Didn't he just have a physical last week?" asked Stuart.

"No," said Althea. "He had a physical last year. Exactly a year ago today. He's very careful with himself."

"Quite the delicate instrument," said Stuart. "I guess I'll just have to talk with him this afternoon. In the meantime, I'd better get some reading done. Keep your ear to the ground for me, will you?"

"Sure," said Althea. "Always."

She went out of his office, closed the door, and then came right back and shut the door.

"I never liked him," she said.

"You never liked who?" asked Stuart.

"Massberg," said Althea. "I never liked him."

"I like him," said Stuart.

Althea shrugged.

"Rick's a little odd," said Stuart, "but he's energetic and with his heart in the right place."

"His heart," said Althea, shaking her head. She started out to her own desk, but before she closed the door, she poked her head back into Stuart's office: "Thank God you didn't go into medicine," she said.

CHAPTER 20

"Who the fuck do you think you are?"

Stuart arrived at the Four Seasons a full ten minutes early, and so walked around the block twice before going inside. Ushered into the dining room, he saw that Herbert Glass was already there, seated at his table.

The courtly older man rose to shake his employee's hand.

"Ah, Stuart," he said. "How are you? Have a seat."

"Fine," said Stuart, nodding, trying hard to read his publisher's intentions. The older man seemed in high spirits.

This must be a good sign, Stuart thought.

The waiter pulled out a chair.

"Let George fetch you a drink," said Glass.

"What are you having?" asked Stuart.

"A Tom Collins," said Glass. "The drink reminds me of the summer," he added, "and so I have it all year. The older I get, the less I enjoy the chill of winter. I suppose it reminds me of death."

Stuart nodded mutely.

"This is not really an adequate adaptation to old age," said Glass, "but it's a good deal less of a dislocation than spending half of my life in Florida."

166

The Publisher and Editorial Director had the look of satisfaction one sometimes sees in men of a certain age who expect never to be surprised again for as long as they live—who expect to live for a long time and near the ocean.

Glass was wearing a full suit. Stuart was in khakis, a shirt and tie (with little wheelbarrows), and a Paul Stuart blazer.

"You want a drink, right?" said Glass. What Stuart wanted was the Editorial Directorship; he ordered a glass of Chardonnay.

"Now," said Herbert Glass, "I have to open with a joke."

"I'm ready," said Stuart, and he moved around in his seat.

"Imagine a good-looking youth, a Harvard graduate," the elder man said, already smiling with anticipation. "He doesn't know what he wants to do with his life. You've never had that problem, have you Stuart?" he said.

"No," said Stuart. "Not really."

Glass nodded thoughtfully. "So our friend, he likes movies. A young woman of his acquaintance suggests he move to California and become a screenwriter. 'You've been to the movies,' she says. 'How hard can it be to write screenplays? The good ones come in at less than a hundred thirty pages.'

"So he moves to California and starts telling people he's a screenwriter. He has the tan. He has the sweaters. He stays at a borrowed house in Malibu. He's bored. He thinks maybe he *will* go to law school. Have you heard the joke?" asked Glass, looking at Stuart.

"No," Stuart said, although he had heard the joke. He'd heard it Monday. From his dear friend Stephen Solon. Today he figures he could hear the joke again. And laugh again too, if necessary. Odd, though, that Solon and Glass moved in the same circles.

"All right, then," said Glass, relishing the buildup, "Our screenwriter is sitting there alone at night, with a drink in his hand. He's discouraged. He hears a noise. Somebody's up in the bedroom, the one our hero's been using as an office; somebody's up there typing." Glass put down his Tom Collins.

At this point, the waiter arrived with a glass and a bottle of Chardonnay. He poured Stuart a sip. Stuart tasted it, nodded. The waiter filled the glass and went away.

"So the screenwriter puts down his drink," continued Glass, putting down his own drink. "He goes upstairs, and he finds a tiny elf, sitting at his keyboard, typing furiously. Now this is not one of your good-looking elves. This is small man, a little man, dirty, and with pointy ears.

"Our hero wants to know what this elf is doing; how he got in. The elf says, 'I love to write. If I can just have the use of your computer, I'd love to write a screenplay. I don't think it will be any good. But if it is any good, it's yours.'

"The screenwriter doesn't have a problem with this. He goes downstairs, has a couple of more drinks, goes to bed. The next morning he wakes up, and the elf is printing out. It's a completed screenplay. It doesn't look any good to our hero. He doesn't read the whole thing. But he does send it to his agent. I mean what's he got to lose?

"Now it's a year later. Our man has just come back to his new house in Malibu. He's carrying the Oscar he won for best original screenplay. He's enjoying his success, all right, but he still doesn't really have anything he needs to write about.

"He unknots his bow tie, kicks off his dancing pumps, and then he hears typing up in the fabulous new office he had set up and decorated with the funds from the elf's first screenplay.

"He climbs the stairs, opens the door to the office. He hadn't remembered that the elf was this dirty. Did the elf smell last time? I mean this is an elf that—in bad light—you could easily mistake for a rat.

" 'I just love to write,' the elf says. 'I have this movie I want to write. If I finish it, and if it's any good—and I doubt it'll be any good—then you can have it.'

" 'Look,' says our hero, 'that last screenplay you wrote, it wasn't bad. I mean it needed a lot of work, of course.'

" 'Of course it needed work,' says the elf.

" 'But still,' " says our hero, "it had some merit. I mean the basic premise had some merit. There was something there to work with.'

"The elf isn't listening now. He's typing feverishly. Totally absorbed in the act of creation.

" 'You want an espresso?' the screenwriter asks, but the elf doesn't look up. 'You want a car, an elf-girlfriend? A bath?'

" 'None of that will be necessary,' the elf says. 'I just want to be left alone to write. I love to write.'

" 'Fine, fine,' says the screenwriter. 'Have it your way.'

"He starts to leave the room. He's at the door, when he hears the voice behind him, familiar, but querulous now: 'There is just one thing you could do,' says the elf.

" 'Sure,' says the screenwriter. 'And what's that?'

"Now the elf is embarrassed.

" 'Now I don't think I should ask,' he says.

" 'Ask,' says our hero. 'Fire away.'

" 'Well,' says the elf. 'If I do finish this screenplay—and I'm not at all sure I'll be able to finish the screenplay—but if I do finish it . . . and if it's any good . . . and if by any chance, they make a movie out of it . . . I mean you'd get all the money, of course. But I wondered, you know where it says, "writer," up there in the credits? I just wondered if right there where it says writer, if you could put *my* name in?'

"What does the screenwriter say?" asked Glass. "Can you guess?"

Stuart shook his head.

"I'll tell you what he says," said Glass. "He says: 'And *who* the fuck do you think *you* are?'"

CHAPTER 21

"I just love to paint."

After Stuart's false laughter had died away, the waiter appeared, and Glass looked up absurdly pleased, still chuckling at his own humor, and having completely failed to notice the insincerity of the audience response.

"George," asked the waiter, "How's the Dover sole today?"

"Delicious," said the waiter.

"Two orders of sole, then," said Glass, looking up at Stuart for confirmation.

Stuart couldn't quite bring himself to speak, but he did manage a nod.

"I want to thank you for doing this," he said, as soon as the waiter was out of earshot.

"No, no," said Glass, "I'm the one who's in your debt." He took a piece of flat bread from the basket, broke it in half, and began to butter it.

"Shouldn't eat this," he said, waving the buttered bread in Stuart's direction. "Don't tell my doctor," he said, and chuckled. Then he took a bite, chewed and swallowed. "You know, of course, that my father never expected to make any money in publishing."

Stuart smiled faintly.

"He made the money elsewhere. He went into publishing because he loved books and writers. But you've made this a going concern. Every single year since you've been Editor-in-Chief, we've been in the black. You've given the house a reputation for probity. Probity," Glass said, as if tasting the word. "Probity turns out to be worth a good deal."

Stuart shrugged. "It's been my pleasure," he said.

Glass nodded and took another piece of bread, chewed hurriedly, wagged his head, as if realizing a problem in his previous statement. He swallowed and began again. "I'm not saying we wouldn't have earned as much with the capital if we'd invested judiciously in the stock market, but then we wouldn't have been part of the cultural life of the nation, which was what my father—a Russian Jew—desperately wanted."

Stuart twisted around in his chair, trying to find a comfortable way to sit.

"When I bought back the publishing house from the conglomerate five years ago, I thought it was an act of hubris. Something done to please my father's shade, and maybe provide gainful employment for my sons—although neither of the boys was even faintly interested. Now it turns out I was brilliant."

He looked Stuart in the eye. "There's nobody else like us. And by publishing a series of esteemed books, you've made Acropolis into an attractive proposition."

"Of course you're the Editorial Director," said Stuart.

"And too damn old to be Editorial Director," said Glass.

Stuart inhaled deeply through his nose. "I *could* do more," he said. "Given time, and a little money, I think I could do more . . ." But now Glass was wagging his head, holding up a finger.

"I'm certain you could," he said. "I have no doubt. Do you know that we only got *The Red Hot Center* because the writer, what was her name?"

"Panela Waters."

"That's right. Panela Waters. She wanted to be published by Acropolis. Random House matched our bid. Did Massberg tell you that? It was your reputation that clinched the deal."

"No," said Stuart. "Massberg didn't tell me that. And besides which, *The Red Hot Center* is not the acquisition I'm proudest of."

Now Glass was nodding. "That's what Richard told me," he said. "Splendid young man that Massberg turned out to be. Almost the son I never had."

Stuart swallowed hard. "Remember who brought him in," he said. "Over *your* dead body," he pointed out and chuckled sourly.

"And you were right again," said Glass. "Now he's a favorite of mine. But I'm not the one who adores him. You know who adores him?"

"No," said Stuart. "Who adores Rick Massberg?" he asked.

"Helen adores him," said Glass.

The fish arrived, and Glass took a bite, smiled quizzically at Stuart, who took a bite, beamed back and nodded. "We had the young Massberg up to the house in Maine last summer, and he looked at Helen's paintings. Of course you know that Helen's been painting since the boys left home."

"I didn't know," said Stuart.

"Very productive," said Glass nodding. "Now, I'm no judge of visual arts, but she does love the work. And the pictures aren't bad to look at. We've had several of them framed and hung."

"Really?" said Stuart, trying vainly to keep the incredulity out of his voice.

"They're seascapes mostly. We set them up around the house. Nobody has ever said anything. I didn't know if this is because nobody noticed, or if our guests did notice and were just polite."

Glass took a big bite of fish, and bolted it down, smiling cheerfully at his guest as he did so. He wiped his lips with the linen napkin.

"Then we invite your friend Massberg to spend the weekend," he continued. "Of course, we've invited you and Andie many times, but it seems you could never break away."

Now Stuart was wagging his head. "Andie's got a murderous schedule," he said.

"I know," said Glass, "And Massberg is a single man, a bachelor. So he came. He rented a car and drove up alone. What's that, fourteen hours? He comes into the foyer of the house and that's where *The Lone Seagull Pines for Its Mate* is hanging."

Stuart nodded and stopped chewing.

"It was as if he'd been shot," said Glass. "He drops his bag, and he's looking at the seagull—I always call the seagull Bradley, because he reminds me of my uncle Bradley—Massberg looks at the seagull, and his mouth falls open. Right away he wants to know who did it.

"Helen is not a retiring woman. She hasn't been coy now for forty years. But she was coy for Massberg. She said, 'A local artist.'

"So then he said, 'Really? Are there other paintings like this one that I could look at?'

"So Helen says, 'Well not exactly. But we do have others by the same artist.' You can tell she's just loving this, having to say that word 'artist' over and over.

"Massberg won't rest until they've been all through the house, and he's had a chance to admire each of her works. She's got six of them on the walls: a lobster boat coming out of the mist, surf against rocks, the lighthouse struck by lightning. I rather admire the picture with the lobster boat. You get the dorsal of a shark cutting the water in front of the bow. Implied menace. In any case, we've seen every H. Greene painting in the house—Helen uses her maiden name for her acrylics, and for the essays."

"I know about the essays," said Stuart.

Glass nodded and went on. "Massberg's bags are still in the foyer. Then he wants to know where this artist exhibits. It seems he wants to buy a painting by this mysterious H. Greene. If he can afford it.

"Well," said Glass, sipping contently on his drink. "I had no idea what a practiced liar my wife could be. She tells him that on Saturday he can visit a gallery that has some of the same artist's work. Which is a lie, of course, because she isn't exhibited any-where. The local places that sell antiques and paintings won't take her work. They say it's too unpleasant. Which is what they always say about true artists, isn't it?"

"I've heard that," said Stuart.

"So they keep putting off the trip to the gallery, and finally he figures it out. And you never heard such praise. I know Helen had never heard such praise. She was Constable in the twentieth century. She was Wyeth with feeling. She was Hopper by the sea."

"Amazing," said Stuart.

"I didn't say anything," continued Glass, using a piece of bread to wipe up the remains of his fish sauce, "but I was thinking, young Massberg's got a Tartar by the toe. He's telling her she should have an exhibition. He's telling her she should have a book brought out. I was thinking, he doesn't know Helen. She's not going to forget.

"So we came back to the city, and he had actually set up an exhibition for her down in Soho. Now Abrams is making noises about a book."

"That is amazing," said Stuart, and this time he meant it.

The waiter arrived. Glass took a second Tom Collins. Stuart refused another glass of wine.

"But speaking of thwarted ambition," said Glass, after taking a long pull on his drink. "I wasn't exactly surprised that your story was selected for the *Best Best Short Stories of the Century*."

Stuart said nothing.

"Have you been writing?"

"No," said Stuart.

"No time?" asked Glass.

Stuart said nothing.

Now Glass was bobbing his head. "Then I've got some good news for you," he said. "Good news and bad news."

"Bad news first," said Stuart.

"Well, actually, I have to sell Acropolis."

"You're kidding," said Stuart. "I don't believe you," he said and meant it.

Glass was smiling genially. "I'm too old for these headaches. Better to give in to the inevitable. Economies of scale and all that."

"But what about me?" asked Stuart.

"Well, there's the good news," said Glass. "We're cutting you free at last. Octopus is buying, and Octopus doesn't want to buy you. Not that you're for sale."

Stuart's throat was suddenly dry. He had a big drink of water.

"I was never comfortable with the fact that all your talent was being wasted on business," said Glass. "Now's the time to go out there and write the novel. Stay at home and write that book we've been hearing about for twenty years. Stop mothering other people's children."

"What about Acropolis?" asked Stuart, still not taking this in.

"Well, Acropolis as you know it will cease to exist," said Glass. "Which is sad, but not all that sad."

Stuart looked mutely at the old man across the table. Glass had a little bit of fish sauce on his chin. Stuart instinctively wiped his own chin.

"When did you decide this?" Stuart asked.

"Yesterday," said Glass, nodding and beaming, fish sauce still on his chin. "You know that if we'd met for lunch yesterday, I would have made you Editorial Director. I would have put you right back up on the high wire. You know that you've been performing against all the odds for five years now. I didn't see any other way to go. Sad as I was, of course, about how you'd probably never write your novel. I'd confided in Massberg a week ago, and he thought I was making the best of a bad situation. Bad for me—keeping all my money tied up. But also bad for you. Keeping you away from your work. Richard's a great fan, you know. Goes on and on about what a talent you are, and what a tragedy it's been for you to have shut down the dynamo of your art."

Stuart swallowed again. His throat was dry, but his water glass was empty. "He did say he liked my story," Stuart said.

"Liked!" said Glass, "He's in awe of your story. And hates like poison that you are forced to waste your substance on business. So Massberg asked if I would mind selling the whole kit and caboodle for the right price. I told him I wouldn't mind. Then he made some phone calls, and up until late yesterday morning, nothing came of his efforts. At the last minute—actually it would have been after the last minute, if we hadn't delayed our little lunch—Octopus comes in with an offer that constitutes a truly astonishing markup. They are able to pay three times what I paid five years ago to bring the firm back into the family. Now that's a tidy profit. And we owe a lot of it to your good work. And I'll insist that you're compensated," Glass said.

Stuart was dazed, and not heartened by this last statement. He knew how this dear old man could squeeze a nickel.

"The imprint—which you've made so valuable—will seem to continue to exist," said Glass. "Rick Massberg has agreed to stay on as Editorial Director."

"But he can't edit," said Stuart. "Who's going to edit the text?"

"Good question," said Glass. "And I've got an answer. Stephen Solon is coming over from Random House to be Editor-in-Chief. He and I had some green beer on Saint Patrick's Day. Everything was tentative at that time, but we agreed on terms. In case a sale was made."

"I thought he was happy at Random House," said Stuart.

"No," said Glass. "They've got him tucked away, working on young adult fiction. He's going wild. Willing to make the jump."

"That's not what he told me," said Stuart.

Glass shrugged. "He sounded definite to me," he said.

"Which makes him a liar," said Stuart.

"I thought you liked Solon?" asked Glass. "You think he's a good editor?"

"He is good," said Stuart, trying to keep the sorrow out of his voice. He reached across the table and picked up Glass's Tom Collins. He took a long pull on the drink.

"I don't know what I'm going to do," he said.

"Now, now," said Glass in fatherly tones. "You'll write. You love to write. You won't have a pension, but I expect to be able to settle more than one hundred thousand dollars on you before we're all through. You'll go home at last and write that novel you've been talking about since you and I first met. What's the matter? You look pale."

"Excuse me," Stuart said, and he stood and walked out of the restaurant. He saw a woman on the street smoking, asked her for a cigarette. She looked at him, recognized the grim pallor, gave him a Merit Ultra Light. She lit it. This he smoked as he walked. He stubbed the cigarette into the sand of the planter outside his building and took the elevator to the ninth floor.

Coming in past the receptionist, he could see Massberg through the glass walls of his office. Rick was on the phone.

Stuart walked up to the door, knocked, and opened it. Massberg saw him, muttered something into the phone. He didn't hang up, but held the receiver against his chest, the mouthpiece muffled.

Stuart came inside the office, but said nothing.

"What?" asked Massberg.

Stuart stood, nodding his head as if he'd just remembered something important. "I should murder you. Murdering you would improve the gene pool."

Massberg shrugged his shoulders. "What are you talking about?" he said.

"You know just what I'm talking about," said Stuart. "From now on," he said, "I'd stay out of alleyways. I'd sleep with a gun under my pillow."

Walking down the hall, he was met by Althea, who looked pale and concerned. "Take this," she said and handed him the plastic bag with the CD player in it. "Can't forget the children."

Stuart nodded, but said nothing. He took the elevator down onto the street and hurried back to the Four Seasons. He got inside just as Glass was being helped on with his coat.

"What's the matter?" Glass asked. "Where did you go?"

"Change it," said Stuart. "Fire Massberg. Retire. Make me Editorial Director. It's the only decent thing you can do."

"And I would certainly do it," said Glass. "If I was going to live forever. If I had no grandchildren to worry about. Octopus will make the family liquid again. I love my sons, but neither of them is ever going to make a living. On the other hand, they've both managed to produce families. And who knows, one of my beloved grandchildren might want to go to college. I have to be able to pay for it."

By now he had his coat on. "I love you," he said, holding out his arms. The two men embraced. "I love you too," said Stuart, "but I'm screwed."

"Go home now," said Glass. "Write that book of yours."

Stuart turned away. He didn't want the older man to see his tears. He walked toward the station. He felt as if both legs were asleep. Inside the main concourse, he checked the schedule. He had half an hour before the next train to Scarborough. He bought a cup of coffee and a copy of the *New York Post*. He fished the new cell phone out of his pocket. He called home. Nobody picked up. "It's Stuart," he told the machine. "Call me."

Then he looked up Andie's new cell number, which he'd written on a piece of paper taped to the back of his own phone.

She wasn't picking up, so he left another message. "It's Stuart. Call me."

He wondered how much Andie would be able to tell from his tone of voice.

Then he went to one of the tables in the downstairs of the station, sat, and tried to read the paper, but he couldn't get the words to stop floating around, so he put the newspaper into the recycling bin. He climbed the stairs and walked around the main concourse. He'd been used to coming there only at rush hour, and so the space seemed empty, lonely. There were still a lot of people about, though, men and women in suits. *Most of them have jobs*, he thought. *I'd guess that most of them have jobs.*

Andie didn't phone back until her husband's train was already in Irvington, most of the way home.

"Hi," she said. "How was the lunch?"

"Are you ready for this?" asked Stuart.

"Ready for what?"

"I'm fired. Glass sold the place to Octopus. He's made Massberg Editorial Director."

"You're kidding," said Andie.

"God, but I wish I were," said Stuart.

"But Glass loves you," said Andie.

"That's what he said," said Stuart. "He said, 'I love you,' and then he fired me. He wants me to stay home and write books."

"He's got a point," said Andie.

"Thanks," said Stuart.

"It's what you've been talking about," said Andie.

"You don't understand," said Stuart. "I fully expected that today I'd be made Editorial Director. Everybody told me that was what to expect. Massberg told me. That cocksucker. Solon told me. You told me."

"Listen," said Andie. "Massberg is a shit. He won't last. He'll fuck up. In the meantime, you'll write that novel of yours. Come back triumphant."

"But Octopus bought us," said Stuart. "They'll never want me. Not after what I've said about those people over the years."

"Maybe you're right," said Andie; then he could hear somebody talking to her in the background. "Can I call you right back?" she asked.

"Who's that?" asked Stuart.

"Warren Beatty. I'd better go now."

"Warren Beatty is calling you at home?" asked Stuart.

"I'm not at home," said Andie. "I'm in the office."

"I thought you were going to stay home today. Protect the children from the big black nanny."

"So did I," said Andie. "Look, I'll call you back." She broke the connection.

Exhausted from his ordeal, and from having gotten up so early, Stuart very nearly slept through his stop, and had to scramble to get off the train.

It was a bright day. He was refreshed by his catnap. The grass still hadn't gone green, but the air was warm and the walk up Scarborough Station Road was not unpleasant. Or it might not have been unpleasant, if his heart weren't broken.

He found Louise and the girls out in the backyard. The nanny had an easel set up so that she could paint the Monticello.

"An imitation of an imitation," Stuart said.

Louise shrugged. "I just love to paint."

CHAPTER 22

"Most novelists fail."

Stuart was still upstairs in his office, and suffering terribly, when he heard his wife's heels on the kitchen tile. It was after seven. He saved his work, shut the laptop, and walked downstairs.

"Welcome home."

"Oh, hi," said Andie, as if surprised to see him. "How are you?"

"Fine," he said, reflexively. "Actually, not fine. I need to talk with you alone."

"Is it about the nanny?" asked Andie.

"No," said Stuart, helping his wife off with her coat. "It's not about the nanny. You look good," he said.

"Thanks," said Andie. "How are the children?"

"The children are fine," said Stuart. "Never been better. It's not about the children. It's about me."

At this point Jane shot past her father, wrapped her arms around her mother's knees. "I love you, Mommy," she said.

"Welcome home," said Louise, and Stuart turned to see her standing in the kitchen doorway. Ginny was at the nanny's side.

"Welcome home, Mom," said Ginny, but without real enthusiasm.

"Let me take you out to dinner," said Stuart.

"I'm sorry," Andie said, patting Janey on the head as she spoke. "I can't do it. I was a nervous wreck all day being away from the children."

"Okay," said Stuart. "But please let me take you out for dinner. We can go to Bistro Maxime's in Chappaqua. I've got a hundred thousand dollars to burn. We can have a glass of wine. Enjoy the last days of Pompeii."

"Alternatively," said Andie, in a voice that indicated no alternatives, "we can give you a break," she said, looking at Louise. "We could take the girls to the Magic Wok in Pleasantville. Jane is always asking if I can make those spareribs for her."

"Sounds elegant," said Stuart.

"We're a family," said Andie. "Let's please act like a family."

"Can Louise come?" asked Ginny.

Andie sighed. "I think we should give Louise ten minutes peace," she said. "Besides which, I want to be alone with my family."

"But Louise is a member of the family," said Ginny. "She lives here."

"She's never had the ribs," said Janey.

"I think you girls should go out with your mother and father," Louise said, and her voice was cool, unfriendly.

"But you'll be here when we get back?" Ginny asked.

"Certainly, I'll be here," said Louise. "I live here," she said. "I'll be in my bedroom. Sketching."

So the biological Crosses put on their coats, climbed solemnly into the Volvo, and drove to Pleasantville.

The Magic Wok was nearly empty, and they took a table near the center of the dining room. When the waiter arrived to take a drink order, Andie asked Jane what she wanted. Jane wanted a Sprite. Ginny wanted a Shirley Temple. Andie and Stuart both wanted gin martinis straight up with olives.

After the drinks arrived, Andie lifted her glass to toast her husband. "Here's to the great American novel," she said.

Stuart clinked her glass, and the glasses of both his daughters. He said nothing.

"Cheer up," said Andie. "You've always wanted to write a novel."

"Yes," said Stuart, "but that was when I had a powerful job. I thought I was popular. Now it turns out I'm not so popular. If nobody's interested in my real-life services, then why should I suppose that they'd be interested in my daydreams?"

"Daydreams are good," said Andie. "All you have to do is start. That's how to start. As for finishing, you've finished up more novels in the last thirty years than any other three novelists have finished up in a lifetime."

Stuart took another long drink. "I want to go back," he said. "I can apologize to Glass. He liked me. He loves me. If I told him I'd work with Octopus, he might insist that I be made Editorial Director. If I still want to write a novel so much, I can do it on the weekends."

"Go to Pipes," said Andie. "Get the largest severance package possible. Hit Glass while he feels guilty."

"It won't be large," said Stuart. "You should have heard the way he said 'one hundred thousand dollars.' You would have thought it was, well, you would have thought it was 1956."

"Well," said Andie, "one hundred thousand dollars is a lot of money."

"Won't pay the taxes on our house for three years," said Stuart.

"All right," said Andie, "write a proposal and two chapters. Get it over to Wallace Stevens and extract an advance. This is your big chance. Take it. When God closes one door, he opens another."

Stuart ate a handful of crackers out of the plastic salad bowl in the middle of the table, took another pull on his drink. He said nothing.

"So you agree?" said Andie.

"It's not like I have a choice," he said.

Andie shrugged.

"There's something I want you to at least acknowledge," Stuart said. "Everybody thought I was going to get this job. You thought I was going to get the job."

"Yeah," said Andie, "actually I did think you'd get the job."

"If I hadn't taken the day off, I would have gotten it."

"How can that be?" asked Andie.

"Because the deal Octopus made hadn't been finalized until Tuesday afternoon."

"How could I have known that?" said Andie.

"You couldn't have known it," said Stuart. "I didn't know it. I just want you to take a minute, take a deep breath, and sympathize with your husband for a career in ruins."

"I do," said Andie, and clinked her glass against his. "I sympathize. I also remember how much my husband wanted to write a novel. Needed to write a novel."

"I also need to make a living," said Stuart.

"Novelists make a living," said Andie.

"Some do," said Stuart.

"Plus, it's not about money, really. It's about what you want to do with the rest of your life. Was all that talk about the novel nonsense? The novel that's been eating your guts out since you first achieved consciousness."

"Not nonsense," said Stuart. "Not exactly."

"Can I order the crispy orange beef?" asked Ginny.

"No," said Andie. "You cannot order the crispy orange beef. You and I, young lady, will eat from the diet menu."

"I hate the diet menu," said Ginny.

"I don't much like it either," said Andie. "But us girls need to watch our figures," she said, and patted her slender belly.

"But you're having a cocktail," said Ginny. "Liquid fat."

"I *am* having a cocktail," said Andie, and nodded.

"Ginny can have spareribs to start with," said Stuart.

"How many orders?" asked Ginny.

"One large order for the family," said Andie.

"Okay," said Ginny. "Daddy," she said. "Will you give me your ribs?"

"Sure," said Stuart.

"Stuart," said Andie. "I'm trying to help your daughter lose weight. It won't work if you're the happy enabler."

"I'm not the happy anything," said Stuart. "Or not tonight, I'm not."

At this point, the waiter arrived and took the family order.

"So when *were* you going to write your book?" asked Andie, when the waiter had finished up.

"I had it all figured out," said Stuart. "A little house on the coast in Maine. A view of the ocean. Both children grown and happily married."

"How old would you have been?" asked Andie.

"I don't know," said Stuart. "I guess about a hundred and fifteen years old."

"All right then," said Andie, "this is your plan exactly. Only the timetable has been pushed up. Write your book. You

187

already wrote one great story. It's one of the best-best of the century."

"That was a million years ago," said Stuart. "I can't remember the guy who wrote that story. Some callow, righteous creature who lived off espresso, cigarettes, and indignation. Writing about Indians. Imagine me writing about Indians. Talk about crust."

"So now you'll write differently," said Andie. "You'll write a mature person's book."

"I'm not certain mature people write books," said Stuart.

"Oh come on," said Andie.

"I don't want to write a book," said Stuart. "I want an office to go to. I want a reason to get dressed in the morning."

"What about me?" said Andie. "I'm not enough of a reason to get dressed in the morning?"

"You'll be out," said Stuart, and finished his drink. Then he gestured violently to the waiter, an old man who walked slowly and deliberately across the room without seeming to notice Stuart's signals.

"You know the tombstone joke," said Stuart. "Here lies a waiter; God finally caught his eye."

"I know the joke," said Andie, but Stuart was standing up at this point, and waving both arms. The waiter saw him.

Dinner was not a conversational success. Andie asked Ginny if she had any homework over break.

Ginny said no, she had no homework over break.

"Is there any extra work you can do to get ahead?"

"No," said Ginny.

"I'll do some extra work," said Janey.

Stuart played and replayed his day's drama. "Knifed in the

back," he said. "One man owes me his job. The other was supposed to be a close friend. They both deserted me."

Andie shrugged. "You'll show them," she said. "You'll show them all."

When the check arrived with fortune cookies, Ginny wanted to know if the girls could each have two fortune cookies, "since you and Daddy already know your future."

"You can have two fortunes," said Andie, "but only one cookie."

When Jane opened her second cookie, she jumped up from the table and waved the little piece of paper in the air. "See, this one already came true," she said.

"What do you mean it already came true?" asked Stuart.

"See," said Jane, passing the tiny piece of paper to her father. "Read it."

Stuart took the reading glasses out of his jacket pocket. "It says here that you will meet a handsome stranger."

"See," said Jane. "I already did. I met a handsome stranger today."

"Shush," said Ginny. "You know he's supposed to be a secret."

"Who's a secret?" asked Andie.

"Nobody's a secret," said Ginny.

Andie turned to Jane. "Who's a secret?" she said.

Jane pursed her lips.

Andie reached across the table and grabbed her older daughter by the wrist.

"I want the truth, young lady," she said, "and I want it now."

Ginny looked as if she were going to cry.

"Janey," Andie said, turning now to the younger girl. "What handsome stranger are you talking about?"

"Don't tell her," said Ginny.

"You'd better tell me," said Andie.

Now Jane began to weep. Quietly at first. Then noisily.

"See what you've done," said Ginny.

It took Andie and Stuart working together an interminable amount of time—probably three minutes—to get Jane to stop shrieking. The waiter was giving them the fish eye. The family that had just been seated at the next table asked to be moved.

Ultimately, Ginny was convinced to talk. Provided, of course, she and Jane each got a bowl of green-tea ice cream.

"We went out today," she said "and Sugar took us to meet her handsome stranger."

"Which handsome stranger?" asked Stuart.

"Sugar's handsome stranger," said Ginny. "That's what she called him, 'my handsome stranger.' He's a magician. He had a deck of cards. I'd pick a card, and then he knew what it was. He said he could swallow fire. He said another time he'd swallow fire for us."

"He was very handsome," said Jane. "He had a tatooey."

"A tattoo," said Ginny.

Andie nodded. She caught Stuart's eye. "*See.*"

After they'd paid the bill, Stuart drove his silent family home in the Volvo.

Then he brought the girls upstairs for a bedtime story. Andie knocked at the door to the maid's quarters.

"Miss Washington," she said. "We need to talk."

"Just a minute," said Louise. "I'll be right out." Then she appeared, but wearing only a blue flannel nightgown, white tube socks, and a black terry robe.

"Come on into the kitchen," said Andie.

"Fine," said Louise. "Anything wrong?"

"Yes," said Andie. "Something is terribly wrong."

"I'm so sorry," said Miss Washington. "Can I help?"

"I think so," said Andie, pulling out a chair and sitting down. She did not suggest that Miss Washington also make herself comfortable.

"Stuart is upstairs with the girls," Andie began. "He's reading to them. Ordinarily we'd talk with you together, but this evening I'm happy to do it alone. You seem to have won him over."

"We like each other," said Louise, standing with her hands on the back of a chair and facing her employer across the wooden table.

"The girls tell me that you went out and met a man," said Andie. "A handsome stranger."

"Yes," said Louise, smiling. "That's right. We ate lunch at the diner across from the Arcadian Shopping Center with an old friend of mine. The girls like him a lot. I call him T. His actual name is Toussaint Louverture. We were very close when I was studying in England. He's been away for a long time. He's working now on a degree at Columbia. He was up in the country for the day to visit the Rockefeller archives in Pocantico Hills. I suggested he meet the girls."

Andie didn't say anything.

"Is there anything wrong with that?" asked Louise. "Ginny had a spinach salad with oil and vinegar. I picked the bacon and croutons out of it. You know she's already beginning to lose weight."

"Here's the problem," said Andie. "And it's a serious problem. Ginny said at dinner that you told her and Jane not to mention the meeting to us." Andie was gritting her teeth, when she said this, her face was paste-white with fury.

Louise seemed unperturbed. "That's correct," she said, pulling out a chair and sitting down. "I told them it was a big secret. Did you ever read *Mary Poppins*?"

"Of course I read *Mary Poppins*," said Andie.

"Do you think Mary Poppins was a good nanny?"

Andie nodded.

"And how much did Mr. and Mrs. Banks know about what went on in their household?"

"Very little," said Andie, "but I'm not Mrs. Banks. Nor can you fly."

"That's true," said Louise, "but I am close to your children. We enjoy each other's company. We are friends. Friends keep secrets together. Not sinister secrets, but secrets. When we went to the zoo I took an apple for each girl. I told Ginny that if she didn't eat anything else, then I would let her see the crocodiles at feeding time. And I added that this had to be our secret."

"Why make it a secret?" asked Andie.

"I don't know if you're fully aware of this, Ms. Wilde, but your daughter's eating disorder is linked to and grows out of the relationship she has with your husband. It is only through the symbolic severing of that relationship that I have been able to get her to think about something other than food."

"Ginny doesn't have a serious problem," said Andie.

"Yes, she does," said Louise. "And you know why? Because you and your husband both think she has a serious problem. Did you know that she was in the habit of coming downstairs at night and making sugar sandwiches with white bread and butter? Three-decker sugar-and-butter sandwiches?"

"No," said Andie. "I didn't know that."

Louise was nodding. "Now you have to promise not to tell her I told you that."

"It's not for me to be making promises to you," said Andie. "I will not tolerate having you tell my children to keep secrets from myself and my husband."

"Of course I had planned all along to tell you what we'd done today," said Louise. "In fact, I expected to tell you about it the first time we were alone."

"Don't do it," said Andie. "Don't ever encourage our girls to keep anything from their parents. I mean that. Don't do it. Ever!"

"Okay," said Louise. "If that's how you feel."

"It's how I feel," said Andie.

"Okay," said Louise. "Fine. Now, since I'm up, would you like me to put the girls to bed?"

"No," said Andie. "Stuart is already doing that. I think my husband can handle his own children for one evening."

At this point Stuart came to the top of the stairs. "Baby," he called, "do you know where my glasses are?"

"Are you still wearing your jacket?" Andie asked.

"Yes," said Stuart.

"Well then," said Andie, ice in her tone, "why not check your jacket pocket?"

"Oh," said Stuart, "you're right," he said, sounding pleasantly surprised. "Thanks, Baby." Then he walked back down the hall and into the girls' room.

"While you and I are talking," said Andie, "I'd like to know your plans for tomorrow."

"I thought I'd take the children to the Metropolitan," said Louise. "I usually start out with the Museum of Natural History, but your girls are precocious. And we're just at the beginning of the spring break."

"I must go to work early tomorrow," said Andie. "I'd much rather you stayed around the house. Mr. Cross will be here. Working at home."

Louise nodded. "Okay," she said. "If that's what you want."

"It's what I want," said Andie.

Louise's face showed a question.

"What?" asked Andie.

"Well," said Louise, "this is a shot in the dark, but I wondered if you knew what had happened to my socks."

"Your what?" asked Andie.

"My socks," said Louise, pointing down at her feet. "I always keep twelve pairs in the drawer. It's a superstitious habit, I have. Silly really, but it's been a habit now for a decade. It's a vice I can afford. Today I found that there were only ten pairs in my drawer. I wondered if you knew what had happened to the other two pairs of socks."

"No idea," said Andie. "No idea." She stood and headed out of the kitchen, pausing at the doorway to look back at Louise. "Never keep a secret from me," she said, "and never leave the house without first writing a note."

Andie then stalked upstairs and found Stuart fast asleep on his elder daughter's bed. Both girls were awake.

"You will have to put yourselves to bed tonight," Andie told the girls, shaking her husband awake. "I'll deal with your father."

"Can Louise come up and read to us?" Ginny asked.

"No," said Andie. "Louise cannot come upstairs and read to you." She led her husband out of the children's room and closed the door.

"I hope we agree on this," she said, as he stepped drowsily out of his pants. "You're staying home. Writing your book. Keeping your little girls out of that woman's clutches."

"No," said Stuart. "Not me. I'm going to phone Herbert Glass and beg."

"Please, please write your book," said Andie.

"You don't care about my book," said Stuart, hanging up his pants.

"Yes, I do," said Andie. "I'm your biggest fan."

"No, you aren't my biggest fan," said Stuart, getting into bed.

"Who is then," said Andie, puckering up for a kiss.

"Rick Massberg is my biggest fan," said Stuart.

Andie came to her husband and tried to kiss him on the lips, but he brushed her away.

"That's the first time," said Andie, "that you've ever refused a kiss of mine."

Stuart leaned forward and kissed his wife lightly on the lips.

"Don't be bitter," said Andie.

"I am bitter," said Stuart.

"Okay, then," said Andie. "Be bitter, but put it in a book."

"I don't want to put it in a book. I want to go back to work."

"What if they won't take you?" asked Andie.

"They'll take me," said Stuart.

"What if the conditions aren't acceptable?" said Andie.

"Any conditions would be acceptable," said Stuart. "They all know me. They all like me. Massberg won't last. Even Althea hates Massberg."

"What about the children?" asked Andie.

"I'm not the least bit worried about the children," said Stuart.

"I'll tell you what," said Andie. "I'll make you a deal."

Stuart inhaled deeply, and then let the air out slowly. "I know about your deals."

"Here it is," said Andie, holding up one finger. "You can return to Acropolis Inc. You can turn your back on the opportunity to write the book you've wanted to write since you first achieved consciousness. You can leave your children in peril. I'll let you do that."

"Good," said Stuart. "I like this deal."

"One thing," said Andie "Will you promise me one thing?"

"I don't know," said Stuart.

"It's reasonable," said Andie. She moved over beside her husband on the bed and began to massage his back.

"All right," said Stuart. "Ask."

"You have to promise first," said Andie.

"All right," said Stuart, and he sighed tragically. "I promise."

"You won't go back on it?"

"I won't go back on it."

"Here's the deal," said Andie. "You'll wait for *them* to call *you*. When they call you, you can beg. You can agree to any humiliation, when they call you. But you can't call them first."

"All right," said Stuart quickly. "I'll give you that much. They have to call me. They don't have to beg me. All they have to do is call. They can call to ask where the key to the filing cabinet is, or where to send my Rolodex. All they have to do is pick up the phone and dial this number."

"You've got a deal," said Andie.

"Waiting is always painful," said Stuart.

"You won't be waiting," said Andie. "You'll be writing. And if you take a break from writing, you can call Wallace Stevens. In fact, you should call Wallace Stevens. Discuss how much you need to write before you sell the book."

"Okay," said Stuart. "But there's something *you* should understand going in."

"What's that?"

"We're probably going to lose the house."

"I don't think so," said Andie. "I bet you're a successful novelist. You know all about novels."

And Stuart sensed an overwhelming lassitude. *The hardest part of being old*, he thought, *is that everybody expects you to know something. No mortal can know anything of importance. The young have an excuse for their ignorance. We have no excuse.*

"Why so quiet?" asked Andie. "You're down right now, which I understand, but you're not going to pretend that you don't know your way around novels."

"That's right," said Stuart. "I do know something about novels. I also know something about novelists."

"Yeah," said Andie. "What's that?"

"Most novelists fail."

CHAPTER 23

"God is in the details."

Having chased his two Chinese-restaurant martinis with five milligrams of Valium, Stuart was understandably groggy Wednesday morning. Still, he was astonished by the alacrity with which Andie fled that big house and her beloved family. The first sound he heard was the click of heels as his wife came down the hall into the bedroom, leaned over and kissed him furtively on the ear.

"Home for dinner," she said. "Don't leave the paragon alone with the girls."

"I have a headache," he said. "Don't you have a headache?"

Andie shook her head prettily, as if checking for aches. "No," she said, "I'm fine." Her face darkened. "But remember: Watch my babies." Stuart nodded uncertainly, as his wife turned, and started away.

"Rats deserting a sinking ship," he called out, as Andie clicked back down the hallway. Then her heels were muffled in the staircase carpet.

It was nine A.M. before the man of the house made it to the first floor. Louise had set up her easel, so that she could paint the yard through the kitchen window. Examining the canvas, he could just make out the lines that would become the frame of the windows. Both girls were in the back room watching cartoons.

"Good morning, Mr. Cross," Louise said, and she was respectful, but there was also a twinkle in her eye. "Would you like coffee?"

"I thought children under your care never watched cartoons," he said, nodding his head in the direction of the great room.

"They never do," Louise said, twinkled, and presented her employer with a cup of coffee. "Hard night?" she asked.

Stuart nodded ruefully. "Ti many martoonies," he said. "And plus I miss my job."

"Spilled milk," said Louise.

"What?" asked Stuart.

"No use crying over spilled milk," said Louise.

"There's that," said Stuart.

"The coffee will help," said Louise. "And solid food."

"And what are the plans for today?" he said.

"I had hoped to take the girls to the city," said Louise. "To the Metropolitan. Give you some solitude to write in. Your wife wants me to stay at home, though."

"She's still a little uneasy," said Stuart. "Move to the suburbs, and the city grows awesome, then dreadful. Maybe we can all go to the museum tomorrow. Together. We'll have to see, though. I am expecting a phone call today. If the phone rings," he said, "grab it and get me. This is important. I don't care if I'm in the shower, the bathroom. Call me."

Miss Washington nodded. "I'll tell the girls to do the same," she said. "And I'd love it if we could all go to the Metropolitan tomorrow. It's one of my favorite places in the world."

"You love the museum because you're a painter?" asked Stuart.

"Actually, it's the reverse," said Louise. "I'm a painter because I so love that museum."

"How's that?" asked Stuart.

"Wait a minute," said Louise. "If we're going to have a conversation, then you're going to have to let me make you some breakfast. Eggs? Oatmeal?"

"Just an English muffin," said Stuart. "Toasted and with a little butter. Now that you've brought the toaster oven back to life."

"All right," said Louise, and opened the refrigerator. "I'm sure I saw some English muffins hiding in here yesterday."

"They're on the bottom shelf," said Stuart. "Mixed in among the vegetables."

"Okay," said the nanny. "I see them now." She removed the package.

"But tell me about the museum," said Stuart.

"I used to go there all the time as a small child," said Louise.

"Your parents strivers?" Stuart asked.

"Not exactly," said Louise. "My mother was a nanny, you know. I told you that. She worked for a family on Fifth Avenue. She had a little girl to take care of. Amanda. My mother used to take Amanda to the Metropolitan. My father would take me to the museum. That was when we could all be together."

"That must have been a bore for you to have to go to a museum when you were a child," said Stuart.

"I had a very strong reaction to the oils," said the nanny. She had halved a muffin, buttered it, and put it in the toaster oven. Now she turned with her back to the counter, and faced her employer. "I used to get sick to my stomach. The crucifixions. Acres of fleshy nudes."

"It is a powerful experience," said Stuart. "If you let it happen."

"That's right," said Louise, "and a lot of people try to protect themselves in museums."

"You do see them with their faces in the literature," said Stuart. "Whenever they come to a new picture, they rush over to the side of it and read the name and dates of the artist. You wonder if they wouldn't be happier staying at home and viewing the catalog. Happier still if the paintings themselves were blacked out, like the faces of men and women in porn videos used to be."

Louise chuckled appreciatively. "We are all a little like that," she said. "Nobody wants to look right into the sun. But a child doesn't have those resources. Children are naked in the world. A child in a museum is in intimate, almost carnal contact with the artists. Yes, the painters are mostly dead, but this seems to heighten the intimacy. There's something terribly compelling about the contact, but also something repulsive."

"I think I understand," said Stuart.

"When I got past the illness," the nanny said, "I began to love the paintings."

Stuart didn't say anything.

"But enough about me," said Louise. "Can't I make you something to go with that muffin?"

"Is there any more of that oatmeal?" Stuart asked.

"Sure," said Louise, "but oatmeal isn't what you really want. What do you really want for breakfast?" she asked.

"How do you know I don't want oatmeal?" asked Stuart.

"After a night out, most people don't want oatmeal," said Louise. "They eat it, but it's not what they want. I had a clue. English muffins don't go with oatmeal?"

"You're right," said Stuart, standing, pouring himself a glass of water, and then going back to the table. "Scrambled eggs with lots of sharp cheddar cheese."

"Coming up," said Louise.

"All right," said Stuart, taking a long pull on his glass of water, "but I also want to hear the rest of your story. How you got to be a painter."

Louise reached down a bowl, and took eggs and a block of cheddar cheese out of the fridge.

"Some of my earliest and most cherished memories are of that place," she said, breaking eggs into a bowl. "I'd go there and sit in my mother's lap. I miss her still when I go back," said Louise. "She died when I was eight. I feel her presence most powerfully when I'm in the museum. The quiet. The murmur of strangers. The smell of wooden floors."

"You must have also seen your mother at home," said Stuart.

Louise shook her head mutely. She was cutting papery-thin slices of cheese. She put the pan on the burner, and then dropped in a chunk of butter.

She saw Stuart's look of concern. "Don't worry," she said. "Real butter won't hurt you."

"You didn't see your mother at home?" asked Stuart. "Your parents were divorced?"

"No," said Louise. "Not divorced. They got along."

"So why didn't you see her?"

"The Fifth Avenue people didn't know that Marcey had a family of her own."

"Why not?" asked Stuart.

Louise poured the eggs into the pan, dropped in the cheese, and began to stir. "They wouldn't have tolerated it," she said. "And it was a good job. The best possible job. So my mother kept the secret. Amanda kept the secret too. Which, when you think of it, is kind of extraordinary. Amanda must have loved my mother very much."

"So your mother lived with the family she worked for?"

"She had her own room. Nobody came in without her permission. She hung her uniform on a hanger on the back of the door."

"Time off?" asked Stuart.

"My mother came home on Monday night. I saw her then. I saw her all day Tuesday. We often spent Tuesdays at the museum. Sunday, we all went to church. During the rest of the week, I only saw her in the museum."

"You know what?" said Stuart. "I just remembered that you were due to have Tuesday off."

"That's all right," said Louise. "I can see when I'm needed. When we all settle down, you'll make it up to me."

"Remind us, though," said Stuart.

Louise nodded.

"Presumably your mother could have worked for an employer that would have allowed her to have a family of her own?"

"I suppose," said Louise, "but it never came up. The Smithsons were generous employers. Marcey liked Amanda. The arrangement is not all that unusual."

"Pretty rare nowadays," said Stuart.

"Not at all," said Louise. "Nowadays a lot of live-in nannies have families in El Salvador or Jamaica. Those women go years without seeing their own children."

"Fascinating," said Stuart. "So you formed an immediate relationship to the visual arts?"

"I guess," said Louise. "It's hard to know, but I suppose being exposed to all that powerful imagery made up my mind for me almost before I had a mind to make up. The two strongest impressions in my life were the smell my mother gave off and the look of those oils. My mother loved the oils. The big ones. The Tiepolos they have now at the top of the stairs. Nicolas Poussin's *The Rape of the Sabine Women*." She turned off the burner under the frying pan.

"Great story," said Stuart.

"Ancient Rome had powerful stories," said Louise, getting down a plate, and putting the English muffins on it. "Boys suckled by a wolf."

"I don't mean the Sabine women," said Stuart. "I'm talking about your own story. It's good. Somebody ought to tell it. If your paintings ever begin to sell, somebody probably will."

Louise bowed her head modestly. "Oh, they sell," she said. "My paintings already sell."

"Good," said Stuart. "Congratulations." And he wondered what sort of horrible this woman's paintings would turn out to be. The fact that they sold was a very bad sign.

"Which brings up some business," said Louise, who now scooped the eggs onto the plate and set the plate in front of her employer.

"Thank you," said Stuart, as Louise gave him a fork, knife, and napkin.

"What business?" he asked.

"I don't know if your wife told you this, but she and I made an arrangement—before I accepted this job—that I would have a place to store my paintings."

"I think she might have mentioned it," said Stuart.

"Is it a problem?" asked Louise.

"No," said Stuart. "Of course not."

"Since we're going to be here all day today," said Louise, "I thought I'd ask my friend to deliver them. If he and the girls and I unload, it shouldn't be too much of a disruption."

Stuart took a bite of egg, chewed, and swallowed. "No disruption," he said. "I'll help."

"You're supposed to be writing today," said Louise. "Not hauling other people's paintings. Ms. Wilde was very clear about that."

"I'll write," said Stuart. "First, I'm going to eat my breakfast."

"Good," said Louise. "Can the girls come in and say good morning to you?"

"Do they have to?" asked Stuart, smiling slyly. "I still feel as fragile as a piece of glass."

Louise nodded. "I'll let you finish up the eggs first," she said. "Then you have to let them in. I'll be here. I won't let anybody jump up and down on your stomach."

"Okay," said Stuart. "As long as you stay in the room. I do have work to do, you know?"

"Of course," said Louise, "now finish those eggs. Let me top up your coffee."

Twenty minutes later Stuart was climbing the stairs alone, a second mug of coffee in his hand, but no song in his heart. *I won't even take a shower*, he thought, sitting down at his empty desk. *I won't shower until I've written the first five pages*, he thought. *How long could that take? Anthony Trollope produced forty-seven novels, most of them while holding a full-time job.* With this in his mind, Stuart went down to the bookcase in the great room, picked out Trollope's autobiography, turned to the page he'd earmarked: "It was my practice to be at my table every morning at 5:30 A.M.; and it was also my practice to allow myself no mercy. By beginning at that hour I could complete my literary work before I dressed for breakfast."

At that rate, thought Stuart, *I'm already behind. That's two-hundred-fifty words per quarter hour. With or without inspiration.* About inspiration Trollope had written, "There are those who would be ashamed to subject themselves to such a taskmaster, and who think that the man who works with his imagination should allow himself to wait till inspiration moves him. When I have heard such doctrine preached, I have hardly been able to repress my scorn. To me it would not be more absurd if the shoemaker were to wait for inspiration, or the tallow-chandler for the divine moment of melting."

Feeling very much like the expectant tallow-chandler—what exactly was a tallow-chandler?—Stuart opened his hand-me-down laptop, turned it on, heard it hum. Waited for the noises of its awakening to subside, and then opened a file, and saved it as "Indian Chief 3/22/2000."

Then, he centered the margins and wrote:

The Last Red Indian.

Then he wrote "By Stuart Cross."

Then he inserted a page break.

He knew that speed was of the utmost importance. When James Thurber was starting out trying to write humor for the *New Yorker*, his wife had told him that he worked over his material too much. She set an alarm clock for an hour, and when the alarm went off, he was supposed to be done with whatever he was working on. Imagine giving up a piece of writing so easily. *That was always the mark of great achievement*, Stuart thought—*not dogged determination, as*

self-help writers would have you believe—but ease and grace, a blessed if
fragile sense of entitlement.

This was it, then. The moment. The first day of the rest of his life. Time to climb into what Yeats called "the foul rag and bone shop of the heart." Stuart looked at his watch. It was nine forty-five A.M. By nine forty-seven he was on his way downstairs again, looking for that briefcase. This was not procrastination. He needed his briefcase. He needed a pen and paper.

Curiously, the briefcase wasn't in its regular spot in the hall closet. Then he realized with a sudden pang that he might have left it at the office. He wouldn't have taken a briefcase to lunch. He hadn't picked it up when he came back to the office to threaten Rick Massberg's life.

He supposed Althea would have noticed and locked it up before she went home that evening. He returned to his desk, sat down again. *I have to start in pen and ink*, he thought, remembering that the entire text of *The Last Red Indian* had been scrawled out in an exercise book with a cheap and leaky fountain pen. *My Mont Blanc is in my briefcase*, he thought.

He walked into the bedroom and picked up the phone. Now he was breathing quickly, almost panting. *Andie will understand*, he thought. *I need my briefcase. This doesn't break my vow.* He dialed Althea's number. The phone rang. It rang again. It rang a third time. He remembered how his secretary played chicken with the office phone. First, she'd take a sip of coffee. Then she'd file a letter, or open a manuscript envelope. The machine was set to pick up after five rings. She never answered before it had rung four times. The phone rang again, and then he heard her voice, his secretary's voice—two boxes of Godiva he'd given that woman every year. And saved her job on more than one occasion. "Acropolis Publishing," Althea said. "Rick Massberg's line."

Stuart dropped the phone to the floor. Then he grabbed it, fumbling, and hung it up, afraid that some ambient sound might identify his person to his former secretary, reveal his terrible, his throbbing need.

He stood and paced back and forth across the bedroom-suite-to-die-for. It all made sense. Massberg would want the big space. That made Althea his secretary. Stuart sat on the bed and waited for his heart to stop racing.

When this happened, he stood, walked back to his desk. He hit the "f" key on the computer, waited for it to wake up. He sat down, looked at the screen. He found that it hurt to breathe. He took another breath. It still hurt. Felt as if he'd been swimming all day. Idly, he pulled open the single drawer in his desk, and then he saw it, the agent's card.

Well, he thought. *This is exactly what agents are for.* He dialed the number. A female voice answered. "This is the Wallace Stevens Literary Agency," she said. "Who would you like to speak with?"

"Wallace Stevens," he said.

"And who can I say is calling?"

"Stuart Cross."

"And what can I say this is in reference to?"

"He'll know," said Stuart. "Just tell him Stuart Cross is on the line."

"Okay," said the secretary, and he could tell by her tone that she didn't believe for a minute that this stranger would get through to the august Wallace Stevens, the delectable Wallace Stevens, the desirable and fabulously busy Wallace Stevens.

"Please hold," she said. So he held. And held. Then Wallace Stevens came on the line.

"Stuart Cross," he said, as if trying the name out for the first time. "To what do I owe the honor?"

"Well," said Stuart, "you said that if I ever needed an agent."

"I said it," said Stevens, "and I meant it. What have you got?"

"It's a novel," said Stuart.

"You've got some writer without an agent?" asked Stevens. "You want me to step in? Give him a deal, but not too good a deal? And which publishing house do you think would be a match? Let's run through the alphabet, starting, of course, with the letter 'a.' Acropolis. Do you suppose Acropolis would make an offer?"

"Very funny," said Stuart, "but you've misunderstood. I'm the writer. It's my novel."

"Oh," said Stevens. "And you don't want to publish it at your own house . . ." he began.

"No," said Stuart, cutting him off. "It's the one I started at Yale. *The Last Red Indian.*"

"Um hum," said Wallace Stevens.

"You know the story," said Stuart.

Wallace Stevens said nothing.

"Only now it's going to be a novel."

"Um hum," said Wallace Stevens again.

"The story *was* just included in the *Best Best Stories of the Century*," said Stuart. "And they put it out in the window of every Barnes & Noble."

"Um hum," said Wallace Stevens. "That's an honor, all right."

"I thought so," said Stuart.

"Do you know how stories make it into the *Best Best Short Stories of the Century*?"

"No," said Stuart. "I assumed there was a board of judges."

"Well, there are judges," said Wallace Stevens. "And they make a list of books that might be included in such a collection. But then somebody else has to come forward and invest in the project. You don't just write a story that is admired and get right into the *Best Best Short Stories of the Century*. Somebody has to kick in a couple of thousand dollars."

"Who would do that?" asked Stuart.

"Sometimes it's a publisher," said Wallace Stevens. "Sometimes it's the writer himself. Or herself. In your case, I suppose it was the Glass family. Unless you ponied up."

"Of course not," said Stuart. "I despise that sort of self-promotion. The look-at-me-now school of prose."

"I thought you'd know about this," said Wallace Stevens.

"Nope," said Stuart. "It's all news to me."

"Most everything's for sale now," said Stevens. "The ads, of course. Which are more and more important. Big books are flogged on television. Then the placement of the books in the chain stores is at least partially determined by how much the publisher antes up. There's even a publication out there now that'll review your book for you, if you pay them two hundred fifty dollars."

"All right," said Stuart. "Enough. But I don't have money. I need money. I'm one of those people who is writing in order to make money."

"Oh no," said Stevens, sounding genuinely concerned.

"In any case," said Stuart, charging ahead. "It's a good piece of work, don't you think? The basis for a full-length treatment?"

"Let me see how well I remember it," said Wallace Stevens. "Don't you liken contemporary American society to the Sioux?

Don't you say that white Americans are all doomed? All dead? We smell of piss?"

"Like that," said Stuart.

"Doesn't seem like *such* a commercial idea to me," said Stevens. "Contemporary readers like to be encouraged. It's Morning in America, you know?"

"Oh," said Stuart. "I hadn't noticed."

"Look," said Wallace Stevens. "If you've already got it written, I'd love to take a look at it. I walk right by your building every evening on my way to the train. Have your secretary run off a copy, leave the manuscript in the lobby, and I'll pick it up today."

"I'm not in the building," said Stuart.

"Tomorrow then," said Stevens.

"I won't be in tomorrow either," said Stuart.

"When will you be in?"

"Never."

"And why's that?"

"I quit."

"You quit?"

"I quit to write," said Stuart.

"You quit your job as Editor-in-Chief in order to write?"

"Yes," said Stuart.

Stevens didn't say anything.

Stuart plunged in to fill the silence. "People have been at me for years to do this. Andie's all for it."

"So you have a movie sale?" asked Stevens.

"No," said Stuart. "Or not yet."

"Wait a minute," said Stevens. "Let me get this absolutely straight. Last I heard you were in line to be the next Editorial Director."

"I quit instead to write," said Stuart. "Everybody I know has been telling me for years that I should quit my job to write."

"I know," said Wallace Stevens. "I've heard that. But then everybody tells me I'm not losing my hair."

"Not the same thing," said Stuart.

"I don't know," said Stevens. "Are you absolutely sure it's not the same thing?"

"Besides which," said Stuart, "it's done. I don't know if your hair is going to grow back, but I'd guess that my job won't."

"All right, then," said Wallace Stevens. "Send me the manuscript. I'll take a look. This week is hellish. This weekend, we're going up to New Hampshire, see what the winter has done to our new roof. You know I worked briefly as a roofer during college?"

"No, I hadn't known," said Stuart, reaching deep within in an attempt to feign interest.

"Yup," said Stevens. "Looking at the bills they've sent me, I wonder if I shouldn't have kept at it. A house is murder on the budget. I'm used to being able to call the super. And this is a cabin. In New Hampshire. How do you keep up with that mansion of yours?"

Stuart didn't say anything.

"Probably middle of next week," said Stevens, "before I get a chance to look at the manuscript. Send it to me right now, though. I'll have somebody else here read it first."

"Can't do that," said Stuart.

"Why not?" said Stevens. "I've got an intern here from Sarah Lawrence. Just a kid, but she's got a good ear."

"I can't send it," said Stuart, "because I haven't written it."

"You haven't written it?" echoed Wallace Stevens.

"That's right."

"Well then, how much do you have?"

"I don't have anything yet," said Stuart. "Except for the original *Best Best Short Story of the Century*."

"Listen old buddy," said Stevens. "Then what, exactly, would you have me do for you?"

"That's easy," said Stuart. "I want you to do what you said Saturday that you wanted to do. I want you to represent me, sell my book."

"Which book?" asked Wallace Stevens.

"The one I'm going to write."

"*The Last Red Indian?*" asked Wallace Stevens.

"You just got through telling me that that wasn't a good idea."

"Nor an outstanding idea," said Stevens.

"I'll write something else," said Stuart. "What do you suggest? What's the market yearning for?"

"Well," said Wallace Stevens. "I suppose if you actually polled the market, the yearning you'd discover would be for fewer books, not more. But in the meantime, I wonder if you've ever thought of a murder mystery? Did you ever work with the police?"

"No," said Stuart. "I never have worked with the police."

"How about the Civil War then?" asked Stevens. "I know Martin Brookstone seems to have that genre cornered, but there's always room in this business for a look-alike. Of course he's put his heroine, Ashley, in the first ranks of Pickett's Charge, so you're going to have to leave Gettysburg alone. She's been to Chancellorsville in the little group of men who fired into the dusk and gave Stonewall Jackson his mortal wound. I think he's working on Antietam now. How about Shiloh? You know anything about Shiloh?"

"No," said Stuart. "Nor would I be comfortable starting right out in my first novel in a woman's voice."

"Umm," said Wallace Stevens. "I hadn't thought of that. Would you consider nonfiction? Nonfiction is easier to sell. Especially in the case of a first book."

"Sure," said Stuart. "I'd consider anything. I'm out of work."

"All right," said Wallace Stevens. "I'll cast about for you. In the meantime, you drub the brainpan yourself. See if there's something you want to look into. You're a literate man. You must have interests."

"Books," said Stuart. "I've always been interested in books. I'm a generalist."

"Yeah," said Wallace Stevens. "I know that. Let's both think, though. See what we can come up with. What about your personal story? Were you molested?"

"No," said Stuart.

"Other personal tragedies?"

"Andie's sister drowned when she was three and Andie was six. Andie's never gotten over it."

"Yeah," said Wallace Stevens, "but that's Andie's story. If Andie wanted to write a book, that would be easy to market."

"I thought you'd come up with an idea for me," said Stuart.

"Oh, I'll work on it," said Stevens. "I'll be thinking. I have to run now," he said. "Toodle-oo," and then he hung up.

Stuart hung up, looked at the computer screen. He could hear the voices of his children coming up the stairs. He could hear his own tortured breathing. He was afraid they'd see how he'd been unmanned. He stood, walked down the hall to the master-bedroom-to-die-for, went to Andie's desk, pulled out its little antique chair, and sat down. He requisitioned a yellow legal pad and a ballpoint pen. Thus equipped, he walked purposefully back to his own desk. At the top of the pad he wrote:

"To every reproach I know but one answer, namely go again to my work. 'But you neglect your relations.' Too true, then I will work harder. 'But you have no genius.' Yes, then I will work harder. 'But you have detached yourself from people. You must regain some positive relation.' Yes, I will work the harder.—Emerson."

Below that he wrote: "A man sits as many risks as he runs.—Henry David Thoreau."

He went back downstairs and got his T.S. Eliot. Turned to the dog-eared page and copied:

"Trying to learn to use words, and every attempt
Is a wholly new start, and a different kind of failure."

This wasn't working. He sat back in the chair. Breathed deeply. Then he heard the sound of tires in the drive. He sprang to his feet. For a moment he thought it must be Andie, coming back to try and cheer him up. Peering out the window, though, he could see that this was a van. A red Ford Econoline with an aluminum ladder strapped to the roof. "Superior House Painters: God Is in the Details" was stenciled on its flank in white Gothic letters.

CHAPTER 24

"Makes the children her own."

Stuart galloped down the stairs. Both girls were in the kitchen. Louise was outside, speaking intently with a small, wiry black man in white painter's pants and an ink-black T-shirt with a package of cigarettes rolled up in the left sleeve.

"Mr. Cross," said Louise, meeting his eye. "There's somebody I want you to meet: Toussaint Louverture," she said. And then turning to her guest, "And T, say hello to Stuart Cross. He's my boss and new best friend."

The stranger thrust out his hand, and Stuart clasped it, noticing that the muscled right forearm had a tattoo of a clock without hands.

The black man was short, five six, almost on Louise's scale. He had blue, blue eyes and an easy smile which he flashed now, revealing small white teeth. "Most people call me T," he said. "My parents named me after somebody out of history."

"I know about Louverture," said Stuart "Didn't he lead a movement on Haiti? They murdered all the white people."

T chuckled pleasantly. "Something like that," he said. "In any case, the name's a mouthful. Which is why people call me T. Easy to spell."

"Glad to meet you, T," said Stuart and he meant it. At this point in his career as a novelist, he would have been delighted by a visit from Charles Manson.

"I'm here with the paintings," T said. "Sugar doesn't like to be one place and have her paintings in another. Where are they supposed to go?"

"Let's look at the attic first," said Stuart. "The basement's dry, but we haven't been here long. Let's see if there's room in the attic."

"If water's a problem, I have a wooden pallet," said T. "We can stack them on the pallet."

"So far," said Stuart, "the basement is dry as a bone. But let's look at the attic first."

So they walked upstairs and through the bedroom-suite-to-die-for, and through Andie's walk-in closet. The back wall of this closet had the door to the attic. "I haven't even looked in here since the inspection," Stuart said. "Supposed to be finished."

The attic wasn't finished, though. No flooring, and the foreground was occupied by a large heating and air-conditioning unit.

"I don't see how this is going to work," said Stuart.

T shook his head mutely in agreement.

"Let's look at the basement," said Stuart, and T followed him out of the closet and into the bedroom. T paused as they crossed this space, and tapped Andie's desk with his index finger. "You know I've seen one of these before," he said. "Beautifully made. And clever."

"Clever?" asked Stuart.

"See this," said T, and he pulled at one of the miniature pillars used to separate the back cubbies. "Secret drawers," he said. "There are four of them in all. Your wife tell you that?"

"Of course," said Stuart. "Of course she did," he lied, and then led T out into the hall and down the stairs into the basement. Stuart sensed that something was wrong even before he took the last step and his boat shoe hit the water. He turned on the light.

It took T a minute to discover that a pipe leading to one of the outdoor faucets had burst. It took him five more minutes to locate the turnoff for that particular faucet.

"The water will go down now," he explained, and together they found a high point on the floor where, with the help of the wooden pallets, the paintings would be dry. When the men went outside, and Stuart saw the van again, he remembered the "red van sought in murder."

"You've got a famous truck," he said.

"Yes," said T, and smiled, but did not elaborate. Nor did Stuart follow up.

Fifteen minutes later, the eight large canvases were out of the van, high and dry and leaning against the wall.

Each painting was wrapped in a sheet, so Stuart didn't see the pictures until they were all in place, at which point he stopped to lift the covering from one of the larger pieces.

It was an oil. He was nauseated. It was a simple idea. The idea was so simple that it was almost a joke. He couldn't be sure if the painter's intention was humorous or serious. The execution was serious and precise. Stuart tasted vomit on the back of his tongue. He was certain. It was good. *Too bad the poor woman will never be recognized*, he thought.

He glanced over at T. The black man was standing beside him, also looking at the painting.

"What do you think?" asked Stuart.

"The Hessians should have seen him coming," said T. "I

218

don't care if it was Christmas Eve, they should have seen him coming."

"There's that," Stuart. "I was talking about the painting, though. What do you think of the painting?"

"Yes," said T. "I think yes." He pulled the sheet back over the picture, and together the two men climbed the stairs to the kitchen. They both kicked off their wet shoes—T had brown loafers, paint speckled. Louise put the shoes near the entrance to the kitchen door.

The girls were at the table, each with a glass of milk. Both men sat down with them.

"You've been peeking," Louise said, and gave her boss a smile.

"Saw a black George Washington Crossing the Deleware," said Stuart "Do you ever sell any of those?"

"Tricky question," said Louise.

"Answer the man," said T.

"I haven't sold many."

"How many?" asked Stuart.

"Two," said Louise.

"And what did they go for?" asked Stuart.

"The first one went for five hundred dollars," said Louise. "The gallery took half of that. Once I was done deducting for materials, and calculated out the hours, I came in well below minimum wage."

"But you should be so flattered," said Stuart. "That's a lot for a painting by an unknown."

"Tell him about the second one," said T.

"And the second painting?" asked Stuart.

Louise moved around the kitchen, tidying up as she served each man a cup of coffee. "The second painting sold for thirty-five. I haven't gotten the money yet."

"Thirty-five hundred dollars? That's a huge amount for an amateur," said Stuart, recalling the twenty-five-dollar check and three contributors' copies of the magazine, since defunct, that he'd gotten for "The Last Red Indian."

"No," said Louise, "thirty-five thousand. The gallery still takes half. So it's really under eighteen."

"Tell her about the museum, Sugar," said T.

"The Museum of Modern Art wants one," said Louise, setting out milk and sugar from which T helped himself.

Stuart took a great gulp of coffee. The liquid was unexpectedly hot and burned his tongue. The room began to swim.

T picked up his mug and got to his feet. "You're all going to have to excuse me now," he said. "That's a borrowed truck. I've got to get a move on. If nobody minds, I'd like to take my coffee outside and have a cigarette with it."

"Do what you have to do, T," said Louise.

"Don't I always?" said T.

"Always," said Louise.

"Look," said Stuart, regaining some composure, "if you don't mind, I'll join you. I mean if you have another cigarette."

"Please don't smoke a cigarette, Daddy," said Ginny.

"Just one," said Stuart, standing and following the other man outside. They both stopped at the door, put on their shoes, and then walked over to a wooden bench, which had been set between two dwarfish pines.

"This will look grand," Stuart explained. "In a decade."

T shook two cigarettes out of his pack, lit Stuart's, and then his own. "Can I look around?" he asked.

"Sure," said Stuart. "I'll give you a guided tour of the stunted plantings."

"They're not stunted," said T. "These plants are just new. They're babies. Give them time."

"Yeah," said Stuart. "I suppose you're right."

At this point, T paused at the shrouded form of his host's motorcycle. He blew smoke out of his nose.

"Can I see it?" he asked.

"Sure," said Stuart, and folded back the tarpaulin.

T whistled. "Nice bike," he said. "I've had bikes, but never one that fine."

Stuart nodded.

"Where do you ride it?"

"Oh, just around. I take a backpack and do errands."

"You do errands," said T and flashed the smile again on his host. "You do errands on a Harley-Davidson Sportster. You *are* a wild man."

Stuart blushed.

"Sorry," said T, and reached out and touched the other man on the shoulder. "I can't ever keep my mouth shut. It gets me in trouble. You'd be astonished how much trouble it gets me into. It's a badass bike."

"Thanks," said Stuart.

"I got some great polish for this bike," T said. "Acme polish. You ever tried it? You put it on wet, just let it be. Dries, but still looks wet."

Stuart hadn't tried Acme polish.

"Next time I'm in the neighborhood, I'll drop it by."

"That's all right," said Stuart.

"No," insisted the other man. "I don't have a bike anymore. What do I need with the polish?"

T turned now and faced the Cross residence. "You've got two

fine little girls," he said. "You thank the Lord for them every single day?"

"I do," lied Stuart. "I thank the Lord."

T nodded. "Sugar says you're a writing man."

Stuart shrugged.

"I write some," said T.

"Oh," said Stuart. "And what do you write?

"Whatever comes along," said T.

"Oh, really," said Stuart, trying with some difficulty to conceal his feelings of superiority. His natural tendency for envy had been inflamed by the conversation with Louise. "Anything I might have seen?"

"Yeah," said T. "As a matter of fact, you *have* seen some of my writing."

"Really," said Stuart. "And what have I seen?"

"I wrote Sugar's résumé," said T, and then he looked away.

"Nice work," said Stuart, and he meant it.

"So you sit here in this great big house and write," said T.

"Yeah," said Stuart.

T nodded. "Sounds like the good life to me," he said. T smiled faintly. "Sugar's happy here," he said, pulling the package of Camels out of his sleeve and lighting a second cigarette for Stuart, before he lit one for himself.

"And we're happy to have her," said Stuart.

T nodded. "Everybody always is," he said. "At first."

"What do you mean by that?" asked Stuart.

T shrugged. "Nothing. I suppose it depends on how you feel about your children. It depends on how important it is to you to be a parent."

"Of course it's terribly important," said Stuart.

"Of course," said T, but he looked away, as if what Stuart had just said were somehow embarrassing.

"Is there anybody who doesn't care about his own children?" Stuart asked.

"No," said T, "everybody cares about children."

Stuart sighed. "As long as we're clear on that," he said.

"Clear as a bell," said T.

"So what were you getting at?" asked Stuart.

"Well," said T. "Louise does have a tendency to take over. Some parents have felt that she makes the children her own."

CHAPTER 25

"That's why they call it work"

Still dizzy from his cigarettes, Stuart returned to his office, switched the laptop back on, opened a second file. This time he left the title blank and wrote only his name and address on the first page. Then he scrolled down to the second page, located the cursor. He could hear the machine humming. Then he remembered that he hadn't had anything for lunch. The cigarettes had given him an upset stomach. It was almost two o'clock.

He went down the stairs and into the kitchen. Janey was on the floor with a jigsaw puzzle. Ginny was seated stock-still at the table, her face frozen, as if in fear. Startled at first, Stuart then noticed Louise behind the island, looking down at her sketch pad, then up at Ginny, then back to the pad.

Stuart came and looked over the nanny's shoulder. He saw a likeness in charcoal, and not unflattering, of his elder daughter.

"Could you do that in oil?"

"I suppose."

"You know Andie has talked about portraits of the girls."

Miss Washington looked pleased. "Very kind of you, Mr. Cross. But I think not."

"Why not?" asked Stuart. "We'll pay you. Not thirty-five thousand dollars, but we'll pay you. And we'll already be paying you, so we'll pay you twice. Why not do it?"

"'Cause you don't really see your children, you know," said Louise. "You can't. You love the girls too much."

"And you don't love them?"

Miss Washington beamed up at him. "I adore your girls. They're not my daughters, though. So I can see them as they are," she said.

Stuart looked again at the drawing. Off Ginny's shoulder, he saw the kitchen window, and through the kitchen window his magisterial lawn. And on the lawn, he saw a stake in the ground with a piece of orange plastic tape nailed into the top. This he hadn't remembered. He walked to the window and looked out. Sure enough, there it was. And a man with some sort of surveying equipment on a wooden tripod was standing near the stake. All of this on Stuart's own private lawn.

He put on his wet boat shoes again and went outside. Walked up behind the man without being seen. "Excuse me," said Stuart. "What are you doing here?"

The man was large, Stuart noticed now, and dressed in khakis and an orange don't-run-me-over vest. He had the face of a bulldog. Not an angry bulldog, but a bulldog nevertheless.

"Laying out a lot," the man said.

"On my property?" said Stuart.

"On your property?" asked the man. "In that case, I apologize. I think I've got this right."

"No," said Stuart. "You haven't got it right. That's my house," he said, pointing up at Tara. "This is my lawn."

The man reached into the back pocket of his khakis and pulled out an envelope, opened it, and withdrew a letter. This he unfolded and read, then he looked back at Stuart.

"Are you Mr. Cross?" he asked.

Stuart nodded.

"Well, then, you know that this isn't your land. Your land stops there," he said, and pointed up to an invisible line halfway between where they stood and the house.

"But this is unbuildable," said Stuart. "That's what I was told."

The man shook his head wonderingly. "I don't know, champ, but I cost money. I don't think they'd pay money to have me out here mapping out an unbuildable lot."

Stuart turned, strode back to the house, and called Joy Gainsborough-Orsini. "Joy's not here now," he was told. "Would you like her voice mail?"

"Sure," said Stuart.

"Joy," he said, when he'd heard the greeting, "it's Stuart. Stuart Cross. They seem to be getting ready to build a house in my yard. Call me. Soon. Now." He hung up. Wagged his head. "Some day," he said aloud. "Some week."

He glanced up and saw that Louise was looking at him. "You're hungry," she said. "Let me make you something to eat."

"Well," said Stuart. "Actually I *am* hungry."

So Louise agreed to make Stuart a tuna-salad sandwich. "With onions?" she asked.

"With onions," said Stuart.

"All right, then," said Louise. "But you go on upstairs now. I'll have Ginny deliver the food."

So Stuart climbed the stairs again. And found, sorrow of sorrows, that it was still not yet three o'clock in the afternoon.

He sat. He breathed in. He breathed out. What was missing?

What was it Cynthia Ozick had said? Stuart went downstairs and pulled *The Courage to Write* by Ralph Keyes out of its spot on the shelf, flipped to the first page.

" 'If we had to say what writing is, we would have to define it essentially as an act of courage.'—Cynthia Ozick."

So what was he afraid of? He ran his tongue around the inside of his mouth.

What had Saul Bellow said about emulation? Something about writing beginning as emulation. Stuart walked along the bookshelves in the great room, picked up *Herzog*. Opened the novel, looked at the first page. Read the first page, then carried the book back upstairs to his office.

Ginny delivered the sandwich. This Stuart ate with elaborate care. He took the plate back to the kitchen. Then he returned to his office. *I'll work until six-thirty P.M.*, he thought. And he worked. And worked. When he gave up at six twenty-four, he had several pages, each with an island of print.

The first page read:

"But for as far back as I can remember, long before we moved to California in search of a different life and our slice of the American pie, I wanted to be a writer. I wanted to write, and I wanted to write anything . . ."

Then there was a line break—and he'd typed "Raymond Carver."

The next page began:

"Was anyone hurt?"

"No one, I'm thankful to say," said Mrs. Beaver, "except two housemaids who lost their heads and jumped through a glass roof into the paved court."

Then a lot of white space. Then—"Evelyn Waugh."
The following page began:

"It is a truth universally acknowledged, that a single man in possession of a good fortune, must be in want of a wife."

At the bottom of this page, he tried out the words "Jane" and "Austen." They had a ring of authenticity.
The following page began:

"I confess that when I first made acquaintance with Charles Strickland I never for a moment discerned that there was in him anything out of the ordinary. Yet now few will be found to deny his greatness."

He ended this page with one letter and two words— "W. Somerset Maugham."
The final page had just two lines of text.

"This is the saddest story I have ever heard."

An acre of white space and then—"Ford Madox Ford."

Stuart felt dreadful. Was the tuna bad? he wondered. Clearly this wasn't working. Although there was that moment between typing out the prose and typing the author's name. It was a little like flying. Flying a very short distance. *More like hopping*, Stuart thought.

At six thirty the phone rang. Stuart stood, darted into the bedroom, and had the phone before it rang again.

"Hi. It's Joy. Joy Gainsborough-Orsini."

"Hi," said Stuart. "And thanks for calling back."

"Did I see you at the appliance store?" she asked. "In the girls' room?"

"Just coming out of the girls' room," Stuart said.

"Oh," said Joy, and paused to see if he was going to explain. Stuart said nothing.

"What's up?" the realtor asked.

"They're building a house in my front yard," said Stuart. "Or at least they're mapping the lot lines."

"In your front yard?" asked Joy.

"That's right," said Stuart.

"Well, that's against the law," said Joy.

Stuart sighed. "You sure?" he asked.

"I'm sure," said Joy.

"Great," said Stuart. "Thanks, then."

"But wait," said Joy. "What do you mean by your front yard?"

"I mean," said Stuart, "the yard that runs down from my house to Route 9. My yard."

"But that isn't all your yard," said Joy. "Half of that belongs to the builder."

"I know, I know," said Stuart impatiently. "But it's not buildable."

"Oh no," said Joy, "it *is* buildable. Who told you it wasn't buildable?"

229

"Nobody told me," said Stuart. "I just assumed."

"Oh, I'm sorry," said the realtor. "Yes, they had trouble getting the variance, but they got permission. This office has the listing."

Stuart didn't say anything.

"They plan to ask a million two," she said. "This will increase the value of your home."

"Yeah," said Stuart, "and cut my lawn in half."

"I'm sorry," said the realtor. "It wasn't your lawn."

Stuart didn't speak.

"I know there will be some disruptions, noise during the construction, but ultimately this is good news. The Manderley is going to be magnificent. It'll add at least one hundred thousand dollars to the value of your property."

Stuart didn't respond to this. He hung up. He went downstairs and made himself a drink. This he took back to his office. He sat in his chair. He couldn't remember ever being this acutely unhappy. Was it the writing that was hurting, or everything else? If the writing was making him miserable, maybe that was a good sign. Thomas Mann had once written: "A writer is someone for whom writing is more difficult than it is for other people."

Maybe I'm a humorist, Stuart thought. *What had Twain said?* "The secret source of humor itself is not joy, but sorrow." But then he didn't feel funny. Absurd, but not funny.

He'd been collecting passages by writers on writing since he grew old enough to read, and many of them, he had to admit now, were gloomy in the extreme. What if these references to melancholy weren't made for dramatic purposes? What if all writers were unhappy? Did he need to get unhappy first? Or at least drunk? Now there was an idea.

So he finished his drink and went back downstairs. Louise was in the kitchen, cleaning up the children's dinner dishes. "You're going to wear out the carpet," she said, "with all that coming down and going up."

Stuart smiled wanly, went by her and into the wet bar, put ice in a glass and poured Wild Turkey over the ice. *As long as you bothered with the ice, you weren't an alcoholic,* he thought.

Back at his post, he sat and looked at his screen, sipped his drink. When he cast his mind back over the lives of writers, the profession—if it was a profession—seemed a truly dreadful prospect. Thomas Cranmer produced *The Book of Common Prayer,* a work so holy that it is rarely used in church anymore. For this, grateful readers burned him at the stake.

Defoe and Dumas both ended their lives in debt. Hart Crane jumped to his death, as did Primo Levi. Virginia Woolf put stones in her pockets and walked into the river. Ernest Hemingway blew his head off with a shotgun. Poe died in agony and madness. John Berryman and Anne Sexton both took their own lives. Nor was despair a long time coming. Sylvia Plath was thirty-one when she gassed herself. Thomas Chatterton was eighteen, when he tore up his work and drank arsenic. Stuart had only been a writer for one afternoon, but he was beginning to understand.

He selected his first two paragraphs and enlarged the font, from fourteen to sixteen. That was better. He tried boldface. That was excessive. Back to sixteen point.

This is foolishness, he told himself. *Writing is a business. Professional writers are encouraged. They are paid. That's what the word professional means.* He needed to differentiate himself from the also-rans—housewives and spirit-broken men—who when they learned that he was an editor had approached him at cocktail parties, on trains, and in airplanes. These people were wild for the affirmation of self:

they were dying, literally dying for the praise they would never hear.

The phone rang. It was Andie. She still hadn't left the city. "Fowler wants to take me out for a drink. Talk about how we're going to reposition our film coverage. Better eat dinner without me."

"Okay," said Stuart, and he tried not to put a lot of venom into it. Andie hung up.

He went downstairs, nodded at Louise and the girls, fixed himself another bourbon on the rocks. Went back to his desk, opened the drawer, and saw again the card Wallace Stevens had put there. He turned it over, saw the home number handwritten with the message "Call me. Please!"

A child answered the phone. "Is your daddy home?" Stuart asked.

"No," said the little girl. "My daddy lives in California. My mommy's home."

"Oh," said Stuart. "Is Wallace Stevens home? Can I speak with Wallace Stevens?"

"Of course you *can* speak with Wallace Stevens," piped the little girl. "The question here is '*May* you speak with Wallace Stevens?'"

Stuart cleared his throat. "*May* I speak with Wallace Stevens?" he said.

The child said nothing, but he could hear the receiver being put down. Three minutes later the agent came on the phone.

"Hi," said Stuart, "It's Stuart Cross."

"Yeah," said Stevens.

"Stuart Cross, remember?"

"Who gave you this number?" asked Stevens.

"You gave it to me," said Stuart. "You wrote it on the back of your card and put your card in the desk in my office. That was Saturday. A week hasn't gone by yet."

"Oh," said Wallace Stevens, "now I remember. But look, don't ever call me at home again. I was just sitting down to dinner."

"Listen," said Stuart. "I have to write a book to keep this family in the black, and I can't write a book without a contract. That's a sucker's game. You gotta help me here."

Wallace Stevens didn't say anything.

"Look," said Stuart. "I think I could write a memoir. About myself. About my love of literature."

"Pardon me while I yawn," said Wallace Stevens.

"Harold Bloom does it."

"But you don't happen to be Harold Bloom."

"I could write about my life in publishing. How to get to the top in publishing," said Stuart.

"Afraid that door's been closed," said Stevens. "But if you want to put together a proposal about being a househusband for a more successful wife, I'll shop that around. We might be able to sell first serial to *Cosmo*, with a couple of your favorite recipes."

"You want a picture of me in an apron?" said Stuart, horrified.

"Might work," said Stevens.

"I can't believe this is happening to me," said Stuart.

"Believe it," said Wallace Stevens. There was a pause, and then the agent said, "You'll have to excuse me now. My pasta primavera is getting cold. My family is also getting cold. Next time you need to call me, please wait until office hours. Call me at work. That's where I work. That's why they call it work."

CHAPTER 26

"I'll Pick You."

By eight our hero was wondering why anyone would want to become a writer. The roller-coaster metaphor was sickeningly apt. Even if you had one success, your life could easily be ruined for you. Take John Knowles of *A Separate Peace*, Robert Persig of *Zen and the Art of Motorcycle Maintenance*, or Henry Roth of *Call It Sleep*. They all wrote one book and then spent most of the rest of their lives avoiding a rematch. Harper Lee wrote *To Kill a Mockingbird* and nothing else. Was she in an agony about that? Not clear. The others seem to have been. As was Ralph Ellison, who wrote *Invisible Man* and then spent his life in its shadow.

Even writers for whom public acclaim remained constant wound up in purgatory. Mario Puzo wrote *The Godfather*, and it was such a success that they kept on publishing him until he died. Until after he had died. *Fools Die* wasn't horrid, but the novels that followed were an embarrassment. For the man who wrote *The Godfather* to try again and come up with *The Last Don* must have been a torture. He'd married his nurse, and she used to let him suck on big cigars, but not light them.

John Gardner got fat and died in a motorcycle accident and then had somebody write a piece in memoriam in which he was described as having looked "like a pregnant man."

Fred Exley was everybody's friend. They all liked *A Fan's Notes.* The other works they weren't so sure about. But many people knew Fred, had a drink with him. When Fred died, there was a feeding frenzy. It seemed he'd never said a foolish thing, made a false move, that somebody wasn't taking notes.

All of this Stuart had known for years, but until this moment had somehow chosen not to acknowledge.

The process, of course, was what mattered. That's what he'd told himself. But the process itself seemed an agony.

The evidence had always been there. Stuart took down a book of quotes he kept. He opened it now: "I sit down religiously every morning," Joseph Conrad had written in a letter to Edward Garnett; "I sit down for eight hours every day—and the sitting down is all. In the course of that working day of 8 hours I write three sentences which I erase before leaving the table in despair . . . I assure you—speaking soberly and on my word of honor—that sometimes it takes all my resolution and power of self control to refrain from butting my head against the wall. I want to howl and foam at the mouth but I daren't do it for fear of waking that baby and alarming my wife."

His quotation book was a black plastic binder into which he'd inserted the pages of his quotation file. He flipped to a quote from H. L. Mencken: "Writing, they all say, is the most dreadful chore ever inflicted upon human beings. It is not only exhausting mentally; it is also extremely fatiguing physically. The writer leaves his desk, his day's work done, with his mind empty and the muscles of his back and neck full of a crippling stiffness. He has suffered horribly that the babies may be fed and beauty may not die."

He'd always felt Mencken meant to be funny. Now he wondered.

He reread the famous Flaubert quote: "Human speech is like a cracked kettle on which we tap crude rhythms for bears to dance to, while we long to make music that will melt the stars."

He'd considered this a grand hyperbole. Maybe it wasn't hyperbole at all. If so, why would you want to tap crude rhythms on a cracked kettle for bears to dance to when you could, well, you could just get a job?

The longing among the people he knew who wanted to be writers now seemed comical. It was as if all the beef cattle out in the west had yearned for a trip to the Chicago stockyards.

Stuart went back downstairs to the kitchen.

Louise and the girls were at the table. His daughters were reading; Louise was sketching.

Janey put down her book, picked up her pistol, and pointed it at her father. "Bang, bang," she said.

"You mustn't do that," said Stuart. "You shouldn't point a gun, any gun at somebody you don't intend to kill."

"Okay," said Janey, sullenly, and pointed the gun at her sister. "Bang, bang," she said.

"Keep that up," said Stuart, "and I'll take the pistol from you."

"Then I'll cry," said Janey. "And you'll give it back. See this," she said. "The orange comes off." She pulled the piece of orange plastic from the end of the toy. "Now it looks like a real gun."

"Yes," said Stuart. "It certainly does look like a real gun. All the more reason not to point. And put that piece back on."

"All right," said Janey sulkily. "But you're no fun, Daddy. Sugar is more fun than you are."

Stuart pulled out a chair and sat with his daughters at the kitchen table.

Louise came around behind him and put a hand on his shoulder. "Want some dinner, honey?"

"No thanks," said Stuart. "I drank my dinner."

"Doesn't look as if it's done you any good," said Louise.

"You don't have a cigarette?" asked Stuart. "I could really use a smoke."

"No," said Louise. "Nannies can't smoke. They'd never get work. I have a friend who was fired because the parents smelled cigarette smoke in her hair. She hadn't been smoking either. She'd ridden on a crowded bus."

"I figured you didn't smoke," said Stuart.

"I tell you what," said Louise. "I'll make you some scrambled eggs with cheddar cheese. And also some toast. While I'm cooking, you talk to me."

"Okay," said Stuart, and he folded his arms on the kitchen table, let his face fall into them.

"So what's the matter, honey?"

"When did you start calling me honey? Andie never calls me honey."

Louise shrugged. "I call everybody honey," she said. "Doesn't mean anything, honey. So what's the matter?"

"Well," said Stuart. "Everything's the matter. I'm out of work now. And so I'm supposed to write a book."

"Yes," said Louise. "I know that."

"I've been up there all day trying to get started."

"You haven't been up there all day," said Louise. "You helped

237

with my paintings. You've spent a lot of time climbing up and down stairs. You've been on the phone. You talked to the man in the yard. You've been drinking."

"Okay," said Stuart. "I haven't been up there all day. It just felt like all day. It felt like all year."

"I don't know about writing," said Louise, "but I know about painting. You have to go somewhere. You have to go somewhere else. Ten minutes there, and it seems like all year. It's not always pleasant."

Stuart nodded. "I think I went there," he said, "and brought nothing out. Except for the memory of having been someplace I'd rather never go to again. Dante without a notebook."

Louise smiled. "Sounds right," she said.

"I had thought I could sell the book first," said Stuart.

"I can see why you might think that," said Louise. "But is that really how it works? That's not how it works in painting."

"I don't know about painting," said Stuart. "But in writing that's exactly how it works. Hundreds of thousands of dollars are paid in advance for twenty-page proposals."

Louise nodded. "That must be why I'm always reading books that were written a hundred years ago," she said. "T is worse. If it's not hard science, he won't touch prose later than the 1890s."

"As fascinating as I find your reading habits," said Stuart, "they are not much of a consolation. I wanted to sell a book. So I called an agent. Wallace Stevens."

"Wallace Stevens?" asked Louise.

"Not that Wallace Stevens," said Stuart. "Did you meet him? He was at the party?"

"Does he spit?" asked Louise.

Stuart nodded. "He spits."

"I met him," said Louise, cracking eggs into a bowl. "He's bald. Fell asleep in the Jacuzzi?"

"That's our man," said Stuart.

Louise didn't say anything, busied herself whisking the eggs with a fork. "I didn't think you liked him," she said.

"He's an agent," said Stuart. "Anyway, I called him. I tried to sell him a novel. Not interested. So then I asked what he would like." Stuart sighed. "You sure you want to hear this?"

Louise nodded. She'd finished beating the eggs and turned now to the stove.

"He wanted to know if I'd been sexually molested as a child."

Louise had poured the eggs into a pan and was now stirring them. She buttered two pieces of bread and put these in the toaster oven.

Stuart was looking at his hands.

"I've known Wallace Stevens for years," he said. "I always thought he could help me out. He told me he could help me out." Stuart shook his head.

Louise took a plate down, filled it, came over from the island, and set the scrambled eggs and toast in front of her boss.

"Thank you," said Stuart. "Thanks a lot."

Louise nodded and then sat down at the table across from Stuart.

Stuart took a forkful of eggs, chewed, and swallowed. "I told him I'd write anything," he said. "Anything he could sell."

"But you didn't mean that," said Louise.

"Yeah," said Stuart, putting a second forkful of scrambled eggs into his mouth and nodding. "I did mean it. Do mean it."

"You must be asking for a lot of money," said the nanny.

"No," said Stuart, "I don't expect a lot of money. I just want a contract. Something to do while I try and put a new life in order. Something to write."

239

"Anything?" asked Louise.

"Anything I can sell," said Stuart.

"You want to write a novel, though," said Louise. "Make a new map of the world?"

"No," said Stuart. "I'd write anything."

Louise got up, poured herself a glass of water, poured another glass for her employer, and came back to the table. She took a sip from her glass and pushed the other one toward Stuart. "You'd better drink that up, honey. All this literary work has dehydrated you."

Stuart smiled wanly and drank off half of the water in the glass.

"Well," said Louise. "Some New York publisher is doing a series. Up Close and Personal with the Arts. Small books like those Penguin Lives biographies. Thirty thousand words. Thirty thousand dollars."

"Not a bad deal," said Stuart.

Louise was nodding quickly now. "They said they want to do one on me," she said. "They asked me if I had a writer I wanted to pick."

"Yeah?" said Stuart.

"Well," said Louise. "I don't know any writers. I told them I'd think about it. Now I've thought about it. I'll pick you."

CHAPTER 27

To Fuck a Novelist

It was after eleven when Andie came home, and Stuart was fast asleep. She undressed, got in bed, lay still for ten minutes, then turned on a light. Sitting up she began to flap noisily through a copy of *Entertainment Weekly*.

Stuart turned over and looked groggily up at his wife.

"Did you mean to wake me up?" he asked.

"Not really," said Andie. "But now that you're up, I'd like to talk. I'd like to know what went on here today."

"You want the bad news first," asked Stuart, "or the bad news?"

"Give me the bad news first," said Andie.

"They're going to build a house on our lawn," said Stuart. "The Manderley."

"I thought that lot was unbuildable," said Andie.

"So did I," said Stuart.

"And the bad news?" asked Andie.

Stuart sighed deeply. "I started my book," he said.

Andie nodded. "Did you at least phone Wallace Stevens?" she asked.

Stuart nodded. "Twice," he said.

"Is he going to handle you?" asked Andie.

"He already has handled me," said Stuart.

"What do you mean?"

"He told me to get lost."

"How can that be?"

Stuart sat up in bed. "How the fuck do I know?" he said. "But that's what Wallace Stevens did. He told me to get lost."

Andie nodded. "And what about the girls?" she said. "Any handsome men in their lives?"

"Actually," Stuart said, "T came over today. We put Louise's paintings in the basement."

"T came over?" asked Andie incredulously.

"Yeah," said Stuart, "seems a nice guy."

"The police phoned me at work today," said Andie.

"I didn't know that," said Stuart.

"Well, they did," said Andie. "They'd spoken with you, but not with me. They think this guy T is actually named Toussaint Louverture."

"That's right," said Stuart. "That's his name."

"Well, he's not going to Columbia," said Andie.

"Who said he was going to Columbia?" asked Stuart. "He seems to work as a housepainter."

Andie bobbed her head angrily. "Louise told me he goes to Columbia," she said. "And that he only came out to Westchester to visit the Rockefeller archives in Pocantico Hills?"

"I don't know," said Stuart. "Maybe he is at Columbia."

"Don't defend him," said Andie.

"I'm not defending him."

"And don't stick up for his doxy."

"His doxy? You mean Louise?"

"That's right. The girl with the .45 caliber pistol in her dresser drawer."

"You told me all about that. But it wasn't a gun, it was a cigarette lighter."

"That's right," said Andie. "She has an illegal switchblade and a cigarette lighter shaped like a gun."

"I don't know," said Stuart. "Maybe it was a gift. That particular lighter is a common item. They used to sell them around Times Square and in those gift shops on Fifth Avenue."

"It's a gun," said Andie. "Unlicensed."

"It's not a gun," said Stuart. "It's a cigarette lighter. A child could buy it. You don't need a license for a cigarette lighter."

"I bet her boyfriend has a real gun," said Andie.

"He's a sweet guy," said Stuart.

"He's a sweet guy who just a month ago got out of prison. Nor was it the first time he'd been in prison. And according to the policeman who called. What's his name?"

"Marks," said Stuart.

"According to Marks, this guy's notorious for violence."

"I like him," said Stuart.

"Marks says he's very bright," said Andie. "Which may be the only reason he hasn't yet been executed. When he was in reform school, they tested him, and his IQ was one hundred forty. So naturally, they gave him every break. So he's always getting out. And everything is fine until somebody insults him. Then he goes after the person who insults him. He's never killed anybody yet."

"That's a relief," said Stuart.

"Nobody that they know about," said Andie. "But they think he murdered the pediatrician."

"I don't believe that," said Stuart.

"Believe it," said Andie. "Apparently he didn't know this pediatrician at all. They had a fender bender, and then your friend Toussaint runs this guy down and shoots him with his own pistol. Because of a fender bender."

"That's speculation," said Stuart.

"Of course it's speculation, which doesn't mean it didn't happen."

"Doesn't sound likely to me," said Stuart.

"He's a killer," said Andie. "That's what Marks thinks."

"Boy, I wish I could have been a killer on Wednesday," said Stuart, "when I went back to the office and confronted that lying asshole Massberg."

"If you could have been him," said Andie, "you'd be in jail right now. Or running from the police."

"No," said Stuart. "I'd be out on bail. But that's another story. Of course you're right, though," he said. "The long-term results of beating Massberg would have been unfortunate," he said, "but it sure is fun to imagine." He was picturing himself upending Massberg's desk, hitting him over the head with the bust of Homer that Massberg was so proud of. He wondered idly what the bust was made of. Probably plaster of paris.

"In any case," said Andie, "You've let a convicted criminal into this house."

"Yeah, sure," said Stuart, "but the man I met was helpful and kind. And I liked him. He was manly in a way I'd forgotten all about. You know the basement had water in it. He figured out how to turn off the pipe that was leaking into the basement. Remind me to call the plumber."

"All right then," said Andie, "I'll remind you to call the plumber."

She turned off the light and put her head on her husband's chest. "If you see him again, you call the police. Promise me that."

"Promise," said Stuart.

"Cross your heart," she said.

"I cross my heart," said Stuart.

"Okay," said Andie, "and there's one more thing you need to remember. I put out a copy of my guacamole recipe for Kika. She's coming by tomorrow to pick it up. You don't even have to be here. She has her own key."

"All right," said Stuart. "And if we are here, we'll be nice. I promise."

"Good boy," said Andie.

Then he could feel his wife's hand in his hair, and her body moving against his. "Let's do a manliness check on you," she said. "I've always wanted to fuck a novelist."

CHAPTER 28

"If Indian Point Blows"

Stuart had woken up at three A.M. and taken five milligrams of Valium. *The housewife's friend*, he thought bitterly, glimpsing his pinched and leathery face in the mirrors of the bathroom-to-die-for. He slept right through his wife's departure for work, and didn't arrive downstairs until it was almost ten A.M.

"I've just brewed fresh coffee," Louise said, "but we've got to get going, if we're going to make it to the museum and see anything before lunch. It's rainy, a perfect day for viewing masterpieces."

Louise was wearing the same blue dress she'd worn to church, and high-heeled sandals.

"Ugh!" said Ginny.

"And that," said Louise, "is the perfect first response. You'll see, baby," she said, patting the shoulder of her younger, but not significantly smaller charge.

"I'd forgotten all about the museum," said Stuart, halfway into an excuse before he remembered that if he didn't go to the Metropolitan, he would have to spend the day writing. "Be good for the girls," he said.

"And I'm so looking forward to it," said Louise, bringing her employer a mug of coffee.

"I've got to make one phone call," said Stuart, took the coffee and went up to the bedroom. He closed the door—didn't want the nanny listening in—and phoned Wallace Stevens.

"I told you I'd get back to you when I had time," said Stevens, when Stuart made it past a wary secretary. "Don't be a bore about this."

"Wait," said Stuart. "I have a book. Remember the nanny? Remember how I said she wanted to paint a picture that would hang in the Museum of Modern Art?"

"The new woman," said Stevens. "Hadn't she just started to work for you on Saturday?"

"Right," said Stuart. "That one."

"Wanted to be a painter," said Stevens.

"Right," said Stuart. "I told you that. Well, it turns out she's much more successful than I could have imagined. They *are* buying one of her pictures. The Museum of Modern Art *is* buying one of her pictures."

"Wait a minute," said Stevens. "Let me make sure I've got this straight. The Museum of Modern Art is buying one of your nanny's pictures? A picture that was painted by the woman who cares for your children?"

"That's right," said Stuart. "The Museum of Modern Art. The place on Fifty-third Street. Between Fifth and Sixth. They're buying one of our nanny's pictures."

"And she still works as a nanny?" asked Stevens.

"So far," said Stuart. "It may not last. She's only just started selling. But that's not the story."

"Sounds like a story to me," said Stevens.

"But here's the deal," said Stuart. "Octopus wants to feature her in an Up-Close-and-Personal-with-the-Arts book. They're putting them out in their prestige line. What's that imprint? Excelsior? They've already told her they want to do it. It's true she's really just starting out, but they wanted a black woman. And she'd said no. But now she's willing to say yes, as a favor to me. She says I can be the writer."

"Okay," said Wallace Stevens. "This does sound like a turnaround. Let me phone Excelsior. I'll call you right back."

Stuart hung up, went downstairs to the kitchen. Here Ginny treated him to a demonstration of her new CD player. He'd lent his daughter the Mozart horn concertos. Now she insisted he install the earphones, turn the volume up, and close his eyes. "Imagine that you're at Carnegie Hall," she said, before plugging the second earphone in. Stuart had his eyes closed and was rather enjoying himself, when he felt Louise's hand on his arm.

"Telephone," she said, when he'd popped out one of the earphones. "It's for you. Boy, those are some tiny headphones. If Ginny hadn't told me, I wouldn't have known that you were listening to music."

"I'll pick up in the bedroom," said Stuart, and ran up the stairs.

"All right," said Wallace Stevens. "I want you to catch the next train. We're meeting Hannibal Artless for lunch. Now let me make absolutely certain I've got this right. What's your nanny's name again?"

"Louise Washington," said Stuart.

"Okay," said Stevens. "Artless is very big at Excelsior. He said he'll close the deal today. You know, they'd already approached the nanny some weeks ago, and she expressed no interest."

"Yeah," said Stuart. "I told you that."

248

"Well, anyway, said Stevens. "This had them wild, since the word's come down from the top that there has to be more diversity in their catalog. But she told you she'd cooperate?"

"That's right," said Stuart. "She'll cooperate." *Or else I'll fire her ass*, he thought, but didn't say.

"You're certain of this?" said Wallace Stevens.

"Yes," said Stuart. "She brought it up."

"Good," said Stevens. "Meet you at the Century Club at noon. Let's get this done."

"What happened?" asked Louise, when Stuart reappeared, beaming.

"We're going to have to put that museum visit off until Monday," he said. "I've got some immediate business."

"The Metropolitan is closed on Monday," said Louise.

"All right, then," said Stewart. "We'll all go to town tomorrow. I promise. But for right now I've got to get dressed and to a train."

"Okay," said Louise, attempting with difficulty to disguise her disappointment. "I suppose we can wait. As long as you're really going someplace. It would break my heart to watch you spend another day marching up and down that grand staircase of yours."

"Break mine too," said Stuart and, fired by this recollection, he raced back up to the bathroom and turned on the shower.

When he came down twenty minutes later in a full suit, the girls and Miss Washington were at the table studying one of the large art books that T had brought when he moved the paintings.

"All right," said Stuart, kissing both daughters. "Be good for Nanny. I should be home by three thirty." Then he turned to Louise. "I'm driving the Volvo to the station," he said. "Ordinarily, I wouldn't leave you without a car, but this is important." He opened the drawer in the kitchen island, reached in, and pulled out a set of keys. "This is the Volvo's second set. If you need a car, go down to the station and get the Volvo. I'll park as prominently as I possibly can. The registration is in the glove compartment."

Louise nodded.

"But you really shouldn't leave the house at all. Just stay here. Unless there's an emergency. And if at any time, for any reason, you were to leave the house . . ."

"Leave a note," said Louise. "I know."

"But don't go out," said Stuart. "Not under any circumstances."

"Not under any circumstances?" asked Louise.

"All right," said Stuart. "If Indian Point blows, you can go out. But only if that happens," he said, and looked meaningfully at Louise.

"If that happens," said Louise, "I'll leave a note."

CHAPTER 29

A Recipe for Guacamole

The weather cleared, and by two, the girls were restless. "Can't we go some place?" Jane asked. "To the city, like Daddy does?"

Louise wagged her head. "Better not," she said. "What if your dad called, and nobody was here to pick up the phone?"

"I'm bored," said Ginny. "I thought we were going to go to the museum."

Louise smiled. "So did I," she said. "Tomorrow."

"I know what," said Ginny.

"What?" asked Louise.

"Let's take the bicycles out," she said. "For the first time this year."

So Louise and her charges hauled the bicycles out of the garage, pumped up the tires.

Janey wanted to ride with her pistol, "like a cowboy." So Louise went inside, fetched the toy pistol, taped it to the right handlebar of the younger girl's two-wheeler.

Then Ginny wanted her crocodile, Hamlet, to come out. "He's been locked indoors for months. He gets blue if he doesn't have enough natural sunlight. He loves to ride a bicycle," she told

Louise. So Louise went inside and fetched Hamlet. Ginny made him sit up in the front in the straw basket.

Janey insisted that she knew how to ride without help, but when she mounted the bicycle, she fell right over on the other side and crashed onto the asphalt, knocking the orange tip off her toy pistol, shattering it into a dozen tiny pieces. The gun was taped back onto the handlebar. Then Janey went all the way around the circular drive with Louise—barefoot, holding her up.

"Okay," said Louise. "You're doing wonderfully, but let's take a rest and watch your sister."

Encouraged by the attention, Ginny managed the entire circle twice. When Louise looked away for a second, Ginny called out: "Look at me, no hands." Wobbling, but keeping control, she managed the circle a third time.

Now Janey was perishing to do the same. Swelling with the magnanimity of accomplishment, Ginny suggested that Janey borrow Hamlet Crocodile.

"I couldn't have done it without him," she said. Starting a victory lap with her hands still off the bars, she took the crocodile by his snout and tried to pull him out of the bicycle's front basket. The animal's tail was trapped in the straw weave. When Ginny yanked at Hamlet a second time, she pulled him free, but found herself leaning precariously in toward the middle of the circular drive. She was, however, an experienced cyclist, and stayed upright—but she overbalanced, speeding off the asphalt, bumping along beside the house for several feet before the front wheel hit a stone. The bicycle veered into the exposed cement foundation. Louise heard the scraping of metal on cement, and then the dull thud of impact.

Ginny's fall might have seemed almost comic, if she hadn't let out a shriek that sounded more like something you'd expect from a wild beast than a child. Louise ran to her. The nanny couldn't determine how badly the girl was hurt and how much of it was surprise and embarrassment. When she tried to help Ginny to her feet, the grimace of pain this engendered was clearly genuine.

"Okay," Louise said, in a voice that sounded as if it wasn't okay at all. "Okay, okay, okay," she said again. "Now sit down, and be comfortable," she said, and lowered the big girl onto the ground. "Don't move. Lie perfectly still. Do you hear me?" she said, and now Ginny was really frightened. She nodded.

"Stay here," said Louise. "Stay still," she said. "Janey will keep you company." Then the nanny tore inside to phone the pediatrician, whose office was said to be just one mile north of the house on Route 9.

"Thank you for calling Washburn and Siller pediatrics," the recording said. "Dial one for insurance information. Dial two for directions and hours. Dial three to make an appointment."

Louise pressed three. "The offices of Washburn and Siller are closed on Friday from noon until one P.M.," she was told. "Leave a message and the date and time of your call."

Louise hung up and dialed 911. "Nine one one," she was told, "and what is the nature of your emergency?"

"I need to get through to the pediatrician," Louise said. "Washburn and Siller."

"Hold while I connect you," the voice said.

And then, miracle of miracles, she heard a deep, masculine voice. "Doctor Washburn here."

"Oh, thank God," said Louise. "Virginia Cross is one of your patients. I'm her new nanny. We had an accident. She fell off her bicycle. Can we come right in?"

"Certainly," said Washburn. "Do you need an ambulance?"

"You're just down the road, right?" said Louise. "We'll be right there." She hung up. Then she remembered that the car she was supposed to use was parked at the station. The station was a quarter of a mile away. She was about to dial 911 a second time, when she heard an engine; somebody was pulling into the drive. It was T in his van.

Louise ran out of the house, reaching the van before it had come to a full stop. "Ginny is hurt," she said. "I don't think it's serious, but I don't know for sure. Can you drive her to the doctor?"

"Sure, honey, of course," T said. "Let's just unload the back of my truck, and we can make her real comfortable. First let me take a look."

He went to Ginny, spoke with her, held her hand, took the girl's pulse. "You're going to be just fine," he said. "But we're going to take you to the doctor, just to make absolutely sure."

Then T and Louise worked furiously, unloading the back of the truck. One of the cans spilled, and black paint ran down the drive.

"Mr. Cross isn't going to like this," said T.

"Clean up what you can," said Louise. "I've got to leave a note."

Janey took the stuffed crocodile over to where Ginny lay on the ground, moaning, but when she handed Hamlet to her big sister, the injured girl tossed the toy away. "He hurt me," Ginny said. The stuffed crocodile caught in the branches of one of the rhododendron with which the builder had meant to disguise the foundation, and hung there upside down.

While T was still mopping up paint, Louise ran into the kitchen. There was a piece of paper beside the phone with something written on it. A Xerox of a recipe. She turned it over and wrote:

"Dear Mr. and Mrs. Cross. DON'T BE CONCERNED. Ginny seems to have sprained—or possibly broken—her ankle. I'm having a friend drive us to Dr. Washburn's office. That's what we're doing now. It's 1:45. We should be home within the hour. If you get here before we do, please phone the doctor's office. Please don't worry."

She signed the note with a flourish.

Then Louise put the piece of paper back where it had been, and put the pen on top of it.

T had seen his share of injuries. He thought Ginny was more frightened than hurt. He wheeled the bicycles into the garage and then got the bottle of "the wet look" motorcycle wax out of the van and went looking for something to leave a message for Stuart with. He found a note pad near the sink, tore off a blank sheet. There was a pen near the phone. When he picked the pen up, he knocked the piece of paper on which it had rested to the floor. T was a conscientious man, so he put the sheet of paper back where it had been, but with the recipe-side up. Then he went out into the garage, found Stuart's workbench and left the wax there with a note.

He and Louise loaded Ginny carefully into the back of the truck.

"Where are you taking me?" Ginny wanted to know.

"To Doctor Washburn," said Louise.

"I hate Doctor Washburn."

"Why's that?" asked Louise.

"He's nice as pie to my face," said Ginny. "But then he took Daddy aside and said I have the classic signs of pre-adolescent obesity. And Daddy was angry at me for a week afterward. And wouldn't buy me the Twix he'd promised."

"I'm sorry," said Louise. "You have to go there. I promise to stay with you the whole time."

"I won't go," said Ginny.

"Yes," said Louise, "you will go."

"Isn't his office right near the diner?" asked Ginny.

"I don't know," said Louise. "Is it?"

"It is," said Ginny. "If you take me to the diner and get me a black-and-white ice cream sundae, I'll go afterward to see Doctor Washburn."

"I'll tell you what," said Louise. "We'll take you to see Doctor Washburn. Then afterward, we can all stop at the diner, and you can have ice cream."

"All right," said Ginny, "but I need my disk player."

"Okay," said Louise.

"And I need my pistol," said Janey.

"Okay," said Louise.

The nanny went into the house, retrieved the disk player, went into the garage and untaped the toy gun from the handlebar of Jane's bicycle.

Janey climbed into the back with her sister. "Don't we need safety belts?" she asked.

"Safety belts would be nice," said Louise, sliding into the front seat, "but right now it's more important to get your sister to the doctor." T pulled out of the development.

Driving north on the old Albany Post Road, the van passed Kika Bourne driving south in her Subaru Outback. Kika pulled into the neighborhood. Leaving the engine running, she darted in through the front door, walked back to the kitchen, took the recipe for guacamole from the exact spot where Andie had said it would be, right by the phone.

CHAPTER 30

Armed and Dangerous

Doctor Washburn established that the ankle was not broken. He considered the sprain sufficiently severe to require an inflatable cast. This he installed, and gave Ginny a pair of wooden crutches. Then T and the nanny and both girls repaired to the diner for the promised treat. The trip from the parking lot to the dining room took so long and required that so much special attention be paid to Ginny that Janey asked Louise if she too couldn't have a pair of crutches.

"Let's wait until your sister has mastered them," said Louise. "Then—if you still want crutches—we can talk."

When the party had settled at a table, Louise borrowed a quarter from T, and went to the restaurant's entrance foyer to call the house. The pay phone had a piece of lined paper, torn from a notebook, which had been Scotch-taped to the coin box: Out of order. Louise stopped at the cash register to ask if she could use the restaurant's own phone for a local call, but the girl working behind the desk was new. "I couldn't give you permission without the manager's okay," she said. "He's out now."

So Louise returned to the dining hall discouraged, but not

overly alarmed. She had left a note. They'd be home within the hour.

In the meantime, Stuart had driven up from the station flushed with victory and two glasses of red wine. He pulled into the drive and was immediately thrown into a panic. There were gallon cans on the lawn, and rags and those sticks used to stir paint. One of the cans had spilled black onto the asphalt. When he had parked, and went to examine the mess, he found that his elder daughter's favorite stuffed animal was upside down in the branches of a rhododendron bush.

"Ginny!" he called. "Jane! Miss Washington!" No answer.

He unlocked the kitchen door, went right inside, and phoned Andie on her cell.

"This had better be good," she said. "I had to come out of a screening to answer the call. The publicist is watching my every move."

"The girls are gone," Stuart said.

"No note?" she asked.

"No note," he said. "Wait, I'll look. Didn't we agree that notes should be left by the phone? No note. And there's paint spread all over the drive. Hamlet the Crocodile has been thrown into the bushes. Ginny wouldn't do that. Hamlet's her favorite."

"Call the police," said Andie. "I'll order a car, and be there as fast as I can."

So Stuart phoned the police, asked for John Marks.

"This is Stuart Cross," he said

"Sure," said Marks. "I remember you."

"Remember Toussaint Louverture?"

"Yeah," said Marks.

"I think Louverture got my daughters," said Stuart. "There seems to have been a scuffle here, and they're all gone. The girls and the nanny."

"What makes you suspect Louverture?"

"I don't know who else it might be. He's her friend. He's a housepainter. There seems to have been some kind of scuffle, and paint's been spilled on my driveway."

"You absolutely positive they didn't go out to the grocery store," asked Marks, "or the zoo?"

"I'm absolutely positive," said Stuart. "When I went into Manhattan this morning, I told the nanny not to leave the house under any circumstances."

"You went to Manhattan today?" asked Marks. "Left that nanny alone with those children again?"

"I know," said Stuart. "It seemed all right at the time." He paused. Marks did not fill the silence.

"So I went," said Stuart. "Can we get past that?"

"Sure," said Marks.

"I left the kids with the nanny. She promised to stay home. She swore that if she did leave the house, she'd leave me a note. We went over this a dozen times."

"All right," said Marks. "I believe you."

"I just came home this instant," said Stuart. "No nanny. No kids here. No note either."

"Have they taken one of your cars?" asked Marks.

"No," said Stuart. "They must be in the van that Toussaint Louverture drives. It's red and has something about God painted on the side. I think it's a Ford."

"All right," said Marks, "we'll start looking. But one thing. Do you trust that nanny? Is she with you, or with him? If this is a kidnapping, do you have any reason to suspect her of being in on it?"

Stuart surprised himself with what he said next. "She's with him. Has been for a long time."

"He's dangerous," said Marks. "She isn't. Right? I mean she's the nanny. That's all she is?"

"Well, actually," said Stuart, "she's also a painter. An artist."

"And what does that have to do with anything?" asked Marks.

"Nothing," said Stuart. "I was just thinking out loud. But she *is* with him. I don't know how dangerous she is, but she definitely is with him. She was writing him love letters when he was in prison."

"Okay," said Marks, "but do you have any reason to suspect her of being dangerous to the children?"

"There's one thing," said Stuart, and he thought with a sudden nausea of Louise's paintings, of the easy unselfconsciousness with which she worked. He remembered her sketching and scrambling him eggs. He recalled the horror of his own attempts at creation.

"Yes," said Marks. "You were saying?

"She keeps a .45 in her dresser," said Stuart, and for the first time since he'd written "The Last Red Indian," the editor felt the thrill of bold, dramatic fiction.

"Why didn't you tell us this before?" asked Marks.

"I didn't know," said Stuart.

"Armed and dangerous," said Marks.

"Armed and dangerous," said Stuart.

CHAPTER 31

"Can't mollycoddle the dead."

When she returned from the failed attempt to make a phone call, Louise found Ginny had surrendered the crutches to her waitress, who had put them near the busing station. The girl herself had settled deeply into the banquette, which was at the back of the diner. Janey was in the seat beside her.

Ginny had put her napkin in her lap and her disk player out on the place mat, inserted the earphones, and turned on the music. Janey had her gun on the table.

"Sit beside me," said Ginny, squinching over and pushing her sister.

"No," said Janey. "Sit with me."

"Well, that's easy," said Louise. "If Janey gets up for a minute, I can sit between you."

This was done, and T took one of the chairs that faced the banquette. Janey picked up her gun and sighted on T.

"Nope," said Louise, taking the toy away, and pushing it out onto the table so that it was beyond the little girl's reach. "You can't play with a gun and eat," she said.

"That's not fair," said Jane. "Ginny has her CD player."

"All right," said Louise. "Ginny will turn off her CD player."

This was done.

The waiter appeared, a stern, pallid young man in black pants, a black vest and white shirt. He distributed menus, and asked, in halting English, if anybody wanted a beverage.

"We're in a bit of a hurry," said Louise. "Give us a second, and we can order everything. What's the soup of the day?"

"Split pea with ham," the waiter said.

"Soup for me, then," said Louise.

"And to drink?" asked the waiter.

"Tap water."

T clapped his menu shut. "Same for me," he said.

Ginny ordered pea soup with a Shirley Temple and then a vanilla sundae with chocolate sauce, whipped cream, nuts, and a cherry.

Janey clapped her menu closed. "Same for me," she said.

After the soup course had been eaten, T asked if he could go outside for a minute.

"To smoke?" asked Ginny.

"To smoke," said T. "I'm sorry," he said sadly. "It's a dirty habit. And don't you ever smoke a cigarette, young lady. You promise me?"

"I promise," said Ginny.

T rose and left the building.

Now the police had spotted the van in the diner's lot. Several squad cars had parked in the lot of the auto parts outlet next door, and three policemen set out to approach the restaurant from behind and on foot, while a fourth headed for the front door.

The group coming in from behind rounded the corner of the building at exactly the moment that T—eyes squinted almost shut— was standing with his back to them, trying to get a match going.

The officers fanned out, and were within yards of their quarry before the sounds of so many leather-soled shoes finally registered, and T looked up.

"Drop it," said the ranking officer. "Hands in the air."

T dropped his cigarettes and matches, wheeled and ran right into the arms of the patrolman who had come around the corner from the front of the building. T put up a terrific if silent fight and managed to blacken one man's eye before they cuffed him, walked him next door, and forced him into the back of a squad car.

One officer stayed with T, while the others, led by the man with the swollen eye, went into the diner.

Louise was sitting with her back to the wall of the restaurant's farthest room, with Ginny on her right and Janey on her left. From where they sat, they looked back into the main eating area. Ginny had convinced the nanny to try the CD player. "It's Mozart. Daddy says he's the best."

Jane objected, but Ginny maintained that a demonstration of the CD player wasn't the same as playing with it.

"That's not fair to me," said Janey. "And she got crutches too." While Louise was still considering how to rule on the pistol, her elder charge inserted the earphones. "It's invisible," Ginny explained. "If you put it under the table," and she did so, placing the unit in her lap, "you can't even see where the music is coming from."

"Now close your eyes," said Ginny and mimed this by blinking her own eyes violently.

So Louise had her eyes closed and her ears stopped, and the volume on the CD player was pushed way up, when the first of the policemen—the man with the blackened eye—came around the corner into the back of the diner. He saw the toy gun and pulled his real one.

"Hands above your head," he shouted.

Jane and Ginny both did as told.

"You too, young lady," he shouted, but Louise didn't hear him. Jane tapped the nanny on the shoulder. Louise looked into the face of her youngest charge, saw how upset Janey was. Unable to hear what was being said, she assumed the girl wanted her toy. Louise thought that under the circumstances this was only fair—and so reached for the gun.

As on Saint Patrick's Day, Stuart found himself peering out of the cathedral windows of his great room, watching the police cars go by. Then an ambulance.

He phoned Kika. Got voice mail. Phoned Andie again, but her cell was out of range. He phoned the police. They would tell him nothing.

He paced. Longed for a cigarette.

Finally, a patrol car pulled into the development and then up to the front door. Stuart rushed out. Both girls were in the back seat. Both crying.

He saw that Ginny had an inflatable cast on her ankle. Other than this injury, though, the girl seemed physically sound. Stuart helped his elder daughter out of the car, up the stairs, and into the house. Janey ran along beside them as they made their way. He set Ginny down on one of the sofas in the great room. He was surprised to discover that his own face was wet with tears.

Both girls were sobbing uncontrollably now.

"It's the shock," Marks explained. "Your daughters have seen more than any child should have to see."

"But they're all right?" asked Stuart.

"They're fine," said Marks. "Been checked over by a paramedic at the scene. If there had been any reason for concern, we would have taken them directly to the hospital."

"How was her leg hurt?" asked Stuart.

"I don't know," said Marks.

Stuart turned and took the police officer's hand in both of his own. "I can't possibly thank you enough," he said. "Both here. Both safe."

"You're very welcome," said Marks. "I'm glad it all came out so well."

"Bless you," said Stuart, going again from one girl to another, kissing them each. The children continued to weep.

A second patrol car appeared, and the man got out with a pair of crutches, which he handed to Stuart. "For your daughter," he said.

"Thank you," said Stuart. "You've all been just great."

"It was nothing," the man said, got back into his car and drove off. Marks lingered in the drive.

"So what happened?" asked Stuart.

"We got both of the kidnappers," said Marks. "And there won't be any mollycoddling done either."

"Good," said Stuart, although his interest was already waning.

"We got enough on Toussaint Nevermind to keep him locked up for life," said Marks. "Assuming the murder charge sticks. And it should stick."

"Yes," said Stuart absently nodding, leaning now on the crutches.

"And as for the other one, she's not going to be mollycoddled much either."

"And why's that?" asked Stuart, thinking of the nanny for the first time in an hour, and recalling the hot indignation he felt when he came home drunk and found the house empty and no note.

"Well," said Marks. "You can't mollycoddle the dead."

CHAPTER 32

"We need a nanny."

Andie arrived within the hour. Kika appeared as if by magic, and the two women decided together to call Doctor Washburn, who closed his office and came to the house. Unified by the crisis, Andie and Stuart worked as a team for the first time in years, but still they had a hellish job getting the girls to stop sobbing. Washburn finally gave each child a sleeping pill.

Going out into the garage to make certain the bicycles were all right—this was at Ginny's request—Stuart spotted a blue plastic bottle on his workbench. This proved to be of "wet look" motorcycle polish, and was holding down a piece of paper. This was a receipt from Bill's Harley-Davidson, of White Plains. A note had been written across the receipt: "Couldn't find the bottle I talked about, so I bought you a new one.

Enjoy!

T."

He and Andie both took pills to sleep that night. Kika stayed over, and took no pills. "In case the house bursts into flames," she said.

When Stuart stumbled out of bed Saturday morning, walked

through the great room, and looked out of the Gothic windows, there were two TV trucks on the lawn and an accompanying huddle of reporters and technicians. He lowered the shades, shuffled into the kitchen and made coffee. He'd finished his first cup, when both girls trooped into the kitchen.

"Hungry?" he asked.

Ginny nodded, so he prepared blueberry pancakes.

Each girl was given a plateful.

"Why do the blueberries always need to be squashed?" asked Ginny.

By the time Andie and Kika woke up, the girls were in the great room, watching cartoons. The adults all settled at the kitchen table, drinking coffee and talking in whispers, as if they might be overheard.

Kika went out into the drive at nine A.M. to fetch the *New York Times* in its sober blue plastic wrapper and the *Citizen Register*, which comes in yellow, and the *New York Post*, which wraps in blood red.

Several reporters called out to her, but she kept her head down and did not respond.

At nine twenty, a young woman led a TV crew up to the front door and rang the bell. Stuart peered out at her through the peephole, but said nothing, nor did he open up.

The phone range almost constantly. Stuart, Andie, and Kika took turns monitoring the answering machine, and taking only those calls they felt they must. Stuart kept expecting somebody to come forward about Louise. A cousin, an uncle. A child that she'd helped raise.

He had been so relieved at first that the girls were safe that it took him some time to even consider the nanny's fate. Death was difficult to understand in any circumstances. He had liked to joke that he still wasn't entirely convinced that his mother, dead these seven years, wasn't simply visiting friends in California. Maybe Louise was with her.

At noon, Kika went into the great room to serve the girls each a grilled cheese sandwich, squinted out through the blinds, and saw a photographer squinting in.

So the children were sent upstairs.

That day the story was on the front page of the *Citizen Register* and in the Metro section of the *New York Times*. The *New York Post* ran a front page editorial which, without actually changing the facts, made it seem as if Louise may have had a real gun.

Stuart and Andie got up at four A.M. Sunday, left their own cars in the drive, and bundled the sleeping children into the back of Kika's Subaru, which had been parked—permission cheerfully granted—in the Woodings' drive. They made it out of the development without being spotted and traveled to the Danbury, Connecticut, Hilton.

Kika remained at Tara, charged with saving whatever she could of the lawn, and making certain that no reporters—looking for keepsakes—broke in.

In Sunday's papers—read assiduously by the Cross family in the dining room of a Brookfield Dunkin' Donuts—the nanny shoot-out had migrated to the editorial pages. Was this one more case of police overreacting—as the *Times* suspected—or was it—as the *New York Post* assumed—justified self-defense with T and Louise presented as a Bonnie Parker and Clyde Barrow in a painter's van.

Early Sunday afternoon there was an apartment fire in Yonkers, which spread into an assisted-living hotel. With the press racing south, the Cross family felt comfortable returning to Scarborough early enough to enjoy a microwaved Lean Cuisine serving of penne pasta with tomato basil sauce while they watched the news for an hour without hearing themselves mentioned or catching a glimpse of their pillared home.

By Monday, Stuart's satisfaction about the safety of the children was giving way to remorse about the death of the nanny. Recollections of her kindness ambushed his thoughts. He replayed the circumstances of the shooting, but couldn't—for the life of him—see how he, Stuart Cross, was responsible.

He'd cooperated with the police. Who wouldn't have? He bought the CD player in order to please his daughter. This he regretted. And those earphones. He'd had a bad feeling about those earphones.

On the other hand, he had paid the woman generously, taken her into his home.

And yet he wished that there was something he could do. He toyed with the idea of hosting a memorial service for Louise himself, but he suspected it would become a political slugfest with the police on one side and activists Louise hadn't known and might not have liked on the other.

He and Andie were heartened and surprised by support from the neighborhood. Men and women they'd never met brought casseroles and pies. George Wooding came over from the Monticello with a tray of Alice's fudge.

"I know who's going to love this," Stuart said, but when he took Ginny a piece wrapped in a napkin, she told him, "No thank you." The girls had been set up again in front of the large-screen TV.

Andie had asked Stuart please to make certain that they watched

269

the Discovery Channel. "At least then they can learn something about animals," she said.

Stuart had switched stations, but when he checked again on the girls an hour later, they were back watching cartoons.

The phone kept ringing, but now many of those calling were not reporters, but people that Stuart or Andie wanted to speak with.

"I assumed that most of these friends were dead," Stuart remarked, after ending a half-hour conversation with the boy with whom he'd edited the *Clarion*, his high school newspaper in Morristown, New Jersey. "Amazing the way Americans pull together in a crisis," he said in the telephone interview he finally relented to that afternoon. This was with the local TV news station. "I've gotten interested in the local news," he explained when Andie asked why he'd turned down NBC for Channel 12. "They are more apt to get it right. I do want to make sure everybody knows that Louise was not armed."

Andie went to work Tuesday. Kika finally gave into the press of business and left Stuart with the girls. There had been a lot of excitement, but alone with his thoughts and the children, it dawned on the man of the house that he hadn't just lost a nanny, he'd also lost a book contract.

At ten A.M. the phone rang.

It was Officer Marks. "I just saw you on Channel 12," he said. "I thought you were happy with the way we'd handled the case?"

"I am," said Stuart.

"That's not what I'm hearing," said Marks.

"I don't know what you're talking about," said Stuart.

"You go on and on about what a great nanny she was," said Marks, "and that it was a plastic gun."

"But she was a great nanny," said Stuart. "And it was a plastic gun."

"All right," said Marks. "But you might want to mention how we saved the children."

"I will," said Stuart. "I'll call Channel 12 and say just that. You did save the children."

"All right then," said Marks. "I appreciate it. I also thought I should fill you in on the investigation," he said. "We've got Levetour on assaulting police officers and on violation of parole, but it looks as if he didn't kill the doctor."

"Who killed the doctor, then?" asked Stuart, alarmed.

"French was a problem," said Marks. "Allegedly, he was selling some of his drugs. The government was after him for that."

"The government didn't shoot him?" Stuart asked.

"No," said Marks. "Allegedly, he was killed by some of the people he was doing business with. He owed money and drugs to an operation that comes up out of the city. They killed him and made it look like a racial incident. I've already told you more than I should. They've got somebody who's turned state's evidence. I don't want you to feel badly about this," said Marks. "Her boyfriend was a criminal, an indigent housepainter. She kept a gun in your house."

"Right," said Stuart.

"You know we'll want to see that, if you don't mind," said Marks.

Stuart paused, felt a thrill of remorse "I looked," he told the policeman. "It's gone. They must have taken it the last time they went out."

Marks paused in his turn. "Figures," he said. "You'd be astonished how often weapons vanish in a case like this."

"I suppose," said Stuart.

"If we need you," Marks said, "you'll testify in court?"

"Of course," said Stuart. "I'm in your debt."

He hung up the phone and sat down at the kitchen table, literally dizzy with the force of the new information. "I always thought T was a nice guy," he said out loud to himself.

Stuart and Andie had both been portrayed favorably in all the press coverage. He'd never had so much and such positive exposure. Nor had he ever felt so entirely undeserving.

He kept replaying the circumstances, like a man probing a loose and painful tooth with his tongue. First, there was no way that he, Stuart, could have known she'd be killed. How often are nannies shot in the line of duty? All he had really wanted to do was make sure that the police rescued his children.

He remembered how forgiving Louise herself had been. What was it she had told him? "No use crying over spilled milk."

Wallace Stevens phoned late that morning.

"Boy have you been in the public eye," he said.

"Yeah," said Stuart.

"I can see you lost your nanny."

"Yeah," said Stuart. "And the subject of my book."

"Whoooooooa!" said Stevens. "Not so fast, amigo. Arguably one of the most prominent up-and-coming black painters in the country. Killed in a shoot-out with police."

"It wasn't a shoot-out," said Stuart. "She was unarmed."

"Are you sure?" asked Stevens.

"I'm sure," said Stuart. "It was a toy gun."

"You wouldn't know that from the TV news," said Wallace Stevens.

"But I know it," said Stuart. "I bought that gun."

"Better still," said Stevens. "She's a martyr."

"Yeah," said Stuart. "I guess that actually she *is* a martyr. But she wasn't all that famous as a painter, was she?"

"Famous enough," said Stevens. "Right on the cusp. More so now that she's killed."

"Not going to do her any good, is it?" said Stuart.

"I can't agree," said Stevens. "People will see her work."

"There's that," said Stuart.

"Are you still on?" asked Stevens.

"What do you mean?"

"Do you want to write this book?"

"What?" said Stuart.

"Do you want to write the book?" asked Stevens.

"I hadn't thought about it," said Stuart.

"Well then," said Stevens, "think about it."

"It feels dirty," said Stuart.

"So you don't want to do it?" asked Stevens.

Stuart didn't respond.

"Will you cooperate then, if I bring in another writer?" Stevens asked.

"Don't put words in my mouth," said Stuart. "I never said that I didn't want to write this book. I want to write."

"If you feel guilty," said Stevens, "you can give half the money to Howard University, or set up a scholarship."

"How much money are we talking about?" asked Stuart.

"A lot," said Stevens.

"I guess I could give some of the money to T," Stuart said. "He's going to need a lawyer."

"Are you in, then?" asked Stevens.

"I think so," said Stuart. "I could honor her. That's right," he said, suddenly engaging with the possibilities. "I could honor Louise. I'd dedicate the book to her."

"You can honor anybody you want," said Stevens. "It's your book."

"Okay, then," said Stuart. "Count me in."

"Okay, then," said Stevens, "we'll be talking."

The agent didn't phone Stuart back until after three P.M.

"You're still in?" he asked again.

"Yes," said Stuart. "I suppose."

"How does half a million dollars sound to you?" said Stevens.

"Sounds fantastic," said Stuart. "Sounds unbelievable."

"Believe it," said Stevens. "You get a third of that at signing. I just got off the phone with Hannibal Artless."

"For thirty thousand words?" asked Stuart.

"No sir," said Stevens. "This calls for a full-length treatment. A great artist. She spent the last week of her life in your home."

"That's true," said Stuart. "Scrambled my eggs. I've got some good material."

"Not good," said Stevens. "It's great. That's what Hannibal Artless said to me at lunch. Great. He's going to phone tonight. By the way, he likes you a lot. He said he wouldn't trust any other writer with this book. You know why?"

"No," said Stuart, "why?"

"Because nobody cares as much about art as Stuart Cross does."

Stuart resisted the impulse to phone Andie at work immediately. Instead, he let the satisfaction marinate. At one point he stepped outside onto his soon-to-be-truncated lawn, looked back at the pillared facade. For the first time ever, he felt that the house looked right. He felt that Tara was his.

He came inside, poked his head into the great room. "I'm going out now," he said. "If you watch Janey and don't fight, I'll bring you a Twix." Ginny didn't respond. He got his helmet and went out on the motorcycle. He stopped at the gourmet take-out, and ordered their most elegant entrée. A young plumpish blonde with a mole on her chin who was working behind the counter recognized him, and threw in a half a pound of whipped garlic potatoes. "The least we can do," she said.

Stuart also stopped at Ben's Ultimate Deli and bought his elder daughter a Twix. He added twenty minutes to the chores with a trip to The Art of Wine in Pleasantville. "I want something pricey," he said. "I want it red. I don't care if it spills. I want to drink it tonight."

Home from his errands at six, Stuart opened the wine, sniffed the cork appreciatively, and fixed his daughters macaroni and cheese out of a box. Then microwaved them each some broccoli with shredded cheese and butter.

The girls sat at the table stern-faced and silent. Ordinarily, he might have threatened punishment, but he dreaded another double-barreled crying jag.

When the children had drifted back into the great room, he gave Ginny her Twix. This she unwrapped, but left unbitten on the arm of the sofa. Afraid that it would melt, Stuart put the candy in a Baggie, put the Baggie in the fridge.

When Andie pulled into the drive at seven thirty, Stuart pranced out to meet the car.

Janey left the TV when she heard the Saab's engine, but instead of rushing out and wrapping her arms around her mother's legs— the move which had been her signature since she learned to walk—

she stood frozen at the top of the stairs, received a dry kiss on the forehead, and then returned to the large-screen cartoons.

Andie might have followed her daughter back into the great room, but Stuart took her by the arm, led her into the kitchen.

He'd set the table with the wedding china, silverware, napkins. Paper napkins, but napkins nevertheless. He had even lit candles. He produced the bottle of wine.

"It's red," she said.

"Let it spill," he said. "It's Bordeaux. The English used to call it claret, but this is a fine Bordeaux. I opened it an hour ago," he explained. "It needed to breathe."

"This *is* wonderful," said Andie. "But what's the occasion?"

"I've got a surprise for you."

"What's that?"

Her husband poured them each a glass. "Up to the brim," he said, "and even above the brim."

"All right," said Andie, "What is this about?"

"Your husband has a book contract," said Stuart.

Andie took elaborate care putting down her glass of wine, but even so, she spilled some, which she licked off of the back of her hand.

"Okay," she said, fixing Stuart with those notoriously sad eyes. "Now the bad news."

"No bad news," said Stuart.

Andie looked dubious.

"You like the wine?" asked Stuart.

Andie nodded.

"This wine cost two hundred dollars. It's a 1985 Chateau Lafite-Rothschild."

"Oh, my God," said Andie.

"Guess how much I got for the book?" asked Stuart.

"I don't know," said Andie, pleased to see her husband happy and reaching around for a lowball that would not dishonor him. "The wine cost two hundred dollars, and you got two hundred thousand dollars," she said.

"Half a million dollars," he said.

"Goodness," said Andie, picking up her glass of wine, taking a sip, and clinking it carefully against his.

"That's right," he said. "Due in a year."

"I knew it would happen," said Andie. "I sensed it. What's the book about?"

Stuart put a finger to his lips. "Shuush," he said. "You'll find out soon enough. For right now, I'd like to keep it a secret."

"You artists," said Andie, but before she could finish her thought, the phone rang.

"The girls are both here and safe," said Andie. "Let it ring."

"I don't know," said Stuart. "I'd better get it." He put his wine glass down and picked up.

"Hello," he said.

"Hello," said a voice. "Is Stuart Cross there?"

"Speaking," said Stuart.

"Celebrating?" asked the voice.

"Yes," said Stuart, somewhat bewildered. "We *are* celebrating. But how would you know that?"

"This is Artless," said the voice. "Congratulations."

"Thanks," said Stuart. "Thanks so much. I won't let you down. This means a great deal to me."

"You're not still at Acropolis?"

"No," said Stuart.

"You can go at this full time?"

"Yes."

"Can you give me a manuscript in six months?

"Six months," said Stuart. "That *is* fast."

"I wouldn't ask you," said Artless, "if it weren't important. Acropolis has also assigned a book. Rick Massberg has thrown a lot of money at the project. You must have known him."

"Yes," said Stuart. "I know Massberg."

"He's all over this," said Artless. "Apparently he knew the woman. He took her death very much to heart. He's brought in two writers. He's got Martin Brookstone, the Civil War novelist, and this woman named Helen Greene. She's an artist herself. They're crashing this. If you give us the manuscript in six months, we can still be first."

Stuart sighed. "That's fast," he said. "And I have this family. Two little girls."

Artless didn't speak.

"Of course I want to do it," said Stuart.

"I need to know if you can do the work in time," said Artless. "I need to know it before we sign the contract."

Unthinkingly, Stuart picked up his glass of wine and took a thirsty pull. "I suppose I can write that fast," he said. Then he heard the cartoons in the back room, thought of the girls and how sad they seemed. "But I do have this family."

"Is the family an obstacle?" asked Artless.

"I guess," said Stuart. "I guess that the family is the obstacle."

"Well then it's easy," said Artless.

"Easy?" asked Stuart.

"Hire a good nanny."

278